"You're more like Scheherezade," Jonathan said.

"Scheherezade?" Damaris repeated.

"Scheherezade. That heathen temptress who beguiled some Oriental king with her stories." Slowly his grip on her wrist relaxed, and his gaze wandered lower. "Saved her own neck with her beguiling, and bedded the king, too, I think."

Damaris was blushing furiously now. Yet, to his surprise, she didn't pull away. Instead her fingers spread and flexed against his chest.

Jonathan stared at the ripeness of her plump lower lip, considering. He slid his hand along the inside of her arm, feeling the pulse at her wrist beneath his thumb. For God's sake, why was he standing on ceremony? Gently he pulled her down.

Dear Reader,

Welcome to Harlequin Historicals. We hope you will enjoy this month's selection.

From Lindsay McKenna comes *Brave Heart,* the story of Serena Rogan, a deeply troubled young woman who discovers a world of love and respect under the gentle care of a Lakota medicine man.

In *Destiny's Promise* by Laurel Pace, Lucinda Chandler hides away on a remote Georgian plantation, but must face her past when she falls in love with her new employer's son.

Ana Seymour's first book, *The Bandit's Bride,* was one of our 1992 March Madness titles. We are very pleased this month to be able to bring you her second book, *Angel of the Lake,* set in Wisconsin in the mid-1800s.

Last, but not least, *Spindrift* by Miranda Jarrett. This captivating romance features the younger Sparhawk brother, Jonathan, from *Columbine* (HH #144), as a shipwrecked seaman determined to unravel the lovely widow Allyn's carefully guarded secrets.

Next month, keep an eye out for *A Warrior's Quest,* the next book in Margaret Moore's Warrior series.

Sincerely,

Tracy Farrell
Senior Editor

Spindrift

MIRANDA JARRETT

Harlequin Books

TORONTO • NEW YORK • LONDON
AMSTERDAM • PARIS • SYDNEY • HAMBURG
STOCKHOLM • ATHENS • TOKYO • MILAN
MADRID • WARSAW • BUDAPEST • AUCKLAND

Harlequin Historicals first edition May 1993

ISBN 0-373-28774-7

SPINDRIFT

Books by Miranda Jarrett

Harlequin Historicals

Steal the Stars #115
Columbine #144
Spindrift #174

MIRANDA JARRETT

is an award-winning designer and art director whose writing combines her love of history and reading. Her travels always include visits to old houses and historical restorations.

Miranda and her husband, a musician, live near Philadelphia with their two small children and two large cats. She is still trying to figure out how to juggle writing, working and refereeing disputes among preschoolers in the sandbox.

For Debra, a dear friend, a splendid colleague and
the perfect partner for lunch.
Here's your book with grown-ups!

Prologue

Off the coast of New England
March 1708

The trap was simple enough. Whether it succeeded or not would depend on the conscience of its victim.

The sloop *Leopard* was twenty-seven days out of Barbados, and for the last three of these she had been forced to run free, with scarcely a scrap of canvas, before a storm that had turned day into night and cast up waves high as houses. But though Jonathan Sparhawk's face and hands were numb from the cold and his eyes ached from sleeplessness, the *Leopard*'s master was a happy man. As the winds died down with nightfall, he knew he was back in his home waters again, knew from the taste of the salt in the air and the way the very wind blew against his cheeks, and from the sixth sense found in every homeward-bound sailor.

"Land, away!" came the lookout's cry from far above, and eagerly Jonathan swung up into the shrouds to see for himself. He was a big man, broad-shouldered, but agile for his size, and he moved through the rigging with easy confidence. His long black hair streamed out behind him, its riband long since blown away. Beneath his boots, the lines were glazed with ice that crackled and shattered as he climbed upward to join the lookout on the foretop. Sweet Lord, but it was cold aloft, he thought as the wind tugged at his coattails, cold enough to freeze the parts a man held most dear. He braced himself between the mast and foretops and steadied his glass on the thin, dark line of land on the horizon.

Point Judith, he guessed, just as the last clouds overhead were torn apart by the wind, giving him the stars and a sliver of a new moon to confirm his bearings. They'd been blown past Saybrook, true, but not so far as Vineyard Sound. He shouted out the orders that would turn the *Leopard* back, toward her home port. With luck, they'd be there by supper tomorrow.

Home. The word sounded good to Jonathan on this bitter night, and he smiled to himself, easily imagining the reception he'd find at Plumstead. The place was really Kit's now, as was right for the older brother, and right, too, because Jonathan had scant interest in a farm seven days upriver from the ocean; the *Leopard*'s cabin was his real home. But there would always be a bed waiting for him in the house where he'd been born, and plenty of good food and laughter, thanks to Kit's pretty wife, Dianna. By now there'd be another babe to join little Tamsin and Joshua, who'd probably forgotten all about their uncle Jonathan in the four months since he'd sailed. No matter; that Noah's ark wrapped so carefully in cotton wool in his sea chest would bring him back in favor soon enough.

The sloop heeled over on her new tack, and hand over hand Jonathan began the long slide down to the deck. Suddenly he stopped, and again lifted the glass to his eye. The tall wave to leeward sank, and there in the dark green valley was a longboat. The boat sat far too low in the water, burdened as it was with a tight mass of men huddled together against the wind and spray, and though the men at the oars strained to pull closer to the *Leopard,* their progress in the rough water was painfully slow.

Twenty men, a merchantman's crew, same as his own. As Jonathan watched, a man in the stern sheets rose to his feet and desperately flapped a water-heavy pennant, his mouth open wide in a hail that was lost in the wind. Quickly Jonathan scanned the horizon for signs of a foundering vessel or a wreck on the rocks off the coast that might harbor more survivors. In this weather a ship could break up and vanish in minutes, and God only knew how long these wretches had been in the open boat.

At once Jonathan was on the deck, taking the helm himself to steer closer to the boat while the men aloft worked feverishly to check the *Leopard*'s progress. A chance misjudgment, and the sloop could swamp or even crush the boat. Members of the *Leopard*'s crew called advice and encouragement to the others in the boat as it drew closer, and at last they were able to pull it safely to the sloop. Exhausted from exertion and exposure, the castaways remained in the boat a moment longer, marshaling their final strength for the climb up the *Leopard*'s slanting side. Slowly, one after another, they appeared on the deck to stand huddled in their coats or beneath makeshift cloaks of blankets, standing tightly together around the mainmast as if they were still in the boat. It was sad, thought Jonathan as he came forward, what losing his ship could do to a man. These poor creatures seemed numbed by their ordeal, unable to speak or even meet the eyes of any of his own men. One castaway, an older man with a beard streaked with gray and a mutilated ear, seemed close to tears, burying his face in a grimy red kerchief to keep his grief private.

The last to board was the one who'd waved, and from the way the others looked toward him, Jonathan decided he must be, or must have been, the captain: a thickset man with a dun-colored beard and a puckered scar that cut through one bristling eyebrow. He wore an overlarge coat with a cape across the shoulders like a coachman's, and he seemed to Jonathan to be as much bowed down by the coat as by his misfortune.

"Jonathan Sparhawk, master of the *Leopard*," said Jonathan warmly as he held his hand out. "We'll do our best by your people, for we're less than a day from port."

The man ignored Jonathan's outstretched hand and squinted up at him from beneath his mangled brow. "And what be that port?"

Around him Jonathan felt the stunned surprise of his crew. No one spoke to their captain like that, not without instantly regretting it. But this time Jonathan bit back the rebuke the man's rudeness deserved. He doubted he'd be too civil himself if he'd just lost both his ship and cargo. "Saybrook, on the Connecticut, though the *Leopard*'s owned by the Sparhawk brothers of Plumstead, near Wickhamton."

"Meanin' yerself, then?" asked the other man sourly.

"Meaning myself and my brother Kit, aye," said Jonathan, his temper sorely tested by the man's surliness. "And who are you, friend, to stand on my deck and inquire? What ship was yours?"

The man's tobacco-stained grin was mean and sudden. "What ship's been mine don't concern us, no more'n what's been yours. Meanin' what's been yours, now be mine."

The man flipped back his coat, and too late Jonathan saw the long barrel of the pistol in his hand....

Chapter One

Aquidneck Island Colony of Rhode Island and Providence Plantations

At midnight, when the tide was highest, the rocks on Nantasket Point offered no shelter. Staring out across the black water, Damaris Allyn drew the hood of her cloak a little higher and tried to shield her face from the wind and the spray.

"We won't be seein' them Dutchmen tonight, Mistress Allyn," said Caleb Turner as Daniel and Seth Reed nodded solemnly beside him. "Leastways not so long as this weather holds. Now, if Master Allyn was here, he'd—"

"But he's not, Caleb, nor will he be, and let that be an end to it," Damaris said, interrupting him, and at once regretting her sharpness. She sighed wearily and shoved a wet strand of hair out of her eyes with a soggy mitten. "Thee knows as well as I—nay, likely better—that Captain de Vere could come any night after the quarter moon. Storm or not, we have to wait."

Caleb set the lantern down on one of the rocks and crouched beside it, blowing into his cupped hands. "Master Allyn ne'er waited on no Dutchmen," he grumbled stubbornly. "'Specially not in no foul blow like this."

This time Damaris let his complaining pass. Another five minutes she'd wait for Captain de Vere, no more. The wet cold had long ago cut through her heavy wool cloak and her quilted petticoats, and her toes, in double stockings, were as numb as her fingers. She doubted she'd ever felt so miserably uncomfortable in her life.

And, of course, Caleb was right about her husband. All the brandy in New Amsterdam couldn't have coaxed Eben away from his fire and his pipe on a night like this. She was the one who'd insisted on this fool's errand, the one who'd worried about offending Captain de Vere. If the fine gentlemen of Newport so wanted to have their brandies and French wines without paying the tariffs, thought Damaris crossly, then let *them* stand out on Nantasket Point in the dark and the rain.

She bent to pick up the lantern herself, and the candlelight glanced off the wide, flat planes of Caleb's face beneath his hat's brim. "Come along, then," she said, with a final glance over her shoulder at the empty horizon as the three men rose stiffly to their feet. "I've kept thee out long enough. Especially thee, Caleb. Thy Ruth will have my head if the damp settles into thy shoulder again."

"Ah, she don't ever say wrong against you, mistress," said Caleb, his mood improving as they headed toward home. He held his hand out to steady Damaris as she climbed from one granite boulder to the next, and his smile flashed white against his black face. "An' not even Ruth can nag th' wind into blowing southerly if it's of a mind to blow north."

"North or south, it still brings good, Caleb Turner," declared Seth, holding his own lantern high over the beach. "There'll be all manner o' wreck an' salvage washed up in the morn. Last storm I found me a whole hogshead o' spermaceti, just as tidy as if I'd called over 'cross the shoals to Nantucket for it myself."

Damaris pulled her cloak more tightly around her shoulders, wishing she were home already. "Thee will be welcome to whatever thee finds come morning, Seth. Now I'd—"

But she paused, frowning, her eye caught by a dark shape against the pale beach beyond the point. She scrambled down off the rocks, her shoes leaving only faint prints across the packed wet sand. As she drew closer, the shape materialized into a man's body, his arms outstretched where the surf had tossed him. For a moment she hesitated, unwilling to be the first to see the drowned man's bloated face. But the sounds of the others following reminded her that if she expected to be their leader she shouldn't shrink back at the sight of some poor corpse. Resolutely she came closer, lowering her lantern to light the man's face, and what she found made her breath catch in her throat.

He was, quite simply, one of the most handsome men she'd ever seen, the line of his jaw strong and firm, his nose straight, his wide, curving mouth made for laughter. The lines that fanned from his eyes were etched deep, and his cheeks were weathered; a mariner then, like Eben. Waxy pale against the dark frame of his long, wet hair, his features were as relaxed as if he slept, his eyes closed and his lips slightly parted. Kneeling beside him, Damaris pulled off her mittens and gently brushed the wet sand from his jaw, his skin so cold beneath her fingers. Foolishly she caught herself wondering what color eyes lay behind the thick black lashes, and what his smile had been like. She guessed his age at thirty, or close to it, not so very much older than her own twenty-six, and too young by anyone's count to die.

"Lord, he be a pretty one, an' not dead long, from th' look o' him," said Seth behind her. "And mark his size, grand as an ox. Wouldn't've wanted no quarrel with him, nay, I wouldn't."

Caleb held his lantern over the man's chest. "Gentry, y'warrant?" he asked doubtfully. "There be lace on his shirt like a lord, an' a good pound o' brass in his coat buttons. But I ne'er seen a gentleman wear a scarlet coat like that one."

"Nay, a pirate, that's what he be!" said Daniel with relish. "I seen the pirates what was hung in Boston, an' the leader wore a scarlet coat bold as this one, an'—"

"Enough of thy nonsense, Daniel Reed!" Damaris rose abruptly, brushing the sand from her cloak and wishing she could put away her sadness at the stranger's death as easily. Foolish, it was, to grieve over a man she hadn't even known. "We'll take him back to the house, and if none come to claim him, we'll see he's buried like a Christian, and without thy tales of pirates and hangings.''

At first she wasn't sure if it was only a trick of the uneven lantern light that made the dead man seem to scowl at her words, or, more likely, her own imagination. Then beside her Caleb swore, fumbling for the ivory charm he wore on a thong around his neck, and the Reed brothers stepped back uneasily. They'd seen it, too, and quickly she dropped down on her knees again, shoving back the tangled mass of the man's hair and his sodden neckcloth, to search for the beating of his heart.

''Take care, mistress,'' warned Caleb, ''afore you go touchin' one that's restin' so uneasy.''

''If he's uneasy, it's because he's still alive,'' said Damaris, ''and we've left him lying here, half in the water and half out. Come, he may still have a chance if we can get him near a fire, and don't thee say it's not what Master Allyn would do, because he would. Now hurry!''

As Caleb and the Reeds staggered awkwardly across the beach and up the dune with the unconscious man, Damaris ran on ahead to the house to build up the fire. Her fingers shook as she gathered the things she'd need to tend him. This was too much like the night last autumn when they'd brought Eben home to her, and then there had been nothing, nothing at all, she could do.

''He's bleeding bad from th' leg, mistress,'' said Caleb as they carefully laid the man on the long trestle table. ''And Daniel thinks he's been cracked on th' head, too.''

Damaris only nodded. He seemed enormous there, sprawled along her kitchen table, still and pale as death, with strands of seaweed snagged on his coat buttons. She could sense the unspoken confidence of the other men as she began to tear away the blood-soaked fabric of the stranger's breeches, and she wished she shared their faith. As mistress of Nantasket, she'd tended her share of cuts and broken bones for her tenants, but that hadn't prepared her for the ugly gunshot wound now before her. Though shipwrecked sailors were often struck by flotsam or rocks, wounds seared with gunpowder were seldom innocent, and Damaris thought again of Eben, how his coat had been red with his life's blood. She remembered, too, what Daniel had said about the Boston pirates, but she quickly thrust the thought away. This man needed her help, not her condemnation, and with her fingers and a thin, long-bladed knife, she quickly set to work retrieving the ball from deep inside his thigh.

Mercifully, the man remained unconscious. Though Caleb and Seth held him down, he never flinched, and the tankard of numbing Jamaica rum that Damaris had set out in case he wakened remained untouched. She set the flattened bit of lead to one side in case he wanted it later as a keepsake, in the odd way men often did. Pausing only to rinse the blood from her hands, she swiftly laid a poultice on the wound and wrapped a linen bandage around his thigh.

After the gunshot, the cut on the back of his head seemed minor enough, a lump the size of a goose's egg and a gash that needed only three quick stitches with an oiled needle to close. With Caleb's help, she stripped away the man's sodden clothes and tossed them unceremoniously in a heap on the floor. Seth was right, he *was* big as an ox, broad-shouldered and powerfully muscled, his chest and forearms dark with curling hair and marked by a score of old scars from knives or swords. Of course, she'd seen Eben without his clothes, but this man was so different, his strength so apparent even as he lay unconscious, that she modestly stopped short of removing what was left of his breeches in front of the others, and motioned instead for them to shift him to the trundle bed she'd pushed near the fire's warmth. Tucked beneath her familiar, worn coverlets, the stranger somehow seemed diminished, unthreatening in a way that Damaris was too tired to consider. With a little sigh of exhaustion, she dropped into Eben's rush-bottomed armchair, her hands limp on her bloodstained apron.

"I'll send Ruth up t' help you, mistress," said Caleb softly as he and the others prepared to go. "It's the world an' more you've done for that rascal already."

But Damaris shook her head. "Nay, Caleb, though I thank thee for thy kindness. There's naught else to do for the man but wait, and I can do that alone."

"You be the kind one, Mistress Allyn," he said with something close to awe, and with a weary smile Damaris watched the door close after him. She settled her chin in the palm of one hand, and with the other traced her fingers across the chair's carved armrest, where Eben's elbow had worn away the wood stain.

Six months had passed since his death, and she wondered when the dull ache of loneliness would ease. Ebenezer Allyn had been her father's shipmate, and she remembered well his round, merry face from her childhood. He had been in need of a young wife to help manage Nantasket at the same time that Damaris had lost her home, such as it was, when the lingering illness finally claimed her widowed mother. She had known Eben would treat his wife kindly and with fairness—even a tall spinster Friend without a penny to her name—while he had judged her to be strong and capable, and a decent cook into the bargain. When they had agreed to wed, both had known it was from friendship and respect, not love, but the affection Damaris had come to feel for Eben in the next five years had been very real.

The storm had blown itself out, and now the first weak light of day filtered through the diamond-shaped panes of the casements. Against the muffled *shush* of the breakers on the beach, she heard the mewing of the gulls wheeling overhead.

Damaris stared down at the unconscious man. His dark hair was stark against the linen bandage, and his thick lashes were sooty upon his cheek. She knew from sad experience that it would take a miracle for him to live. He had spent too much time in the icy water, lost too much blood, and though she'd drawn the pistol ball itself, she'd likely left enough bits of fabric to bring on the inflammation and fever that killed even the strongest man, even one grand as an ox.

Suddenly the man's eyes opened, and he stared up at her, unseeing, as his mouth curved into a shaky, unexpected grin. "Ah, you're here then," he said thickly. "My pretty little vixen!" Then, as quickly as his face had brightened, the animation vanished, and his eyes once again fell shut.

For one awful moment, Damaris thought he had died. But the faint pulse remained, and the almost imperceptible rise and fall of his breathing continued minute by agonizing minute. She reminded herself sternly that it was only the first stage of the inevitable delirium that had caused him to mistake her for another. Only the surprise of his outburst could have left her cheeks so warm and her heart fluttering within her breast.

But his eyes were green, the greenest she'd ever seen.

And no one, especially not Eben, had ever before called her his pretty little vixen.

Chapter Two

"Jonathan Sparhawk."

The woman made a statement of it, not a question. Her voice was soft and low, and intriguing enough for Jonathan to make the effort to open his eyes. When he did, he wished he hadn't. The room reeled crazily around him, and though he clutched at the sheets at his sides, he couldn't seem to stop the spinning. Breathing hard, he squeezed his eyes shut again, and gradually the motion slowed.

"Jonathan Sparhawk," the soft voice said again, though this time he wasn't lured into seeking the woman behind it. "That is thy name, isn't it? I found it marked in red stitches on thy handkerchief."

The name might be his, or it might not. Right now, he didn't know, and he didn't care. Sweet Lord, what *had* he drunk last night, to make him feel like he had a dead polecat in his mouth, and all its relatives come to mourn in his head?

As if she understood, the woman laid a cold cloth across his closed eyes. "It would seem strange to learn thy name was otherwise," she continued. "For a fortnight now thee has lain here, and all that time I've called thee Jonathan, and nothing else. It favors thee, I think.''

Her meaning cut through the soft words like a knife. ''A fortnight?'' he croaked, his voice raspy from disuse, and he heard her gasp with surprise. Clearly, she had not expected a reply.

''Aye, a fortnight,'' she said stiffly, her informality gone. ''Thee has been very ill, and only God's mercy has brought thee through thy adversity.''

Her old-fashioned speech confused him more. How had he come to spend two weeks—two weeks he had not the slightest memory of—in the bed of a woman who canted like a preacher? He shifted toward her, and a bolt of unbelievable pain shot through his leg. He gasped raggedly, feeling the vertigo come swirling back again.

''Here now, drink this.'' Unprotesting, he let her lift his head and tip the syrupy liquid, tasting both of honey and of something bitter, into his mouth. Almost at once, the dizziness began to recede, and he felt himself relaxing, drifting into a state of pleasant well-being.

Damaris sat back, thankful that she'd thought to mix the caudle the night before. When the man's fever had broken, and true sleep had replaced his delirium, she'd known this moment would come. She'd known, too, that she should be grateful for a recovery that was as close to a miracle as her kitchen would ever see, and yet, deep down, she knew that, selfishly, she wasn't.

For two weeks he had been company, hers to nurse and worry over. She had come to know every inch of his powerful body as she'd bathed him to lower the fever and watched with concern as the illness slowly gnawed away at his strength, leaving him even leaner, the knotted pattern of muscle across his chest and back even more evident. She had seen the black beard grow to hide his cheeks and the line of his jaw, and listened as, delirious, he'd muttered sailor's calls and the names of people she didn't know. Unconscious, he had been only a human being who needed her, and someone to talk to in her empty house. But awake, he was a man, a very large man of very real flesh and blood, and having him here could bring her nothing but trouble.

"So thy head grieves thee, too?" she asked, absently rubbing her thumb around and around the rim of the now-empty cup in her hands.

"Aye, lass, it does. Or did, before that marvel of a potion." He fought against the drowsiness that came with the drug, determined now to open his eyes again. If only for a moment, he wanted to know what she looked like.

"I thought that once the fever left thee, and the poison left thy leg . . ."

"It's been nigh on five years since I broke my leg chasing that boy's damned monkey 'cross the foremast shrouds," said Jonathan irritably, "and if I'd been carrying around any poison since then I'd have been dead long before this."

He moved to sit, and there again was the pain, as fresh and sharp as it had been that day, when the line had given way and he'd dropped twenty feet to the deck. It made no sense, no sense at all. He swore under his breath, and with shaking fingers reached down to touch the bandage around his thigh. The soft linen strips were as real as the pain, yet he'd have staked his life that all this, or something very much like it, had happened five years ago. Though there'd been no woman then, no soft-voiced temptress. He yanked away the damp cloth Damaris had laid over his eyes and braced his arms on the narrow trundle frame, determined to rise.

But even that small movement exhausted him, and when Damaris reached out to gently press him back, he dropped weakly down against the pillows, his face glazed with sweat.

"Thee must rest, or the fever will return," she chided. "I don't want to have brought thee this far from thy grave only to have thee leap back into it from thy own stubbornness!"

"The devil take your fever!" He caught her wrist with unexpected force, trapping her hand against his bare chest. His eyes were open wide now, with no hint of dizziness to dilute the anger that blazed out at her. "What game are you playing with me, lass?" he demanded. "What jest, eh?"

"Hush, thee makes no sense—"

"You're the one who makes no sense, stringing me along with tales that wouldn't fool a child!"

"Thee has no right to accuse me of anything," she said defensively. "I'm not without faults, but I do not lie, not to thee, not to any man or woman."

Yet her hand remained caught in his, and though she reminded herself that the man was still too weak even to sit upright, that she should pull away, here she foolishly stayed, more trapped by his gaze than by his grasp as her fingers tangled in the curling hair of his chest. She had thought him a handsome man before, but dear Lord, how he looked now, his whole face ablaze with the angry fire in those green eyes! Beneath her palm she could feel the pounding of his heart and the labored measure of his breathing, and her cheeks grew warm as his eyes narrowed, studying her. He made her painfully aware of how she'd hurried to his side from her bedchamber in no more than her night shift and a shawl, her hair shamelessly unbraided and uncovered beneath his scrutiny.

Despite his anger and frustration, what Jonathan saw intrigued him. Even by the unsteady light of the single candle, her face held all the beauty that her voice had promised. She was tall and slender without being delicate, and her skin was fair but sun-burnished, and warmer in color than was the fashion. Her mouth was very red, her lips were still parted with surprise, her eyes were wide and very blue, and her hair slipped across her shoulders like poured honey, shining dark gold.

"Ah, I said you'd spun tales, not lied outright, and there's a world of difference between the two." She wouldn't be capable of a falsehood, not with those eyes. Instinctively he knew she'd spoken the truth, but his head was too muddled for him to admit it gracefully. "You're more like Scheherazade."

"Scheherazade?" repeated Damaris, trying vainly to place the name in the Old Testament.

"Scheherazade. That heathen temptress that beguiled some Oriental king or t'other with her stories." Slowly his grip on her wrist relaxed, and his gaze wandered lower. The neckline of her shift was thick with Flemish lace, and he could see the rounded curves of her breasts through the cutwork, their fullness clear beneath the sheer linen as she leaned over him. "Saved her own neck with her beguiling, and bedded the king, too, I think."

She was blushing furiously now, her discomfiture so plain he almost laughed. Yet, to his surprise, she didn't pull away, as he'd expected. Instead, her fingers spread and flexed against his chest, and he would have wagered what was left of his life that she was doing it unconsciously. She was a full-grown woman, no doubt, but somehow she'd kept the appealing innocence of a young girl unaware of how very pretty she was.

Maybe, thought Jonathan, just maybe, it was because she wasn't any more real than the rest of this crazy fever dream. He slid his hand along the inside of her arm, feeling the pulse at her wrist beneath his thumb. She certainly seemed real enough, soft flesh and quickening blood and the sweet musky fragrance of a woman roused from sleep, all enough to make his poor head spin even more.

He stared at the ripeness of her plump lower lip, considering. For God's sake, why was he standing on ceremony? He was already lying naked in the woman's bed, and had been for two weeks. She'd said so herself. Gently he pulled her down, and she bent over him, as pliant as a willow.

Damaris felt her breasts crush against his chest, and a growing heat between their bodies that had nothing to do with fever. Her conscience screamed that this was madness that must stop now, but still she seemed unable to protest, let alone retreat. She was a good woman, Ebenezer Allyn's widow, not a... not a...

She lost the thought of what she wasn't as his fingers moved along her throat, tracing the curve of her jaw, and she shivered beneath his touch as their lips met. He teased her first, barely feathering across her parted lips in a way that made Damaris's breath stop from anticipation, both dreading and hoping for what would come next. Then the fingers of both hands tangled in the honey silk of her hair as he pulled her closer, and his mouth moved surely, seductively, across hers. Her limbs seemed to turn soft as butter, and her heart pounded wildly as her whole body felt on edge with new sensations.

Oh, aye, she was real enough, decided Jonathan as he kissed her—delightfully, achingly real. The taste of her mouth cut through the haze of drugs and pain with an intensity that stunned him. How close he must have been to death, for him to respond like this! Here, now, was life again, all the passion and fire of it in this one woman's kiss, and hungrily he moved deeper, into the softest places in her mouth. But even as he did, he felt the weakness returning. A woman like this deserved more than he could give her this morning. Reluctantly he broke his mouth away from hers, and his hands fell back on the coverlet. Still she hovered over him, her lips still parted and her eyes closed, and her quick, short breaths warm on his cheek.

"My regrets, sweetheart," he whispered ruefully, with a sorry attempt at a smile. "Next time I swear I won't leave you wanting. But then I expect you know that of me already, don't you?''

He reached up again to brush her cheek, and she opened her eyes. "My sweet Scheherazade," he murmured drowsily. God, how he wished he could remember more about her.

Abruptly Damaris pushed herself away and sat upright. Appalled by her own behavior, she pressed her hands to her mouth, only to feel the warmth of his kiss still on her lips, lips that were eager to betray her again. She was shaking, her whole sense of herself tumbled apart. Never before had she acted so thoroughly on impulse, without reason or thought for the consequences. Yet the way this man had kissed her was so different from what she had known with Eben, who'd as soon have kissed her cheek as her lips. No wonder he kept comparing her to this wicked heathen Scheherazade!

She pulled her shawl tight around her shoulders and over her breasts, and struggled to regain her composure. The man was still gravely ill. Perhaps he wouldn't remember what had just passed between them, or would think he'd only dreamed it in the fever. If she could pretend it had never happened, maybe he would believe it, too. She took a deep breath to steady herself, and prayed her voice would stay level. "Could thee tell me the names of thy kin or thy friends, so I might let them know thee is safe?"

He closed his eyes and lay there silently for several long minutes, frowning to himself. "I can't tell you, lass, because I don't know myself," he said at last, so softly that she had to bend close again to hear him.

"It's like there's some fog or squall clouds in my thoughts, hiding the truth away from me. There's bits and pieces, but nothing real, nothing I can grasp and swear to."

He laughed to himself. It was an odd, humorless rattle. "It's that witches' potion you've given me, aye, that's it," he muttered hoarsely, and there was an edge of desperation in his voice that startled Damaris. "Your draught's addled my wits."

"'Twas but honey and tansy to ease the dizziness, nothing more." Troubled, Damaris drew her shawl more closely over her shoulders. She'd heard of men who'd lost their memories from a blow to the head, but she'd never seen it herself. "Thee said thee once broke thy leg chasing some boy's monkey on a ship. Can thee recall the boy's name, or the ship's?"

"Hell and damnation, I can't remember a single, blasted thing." But there was no fire to his swearing, only a forlorn desolation that echoed too closely her own loneliness. His words were slurring clumsily now, and she knew that finally the caudle was claiming him. "I don't know my own name, nor my father's, nay, nor even my mother's. And you, lass. I can't even thank you by name."

"Damaris," she whispered urgently. "It's Damaris Allyn, and thee never did know it."

But he'd already slipped away into unconsciousness, and though he'd likely sleep through this day, and the night ahead, too, she couldn't risk him waking alone when she would be out with the others at the point, waiting for de Vere. She'd have to ask Caleb's wife, Ruth, to stay with him while she was gone; if anyone could deflect his questions, it would be Ruth. Quickly Damaris dressed, banked the kitchen fire, and, with a final glance at the sleeping man, closed the door softly as she left.

As the sun rose higher over the water, she turned back to look at her house, trying to turn her thoughts to anything other than the man who lay sleeping in the kitchen. For six years this house had been her home, and it was impossible now to imagine living anywhere else. Eben's father had built it after the last Indian wars, when King Philip's warriors had burned the old farm to the ground. The front of the new house was narrow clapboard weathered to a silver-gray, two stories high, with a tall peaked gable in the center over the door. There were nine windows with leaded-glass panes shaped like diamonds, brought especially from London, and rare enough at the time to make the neighbors gossip of the Allyns' pretensions. The north end of the house was fieldstone, rising into a massive, elaborate chimney before slanting sharply back to the one-story kitchen in the rear.

Behind the house was a small barn, the well, a hen-house, and the kitchen gardens in their raised beds. Wide stone fences enclosed the yard and served to protect the summer flowers—hollyhocks, roses and asters—that Eben had ordered from England for Damaris.

Damaris smiled wistfully, thinking of the flowers and thinking of Eben. Even though Nantasket had always belonged to the Allyns, Eben had never really cared for it, not the way she'd come to. She had lived most of her life in the uneasy balance of charity and poverty, crowded with her widowed mother and three nieces into a drafty, noisy room over her uncle's shop in Newport. For Damaris, the seventy-five acres of the Nantasket grant had seemed more than she could ever desire or deserve.

But a well-traveled mariner like Eben had felt tied down by the farm's responsibilities from the day he'd inherited it from his father. Smuggling had became the quickest—and the most profitable—way to relieve his boredom. With the money from the Newport merchants who bought his untariffed liquor, he could afford to sell off the sheep herd and let the land turn fallow, and to gently scoff at Damaris's worries for his safety.

And then had come the night last autumn when Eben and his men had met with another boat in the fog—fellow smugglers, or pirates, or excise men, they had never learned for certain—and Eben had been dead in an instant, shot. Lost in her grief, Damaris had sworn to put an end to the smuggling.

Or had until the lawyer had ridden out to call on her the week after Eben's burial. True, Eben had left everything to her and her heirs, but he'd also borrowed so heavily against the land that the lawyer had advised Damaris to sell the farm, the house and the slaves as the only way to pay off Eben's debts. Return to Newport, he had urged her, and find some humble widow's lodging within her means before the creditors seized Nantasket and left her with nothing.

In silence Damaris had listened, fear tightening around her fresh grief. With Eben gone, Nantasket was all she had left, and she couldn't bear the thought of losing her home, as well as her husband. Too well she remembered how it felt to be poor and dependent on others, and when Captain de Vere had returned in November, Damaris had been there on the rocky beach to meet him. Carefully she returned all her profits back to the farm, and prayed for the day when they would be self-sufficient again, while praying, too, that no other men would be killed serving her in this risky trade.

But now had come this stranger to complicate things all the more. As Jonathan grew stronger, Damaris knew his questions would grow sharper, too. She wouldn't lie outright, and she was wretched at dissembling. It wouldn't take a man like Jonathan Sparhawk long to discover the truth about how she spent her nights. And then what? Would he turn them all in to the customs men for the reward, or would he demand a price to hold his silence?

And as for the kissing, there would be no more of that, pure and simple. Her face grew hot all over again at the memory of what she'd let him do—no, what she'd done, too, and brazenly—and she welcomed the chilly wind off the water on her face. She'd never be able to look at the man again without feeling ashamed. With a sigh, she poked a strand of hair blown free by the wind back up under her cap, and turned toward the path that ran along the beach.

The Turners' house was not far, and she soon saw their chimney, and the pale smoke that rose from the soot-blackened bricks. The house was much smaller than hers, with only a kitchen, a small hall, and a sleeping loft above. The outside walls were covered with rough shingles in place of clapboard, the floor was packed earth, and the few furnishings had been made by Caleb himself, not London cabinetmakers.

Yet it was still better than tenants expected from their masters, and far beyond what most masters would grant to their slaves, a fact that Eben had always been quick to point out to Damaris. To Eben, Caleb and Ruth and their sons were property, as much a part of Nantasket's livestock as the cows and horses, while to Damaris they were people, and her insistence on treating them that way had rankled Eben's rigid sense of social hierarchy. Although she had known he wouldn't have been pleased, her one change on the farm after Eben's death had been to give the Turners their freedom, transforming them from slaves to free-holders. That act had cut the value of Eben's estate by several hundred pounds, but not once, thought Damaris as she knocked at the Turners' door, not once had she regretted it.

"So ye have come for my help with layin' out yer castaway at last, haven't ye, mistress?" said Ruth as she wiped the chin of Eli, her youngest boy, who was squirming in her lap. She placed the baby in Damaris's outstretched arms and scrubbed at the porridge that he'd spattered on her apron. Ruth was a handsome woman, strong and straight, with flawless dark brown skin and angled eyes of a gold like amber. Though from habit she still called Damaris her mistress, the bond between the two women went far deeper. "From how bad Caleb said he'd been hurt, I'd of thought ye would have been here sooner."

"Nay, Ruth, for once thee is wrong." Damaris smiled as she took the baby from his mother and curled his little body in the crook of her arm. The other three Turner boys were nearly men themselves, and were out in the fields with their father. Eli's arrival five months before had been something of a surprise, but, as Ruth proudly noted, he was the only one of them born into freedom. "The man's fever broke last night, and I think now he'll live, God willing."

Ruth's eyebrows rose. "So what do ye be wantin' of me, then? Ye've done yer nursin' well enough without me, if ye managed to save his raggedy, wicked soul."

"Thee doesn't know if he's wicked or not, Ruth," chided Damaris, "and neither thee nor I have any right to judge him."

"He's not one o' yer gull chicks with a broken wing, that's for certain." With both hands Ruth picked up an empty kettle and hooked it on the jack over the fire, letting it swing with a clang against the brick fireplace for emphasis. "To my mind, ye would have done better t' leave him to meet his end out on the beach."

Eli gurgled in Damaris's arms, and she gave him her knuckle to chew on. "Thee knows I couldn't do that, Ruth. 'Twould not be Christian to leave some poor stranger to die...."

Ruth snorted. "Yer Christian ways will be bringin' us naught but trouble this time. Ye order my Caleb an' the others t'go riskin' their necks for ye—"

"I *ask* Caleb," said Damaris warmly. "I don't order him."

"Aye, mistress, he'll do whatever ye wish, no matter if it be askin' or orderin'," said Ruth crossly. "He loves ye too well t'ever do otherwise. That be what I'm sayin', if ye would but listen. Ye will be the one t' suffer most if the excise men come pokin' their muskets 'round Nantasket. An' here ye be, lettin' yerself get all hollow-eyed an' gaunt, sittin' up with some weasely rogue that could hang us all!"

Even as Damaris's chin rose defensively, she caught herself wondering if she looked as ill as Ruth said. Not, of course, that such vanity mattered. "I asked thee not to judge him, Ruth. Thee doesn't know for certain he's a rogue."

"Has he told ye otherwise, then?"

"He hasn't told me much at all. The blow to his head has taken his memory, and he can't even recall his own name, poor man."

"'Poor man'!" scoffed Ruth. "The devil take yer poor man! Ye don't accept the rascal's tale, do ye?"

"Aye, Ruth, I believe I do," said Damaris softly, stroking Eli's velvety cheek as his eyelids began to droop. "He is, I think, quite lost."

"An' so will ye be, Mistress Allyn, an' don't dare say I didn't warn ye from yer folly." Ruth shook her head solemnly as she poured water from a bucket into the kettle, and Damaris looked down at little Eli, praying her folly didn't show on her face already. "But ye came here with a purpose beyond hearin' advice ye did not want, didn't ye?"

Carefully Damaris laid the baby, now asleep, in his rough-hewn cradle. "Tonight I'll wait with the others again for Captain de Vere. If thee can, I would wish thee to stay with Jonathan.''

"Jonathan, is it?" said Ruth shrewdly. "I thought ye said he'd lost his wits.''

Feeling well caught, Damaris flushed again. "His handkerchief was marked with that name, and it serves as well as any other.''

"And is he still as comely as Caleb said, or has th' illness robbed him of his manly beauty?''

Damaris's cheeks grew hotter still. "I haven't noticed.''

Ruth snorted derisively. "The day a woman stops noticin' if a man be handsome or not is the day she be dead.''

"Oh, then, aye, most women would call him a handsome man," said Damaris in a rush, wishing Ruth weren't quite so forthright. "But thee can come see for yourself. I wish thee to stay with him tonight in case he wakes, and put him off if he asks where I am.''

"Aye, Eli an' I will keep him company." Ruth grinned, pleased as much by the rare crack in Damaris's calm demeanor as by the prospect of viewing the stranger. "He'll learn no secrets from either o' us.''

"Then I thank thee, Ruth." Damaris rose to leave. "Tell Caleb I'll see him tonight.''

"Mistress, wait." The older woman's teasing smile faded as she touched Damaris's sleeve. "Truly ye don't believe this man t'be a rogue, even coming to ye in a scarlet coat with a bullet in his leg an' his chest all scarred by swords?''

"I won't believe it until he convinces me otherwise.''

"Faith, mistress, what rogue would come out an' tell ye he be wicked?"

"Ruth, thee listens too much to Daniel Reed's folderol about Blackbeard and Henry Morgan and heaven knows who else," said Damaris in exasperation. "All Daniel knows about pirates he learned secondhand in a rumshop."

"Then this Jonathan be neither rogue nor king's man from th' customs house?" Ruth looked at her doubtfully. "Ye don't be scared by him, even a tiny bit?"

"Nay, Ruth, I am not," Damaris declared firmly. "I'm not frightened at all by a poor lost man like Jonathan Sparhawk."

But as she walked home alone, Damaris knew she hadn't been entirely honest, not with Ruth, and not with herself. Of course she was worried by the castaway and the havoc he could bring to her life, but she could deal with that. After all, if she had to, she could call off the smuggling until he was well again. He could be gone next week, and that would be the end of it.

No, it wasn't Jonathan Sparhawk that truly frightened her. It was something much harder to admit, some weakness deep inside herself that she couldn't have named. She remembered how he'd smiled at her that first night and called her his pretty vixen, and she remembered how he'd looked at her today as she'd let her hand stray across his chest, the feel of his warm skin and his curling hair and his heart, beating beneath her fingers as their lips met.

Fiercely she told herself she must not care, that women like her were above dalliances, beyond flirtations and the silly names sailors called the doxies outside the taverns. She had other, better virtues than those giggling wenches, virtues that had made Eben proud to call her his wife.

But within herself she knew that her lonely heart would hear what her pride denied. This Jonathan Sparhawk would tell her the promises that men in scarlet coats told women, and because she'd never heard them before, she would listen. *He* would be *her* Scheherazade. Then his leg would heal and he would leave, and never once look back at a foolish, lonely widow.

She was almost running now, the tall, dry grass slashing at her skirts as she tried to flee her own thoughts.

He could not be gone soon enough to save her from herself.

Chapter Three

Deep beneath the heavy folds of her cloak, Damaris kept her fingers curled tightly around the small leather bag in her pocket as she watched Johannes de Vere come splashing through the shallows toward her. He was scowling down at his boots to avoid looking up to where she stood waiting on the rocks above the beach.

She knew well that the Dutchman didn't like dealing with her any more than she did with him. For reassurance she felt the coins through the soft leather, the gold and silver that were the only reason he kept coming back. The gentlemen in Newport always paid her in hard money, and de Vere was so eager for coins that he'd overlook the insult of having to bargain with a female. Still, he always tried to cheat her, not believing that a woman could add her figures as well as a man, and when she questioned him his pale blue eyes would drop suggestively to her breasts in a way that discounted everything she said, and made her glad to have Caleb and the Reeds nearby. He would never have dared do it while Eben lived, and the Dutchman was one more reason why she longed to be done with smuggling. Eben had told her that de Vere kept one wife, blond and Dutch like himself, in Hempstead, and a second, an Abenaki squaw, in Falmouth to the north, and Damaris had always wondered that there were even two women in the world who would tolerate the man.

"Thee has kept me waiting more than a fortnight, Captain de Vere," she said coolly.

"Thank your heathen Quaker god I'm here at all, woman." At last he raised his face to look at her, his eyes half-lidded. "I don't know why I bother risking my neck, aye, and my men, too, hauling your miserable excuse for a cargo."

Knowing better than to rise to his taunts, with an effort Damaris ignored them instead. "Did thee find the canary wine I asked thee for last time?"

"Oh, aye, but you'll pay dear for it, Mistress Allyn. Canary wine! Sometimes the gentlemen like it fancy, don't they, and sometimes they like it plain." He leered to make clear his double meaning, but Damaris steadfastly kept to business.

"I'll pay thee what the wine's worth, not a farthing more, and if thee believes otherwise, thee can just haul it back to thy ship."

Crossly de Vere barked an order in Dutch back over his shoulder to the seamen straining to pull the boat up onto the beach. Damaris nodded, and Caleb and the Reed brothers left her side to head down to the water to help unload the pipes and casks that were hers. De Vere was right—it didn't amount to much of his cargo. Her entire shipment would be brought from his ship in two trips of the boat, but the spirits she bought—

canary and port and the finest brandies—were likely worth more than all the cheap rum that filled his hold.

She watched as the men hoisted the barrels on to their shoulders and carried them up the beach, their feet sinking deep in the sand beneath the extra weight, and across the rocks to the waiting wagon. As always, Damaris would make a great show of driving the horses across the fields to her barn while de Vere and his men rowed back out to their ship. But once the ketch was out of sight, Damaris and the others would quietly lead the wagon back to the beach and down to the cave that served as their true storehouse. The cave's entrance was overgrown and hidden with scrub bayberry bushes and brambles—and Eben had sworn that no one outside the Allyn family knew it existed— but Damaris insisted on being careful, especially around de Vere.

De Vere came to stand beside her on the rocks, and Damaris resisted the impulse to move away. He turned his back to the breeze off the water and cupped his hands around the flint as he lit his pipe. The sparks caught, and for a moment the light flared across his full cheeks as he puffed furiously.

"You're lucky to see any of this tonight," he said again. "Times are hard for poor sailors."

"If thee means the last gale, that was fifteen nights ago," said Damaris evenly. She'd counted every one of the fifteen nights and days since the storm had brought Jonathan Sparhawk to Nantasket. Was he awake now? she wondered, then tried to forget the image of his dark, bearded face against the white pillow. "Fifteen days ago thee still would've been in

Hempstead. Thy hard times must grow much harder than that before I'll pay you more."

De Vere snorted with disgust, tobacco smoke shooting from his nose. "Fah, woman, I didn't mean that puny storm! That wasn't wind enough to cool my soup! Nay, I mean the murdering thieves and bastards that try to steal an honest man's livelihood. I mean pirates."

"Pirates!" Damaris's voice rose with disbelief. "Not thee, too, Captain de Vere! All I've heard this winter is pirates this and pirates that, as if our Aquidneck's become no better than Port Royal itself! Pirates! Next thee'll be with Daniel Reed, seeing the great hoary ghost of Blackbeard, or Bluebeard, or whichever beard it was, walking out of a Thames Street tavern! Pirates, for the love of all!"

"You wouldn't talk so free if you'd seen what I'd seen, Mistress Allyn," said de Vere doggedly. "Ships limping into Boston with their rig in shambles and the blood dark on the deck. And that's the lucky ones that got away. More often they don't, and every last Christian's slaughtered where he stands. They're in these waters, no mistake."

Damaris glanced at him uncertainly. "Thee isn't lying?"

"Why should I? I've nothing to gain by it, and maybe much to lose." His voice dropped lower, more confidential, and though his eyes were hidden in the shadow beneath his hat, Damaris felt his gaze roam across her body as if the layers of wool and linen had vanished. "The world knows your husband did well for himself. I'll wager there's plate on your mantel, isn't there, eh? Allyn always paid hard money, and so do you. That's enough to tempt a pirate to thieving ashore. And then there's you, little widow. Young and sweet and all alone in a house near the water. Pirates are men first. If they found you here alone, you'd wish you were dead when they were done.''

''Thee *is* lying!'' said Damaris indignantly, angry with herself for listening to him. ''There aren't any pirates, only thy own foolish tales....''

''Nay, mind me, the pirates are real enough.'' Damaris realized, to her surprise, that he was speaking in complete seriousness, perhaps for the first time since she'd taken over for Eben. ''You pay me well, hard money, and you'd never call me out to the customs house. You let yourself get hauled off and sold to some brothel, and I'll never see your gold again. So you mind me, eh? You keep your own eyes open, and keep clear of strangers.''

Damaris nodded gravely, her hands folded across her chest. She still wasn't sure whether to believe him or not. She didn't want to. For although, like de Vere, she watched the men unloading the boat, what she saw was the scarlet coat with the brass buttons, newly washed and pressed, that now hung on the back peg of her keeping room door.

Ruth was waiting at the window, silhouetted by the firelight, when Caleb finally brought the wagon into the yard, and seeing her there, Damaris jumped down from the seat before the wheels had stopped turning. The older woman's face was grim as she met her at the door, and beneath her cloak Damaris's hands were knotted into tight fists at her sides.

"He died, didn't he?" she asked, her voice emotionless. "I knew if I left—"

"Save yer pity, mistress, th' man's as fit an' alive as when ye left him," said Ruth dryly. "He never woke once, sleeping as peaceable as th' babe."

Damaris's stiff composure melted with relief, and impulsively she hugged the other woman. "Thank God, and thank thee, too, Ruth, for watching over him."

"It's watchin' over you that troubles me more, an' th' more ye babble on, th' more I see ye need me." Ruth stepped outside and pulled the door shut behind her. "If he wakes, I don't want that man hearin' what I have t' say."

Ruth's face was lost in the night shadows, but there was no mistaking the urgency in her voice. "He'll bring ye trouble, mistress, nothin' but sorrow, an' ye best turn him out, soon as ye can."

Damaris sighed impatiently. "Ruth, I told thee before that I don't believe Jonathan is one of thy pirates."

"Pirating be the least o' yer grief from that one! Oh, Caleb said he was comely, but sweet Lord, mistress, one look at him an' I felt my heart drop for ye. This Jonathan be finer, handsomer, than any man I ever seen, an' you think so, too, from th' way ye dither on about him."

"Ruth, I'm not some giddy maid to have my head turned by a handsome face!"

"True enough. But ye do be a widow that's gone six months without a man's comfort, an' that be a deal worse." Her tone softened, and she took Damaris's hand gently in her own. "I know ye didn't marry Master Allyn from love. He was kind t' ye, an' ye was fond o' him, I saw it, but he was stout an' bald an' half a head shorter than yerself, an' he treated ye more like his daughter than his wife. Now this handsome creature drops into yer life—nay, into yer own kitchen. He's young an' a pleasure t' look upon. When he finds his legs again, he'll be strong an' randy as a three-year bull. He'll be after ye, no mistake, an' I won't blame ye if ye let him. But what will ye do if he fills yer belly with a babe, eh?"

"Thee should know there's scant chance of that, Ruth," said Damaris stiffly.

"What, because ye won't lay with him, or because ye were Master Allyn's wife for six years with no child between ye?" Ruth shook her head. "'Tis not only women that be barren, mistress. Sometimes it's th' man's seed that be at fault."

"Ruth, please!"

"The truth of it be that yer too kind by half fer a man like that, an' when he leaves, ye'll be left heartsore an' hurt," said Ruth firmly. "An' I don't want t' see that, whether he be pirate or not. Send him away soon as ye can, mistress. Send him away before he grieves ye!"

"It won't be like that, Ruth, I swear to thee," answered Damaris, thankful that the night hid her blushes. "How could I come to care for a man who is—who is as thee says this one is? When he leaves, I'll wish him Godspeed, but he'll go without my heart.''

Inside the house, the baby began to cry—it was a muffled, sleepy wail—and Ruth went to him, leaving Damaris outside. When she returned, her shawl was wrapped over her head and shoulders for the walk home, and little Eli was bundled warmly in her arms.

''Good night t' ye, Mistress Allyn,'' she said evenly, pausing at the doorway before she joined Caleb. ''Yesterday ye said ye weren't a bit afraid o' that man in there, an' I believed ye. Tonight I believe you'll be sorry if ye aren't.''

It was morning again when Jonathan woke, and the sun from the east spilled through the casements into diamond-patterned shadows on the scrubbed pine floor. For the first time he saw the room in daylight, and he realized to his surprise that he lay in a kitchen, not a bedchamber. Like some poor, puling invalid tucked beside the chimney, he thought with disgust as he tried to push himself up on the pillows. He was still weak—God in heaven, he was weak!—and his arms shook from the effort, but at least the dizziness seemed gone.

The kitchen's fireplace wall was gray stone, the hearth itself big enough to roast a deer, and the lavish assortment of imported iron pots and skillets would be the envy of most cooks. But the fire in the hearth was small, barely enough to take the chill from the air, and the pots and skillets sat idle and empty. Equally empty, Jonathan's stomach rumbled loudly in complaint, and with a heartfelt sigh he imagined hot oatcakes with maple syrup, and squash pies plump from the oven, and bacon spattering in a skillet the way it always had when—when what? When he was a child?

"So there thee is, awake to join the world at last," said the woman behind him. "I felt sure thee would sleep clear through First Day, too."

Eagerly he twisted around, toward her voice, squeezing his eyes shut as pain sliced through his leg with the movement. He forced himself to breathe evenly, to ride it out until the pain faded to a dull ache, before he opened his eyes again and was able to manage a shaky smile. Although he feared she'd seen far worse from him when he was unconscious, now that he had some control over himself again, he'd be damned if he'd let her see him wince and whine.

But the woman before him was very different from the one he'd kissed. Not that he doubted that she *was* the same one, but in place of the lace-trimmed nightgown was a dark gray bodice laced high over her breasts, with a thick white kerchief tied over it for good measure. Her sleeves were straight and plain, her linen cuffs were untrimmed, her skirt was more of the same gray woolen, without a hint of tucking or flounce. Her hair—all that beautiful, silky, honey-colored hair—was drawn back so severely from her face that not one tendril or wave would dare escape from the white lawn cap. She sat stiffly upright in a straight-backed chair that was as unyielding as her clothing, and open in her hands was a small Old Testament.

"You're a Quakeress, aren't you?" he asked softly, his chagrin and regret oddly equal.

"A Friend, if thee pleases." Her fingers slid blindly down the page, across the dimpled words marked on the paper, and with a little sigh at her own frailty she closed the covers. Now that he was at last awake, she would stop pretending to concentrate on the scriptures. How could she do otherwise, with him lying there watching her with those green cat's eyes?

Jonathan's sigh echoed hers, but for very different reasons. "I liked what you wore last night far better, you know."

Damaris blushed, but her gaze held his evenly. Just because he remembered what she had worn, that didn't mean he remembered kissing her, too. "That was my husband's fancy, and I wore it only to please him. My own taste is less worldly."

"Ah, your husband." What did he expect? Quaker or not, women this pretty were always wedded. "I must thank him for his hospitality."

Damaris looked down to the book in her lap. "Thee can't, though it would have pleased him to hear thee say it. My Eben died in October."

"I'm sorry," said Jonathan gently, and he meant it. Her grief was too new and real to leave him untouched. And in that moment he knew for certain that, however he'd come to her house, he'd never shared her bed.

"I thank God that it was sudden, an apoplexy. He was too good a man to suffer." Damaris rose quickly to mask her agitation, and crossed the room to lay another piece of wood on the small fire. The doctor she'd called from Newport, one of the gentlemen who were so fond of untaxed brandy, had concocted the story of Eben's death that the world had accepted without question, but it still bothered her to repeat it. "The doctor said a younger man might have survived, but Eben would have been fifty-three in December."

At least her husband had died happy, thought Jonathan wryly as he watched Damaris's tall, graceful figure across the room. The quick flurry of her movements wasn't encouraging, but Jonathan persisted. He did, it seemed, owe the woman his life. "If I can't thank your husband, at least I can try with you, Mistress—?"

"Allyn. Damaris Allyn," said Damaris automatically, then wished she hadn't. She didn't need his gratitude any more than she wanted his sympathy.

"If thee is well enough for all these pretty thankyous," she said brusquely, "then does thee now remember who thee thyself might be?"

Jonathan shook his head, and saw how her brows drew grimly together. Lord, he never should have teased her about the nightgown, but how was he to know she was a new widow, and a Quaker widow at that? She certainly hadn't acted like one last night, and that was likely why she was so shrewish this morning. "Mistress Allyn, I've no more wish to remain here than—"

"Thee must not call me 'mistress,'" Damaris told him crossly. "Ruth and the others do so from my husband's habit, but to my mind it's false pride to set oneself above others with a title."

Jonathan eased himself farther up against the pillows, until he was almost sitting upright, taking care not to move his leg. God in heaven, he'd never before run afoul of a woman for being overly respectful! "Would it be too prideful, Damaris," he asked with exasperated politeness, "to ask if there's any breakfast?"

Damaris glanced at him sharply. Hearing her name on his lips was worse than being called "mistress," and far worse than that was the way he'd let the coverlet slip down to his lap, until the broad expanse of his shoulders and chest were bare except for the whorls of black hair across the sun-browned skin. His lack of modesty irritated her further, and for once she made no effort to control her temper. Maybe if she was angry enough with him, she'd stop noticing things like the width of his shoulders, or the way his smile cocked up higher on the right side.

Without a word, she retrieved his laundered shirt from the peg on the door and flung it at him, turning her back before he could thank her. She'd have to do something soon about breeches for the man, for the ones he'd worn were beyond repair. Since Eben had been a smallish man, and stout through the waist, his were out of the question. She'd have to remember to ask Ruth for a pair of Caleb's. "I've made thee a thin chicken broth to build thy strength, and that will be breakfast enough for now."

"Chicken broth!" Grimacing, Jonathan pulled the shirt over his head, his visions of bacon and oatcakes fading fast. "There's precious little strength in chicken broth, except perhaps for the old hen that went into it!"

"Then thee can have the beans and corn bread I put by for supper, and I'll not answer to the consequences if thy fever returns." Furiously Damaris pulled the crock from the cupboard and scooped the cold beans into a wooden bowl.

"What's it matter to you, anyway?" demanded Jonathan, his patience finally exhausted. "Nothing would make you happier than if I keeled over dead right here on your hearth!"

Damaris gasped. "Thee is the most ungrateful creature! How dare thee talk to me like—"

"I'll talk and you'll listen, Sister Holier-than-Thee." His voice rumbled so loud and deep from his chest that she had no choice but to hear him out. "Wherever I am, I didn't well ask to be here, and I'm certain as hell I didn't ask to be indebted to you. I'm tired of you fussing over me like some blasted nursemaid, and you can't even let me thank you without launching off onto another of your infernal sermons."

He lowered his chin to his chest and glowered at her from beneath the single black line of his brows. "And if all this racketing on your part comes from kissing me last night, well, mistress, it didn't amount to a speck of dust to me, and you'd be wise to feel the same." Here Jonathan's conscience nagged him. Kissing Damaris Allyn had been quite extraordinary, whatever the reason, but if she needed absolution from him to be civil, she'd have it. "Not a blessed speck of dust!"

"*I* didn't kiss thee, and thee knows it!" cried Damaris indignantly.

"Thee, thou, or me, it makes precious little difference, doesn't it?" Jonathan shrugged carelessly. "And tell me, Damaris—since you find me so damned indecent now, did you look your fill when I couldn't notice?"

"Oh— *Oh!*" Shocked speechless, Damaris grabbed a knife and spent her anger on the fat cake of corn bread. *Whack!* How dare he mock her for her plain speech? *Whack!* How could he accuse her of—of *ogling* him when he'd been unconscious? Whack! And how could kissing her be as meaningless to him as a speck of dust?

She shoved the uneven chunk of corn bread on top of the beans, stuck a spoon in the beans, and marched across the room to thrust the bowl into Jonathan's hands. "If thee wishes to poison thyself further with hot food, thee will just have to wait until sundown," she announced as he stared down at the shiny mass of cold beans. "I keep First Day with reflection, not kitchen tasks."

With her head triumphantly high, Damaris returned to her chair and her Old Testament. She was certain he'd find the cold beans unappetizing, but she hadn't reckoned on a sailor's ability to eat almost anything unheated when high seas shut down the stove. At once Jonathan ladled a dripping spoonful into his mouth.

Cold or hot, Damaris's cooking was far better than Jonathan would have dreamed possible, and he gave a little groan of pleasure as the flavors melded on his tongue. Molasses and salt pork, thyme and pepper, and maybe a hint of maple, too. But he was too hungry to really savor the food, and he ate quickly, using the corn bread to soak up the last bits of sauce. Stubborn woman, he thought indulgently as the food mellowed his temper. No wonder her poor husband had died of apoplexy!

Over and over Damaris's eyes crossed the same passage without reading the words. She listened to Jonathan's sigh of contentment, and the scraping of the pewter spoon against the wooden bowl, and was able to order herself not to look up until she heard the empty bowl clatter to the floor, and the oath that followed. But her reprimand vanished when she saw how pale he was, his forehead slick with sweat, and how he'd slid back down against the pillows.

"Seems a decent meal's all it takes to make me clumsy as a bear," he said, his smile weak. A decent meal, and bellowing at the cook. Lord, at this rate he'd be her unwilling guest for weeks. Self-consciously he brushed corn bread crumbs from his beard, and with concern Damaris saw how his hand shook. "Likely look like one, too, with these whiskers."

"I can get Eben's razor, if thee wishes," said Damaris softly as she picked up the dropped bowl. It was impossible for her to stay angry with him when he looked this ill, and she blamed herself for letting him eat so much so soon.

Jonathan shook his head ruefully, and held out his unsteady hand for her to see. "You'd be rid of me soon enough if I tried putting a blade near my throat today."

"Nay, I mean to do it for thee." Quickly she hoisted a small kettle of water to heat over the fire, and ran upstairs to gather a towel, soap, and the razor. The wariness on his face when she returned made her giggle with a girlishness that he found enchanting. "Oh, be easy, I won't slit thy throat. I did this often for Eben, and never spilled his blood."

She perched on a stool behind the head of the trundle and tucked the towel around his chin. He liked having her bend over him this way, her round-cheeked face upside down above his and her lips pursed with concentration. It reminded him of last night, and of kissing her. Would it be as pleasurable now that his head was clear? He could remember other women he'd known, laughing, lovely faces and willing bodies, but there seemed no one in particular that he'd cared for, and certainly no one who had been anything like Damaris Allyn.

"What date is it?" he asked abruptly, trying to steer his thoughts away from the sweet fragrance of her skin.

"The seventh day of Fourth Month, though it's really First Day."

"Meaning that it's April the seventh, and a Sunday?"

Damaris nodded as she stirred the soap to a froth. "Aye, by worldly calendars."

"For people professing plainness, you Quakers make things more complicated than any other godly folks."

Damaris had heard such comments too many times before to rise to his taunts. "And thee must be a Massachusetts man, to see right and wrong so clearly where the rest of us can't."

He frowned, and Damaris saw the desperation flicker again in his eyes. "Do you know for certain that's where I'm from?"

"Nay, I don't, but thee does speak like men from Boston." She spread the soap over his whiskers. "Now thee must be quiet while I do this, or thee will learn for thyself why barbers and surgeons are often one and the same."

He grunted, but didn't argue with the long, straight blade in her hand.

"I'll tell thee all I know about thee," she continued, "and perhaps thee can recall the rest. I found thee on the beach after a storm, and had thee brought here, to Nantasket Farm. We're five miles from Newport, on the west shore of Aquidneck Island, in Providence Plantations. Thee had nothing else on thy person save thy handkerchief to tell me who thee is, but I believe thee is a mariner from thy hands and the pale lines around thy eyes."

"Aye, you're right," he said excitedly. "I remember a ship—"

"Hush now! Thee must not move thy mouth!" Damaris scowled down at him, and Jonathan obediently fell silent. "From thy darkened skin in winter, thee has likely been to the Caribbean, and from the way that orders fly so quickly to thy tongue, thee must be an officer, maybe even a captain. Thy clothing is costly, too, not that of a common seaman."

As the razor scraped across his upper lip, Jonathan considered what she said. On some level he sensed she was right, though he couldn't have said how or why. He *was* a mariner. He had known immediately where

Aquidneck lay, at the top of Rhode Island Sound, and he vividly remembered clearing Barbados, standing shirtless in the hot sun on the deck, with the clouds of canvas stretched taut overhead. But what had become of that ship, and his shipmates?

"What else?" he asked tersely.

"What else?" she repeated uncertainly. There was the flattened bullet she'd taken from his leg and the pale scars on his chest and arms, as well as de Vere's warning, and Daniel's gossip. But when she looked down at Jonathan now and saw the lost look that he was trying so hard to keep from her, she couldn't believe he'd bring her harm. *Can't*, her conscience asked, *or won't?*

"There is nothing else, except what thee may tell me," she said firmly. "I had one of my tenants ask in Newport. There were no ships lost or other men found after the storm, no one who knew of thee. I've sent word to Boston, too, but no reply's come yet."

Her voice dropped lower, to a fierce, low whisper. "Thee may think my fussing is a trial, but mind, thee is quite free to leave whenever thee wishes. I have done for thee what I would do for anyone in need, and thee must not feel in my debt."

Damaris said nothing more, concentrating instead on shaving the last whiskers from his jaw. For Jonathan, her silence was painful. He wanted and needed to hear her voice, if only to drown out the questions that clamored for answers within his own head. She was here and she was real, and she was, for now, all he had to trust.

"If this is your Sabbath," he said abruptly, blurting out the first question that came to him, "then why aren't you at your meeting?"

"Because I'm not welcome there." Carefully Damaris wiped away the last of the soap. "Eben was not of the Society. When I wed him, I willfully transgressed against the Society's rules, and I was expelled from the meeting."

Six years had passed, but she hadn't forgotten the humiliation when the stiff old men and women of the Society's committee had refused her permission to wed, and accused her of misconduct for even asking. She had prayed to God for guidance, and married Eben in his church, alone, without a single friend of her own to wish her happiness.

Jonathan listened, incredulous. "But now that he's dead..."

Damaris shook her head. "Nay, it doesn't matter. I was at fault. Unless I come before the meeting and admit I was wrong and ask forgiveness, I cannot come back. And I won't do that. I'm not sorry, and I won't lie, not to please those who twist God's words into their own." Her smile was quick, and tinged with bitterness. "Even now, in Newport, none of the women's meeting will speak to me."

But it was the forced little shrug of her shoulders that told Jonathan the rest of the story. That gray shroud of meekness couldn't begin to hide her spirit, and he hoped old Master Allyn had appreciated what she'd done for him. She was a proud woman, and wouldn't give either her love or her loyalty lightly. Yet how incredibly lonely she must be, living out here by herself!

He reached up and brushed her cheek with the back of his fingers. "Like it or not, my Quaker Scheherazade," he said gently, "it seems we're both of us castaways, doesn't it?"

Chapter Four

Damaris felt the odd quickening of her blood when Jonathan touched her, his callused fingertips rough on her cheek. Briefly she let herself give in to sensation, wondering at the pleasure such a tiny caress could bring. It would be so easy for her to bend lower, and once again feel his lips on hers.

He was right, they were both castaways. She had never thought of things that way. And it was how he'd said it, too, that had nearly undone her. She hadn't heard gentleness like that in a man's voice since Eben had died.

But Jonathan wasn't Eben. He wasn't even a friend, let alone a husband, and he might well be an enemy. To kiss him once had been foolish. To do it again would be inexcusable. Swiftly she rose to her feet, concentrating on wiping the razor clean to avoid the question she felt sure would be in Jonathan's gaze.

"Thee must rest now," she said, sounding to her own ears every bit the nursemaid he'd accused her of being. "If thee's still better tonight, perhaps I'll fry thee ham and onions, since thee has eaten thy supper for breakfast."

Worse than a nursemaid, she thought glumly, bartering a treat for good behavior. She hurried so quickly from the room that the soapy water sloshed over the sides of the bowl in her hands, spotting her skirts and leaving a sloppy trail across her floor. She tossed the water near the wall and rinsed the bowl from the bucket at the well. Though the morning was bright and sharp, and too chilly for her to be without a shawl or cloak, Damaris welcomed the excuse to be outside and away from Jonathan. What was it about him that made her behave so oddly? Sanctimonious or slatternly, neither one was how she saw herself.

She sighed, absently twisting the ends of her neckerchief between her fingers. The gray-speckled guinea hens had come running from the barn when she'd appeared, and now they clustered around her skirts, squabbling and pecking at the nonexistent food they expected to be there. At least they showed the good sense to ignore the rooster in their midst, which was more than could be said about her.

She heard the galloping horse before she could see it, and, frowning, she stepped up on the stone wall to look over the hill to the path below. Few visitors came to Nantasket, fewer still by horseback. The rider saw her and waved, and though his face was still too far away to recognize, Damaris knew at once from the highbred quality of the bay stallion that the man was Eben's brother, Roger. Her mother had always claimed that trouble came in threes, and here, thought Damaris unhappily, was the proof: pirates, Jonathan, and now Roger.

Slowly she stepped down from the wall, wishing she hadn't shown herself and could pretend she wasn't home. She hadn't seen Roger since Eben's funeral, and she couldn't imagine what had brought him here today. There had never been much love between the brothers—half brothers, really, for Roger's mother had been the second Mistress Allyn, and twenty years separated the two men.

Yet more than age had separated the brothers. Like Eben, Roger had left Nantasket as soon as he could, but while Eben had gone off to sea, Roger had traveled no farther than Newport, and had prospered as a merchant there, marrying into one of the town's wealthier families. Eben had always dismissed Roger as good-for-nothing and vain, and when he'd called him a peacock, he'd emphasized the second syllable in a way that made it embarrassingly clear even to Damaris that the insult had more to do with Roger's virility than with his taste in clothes.

Yet if only a difference of temperaments had kept the brothers apart, Damaris would have been willing to end the quarreling with Eben's death. Since her own family refused to acknowledge her, she would have welcomed what comfort she could find among the Allyns. Except, however, for two small facts: Roger held an appointment from Queen Anne herself as chief magistrate for the naval court in Newport, and Damaris, thanks to Eben, made her own livelihood avoiding the same tariffs that Roger was sworn to collect. How much Eben had relished driving the wagon full of de Vere's brandy straight beneath the windows of Roger's elegant new house!

Damaris longed for a measure of her husband's nerve and daring as Roger drew closer. Why had he come clear out to Nantasket, anyway? Anxiously she thought of the rows of barrels stacked neatly in the cave near the beach. Eben had always sworn that as a boy Roger had never discovered the cave for himself, and had never known it existed, but now Damaris's uneasiness grew. Family or not, smugglers could be hanged, or at best left to languish in gaol. She would lose Nantasket for certain, and even if the Reed brothers and the Turners weren't arrested with her, a new landowner would likely turn them out in favor of his own people. Why, why, was Roger here?

Coming around the walls into the yard, Roger plucked off his hat and waved it with a flourish. Damaris's frown deepened. Such gallantry likely played well in Newport, but Friends doffed their hats to no one, and the gesture irritated her. He turned the horse neatly before her, the chickens scattering on either side. With his three-cornered hat still in his hand, he slid gracefully from the saddle.

"Sister Damaris, good day to you!" he began heartily, ignoring her obvious lack of a welcome. He was more handsome than Eben had been, with shrewd dark eyes and a lean, angular face above his immaculate neckcloth. His coat was dark purple, with a pale blue sash across his chest, and he wore fawn-colored boots fit for riding and little else, with heels that gave him height nearly equal to her own. "It's been far too long since we've seen you in town, my dear."

"Good day to thee, too, Roger," she said gravely. It was small of her, she knew, but she couldn't help hoping that beneath his long, curled wig, Roger's hair had fallen out on top like Eben's. "If thee has looked for me in Newport, perhaps thee forgets that I still grieve for thy brother, and the pleasures of thy town hold little interest to me."

While another man would have felt the barb in her words, Roger only shrugged them off. "You've kept yourself hidden away out here all winter. You know old Ebenezer wouldn't have wanted you to be all sad and mournful on his account."

His manner shocked but did not surprise her. "Thee forgets then, too, that even before Eben's death I had no interest in worldly pleasures."

"Calling at our house would hardly send you into the devil's hands, Damaris. Evelyn asks after you often, and would welcome you to share a dish of tea." He was looking past her, at the house and barn and outbuildings, and she could see the contempt in his gaze as clearly as if he'd spoken. "God, this place really is as bleak as I remembered! How you can stand to be out here with only that pack of black-skinned monkeys for company—"

"If thee means the Turners, then thee is insulting both my tenants and my friends," she told him, her voice frosty.

"They should be your property, too, if you hadn't been fool enough to counter my brother's wishes," he fired back, his eyes hard as flint. "Like tossing gold off a dock, what you did."

Working hard to control her temper, Damaris hoisted the bucket off the top of the well and set the water down for his horse to drink, scratching the animal between his ears as he drank noisily. It was thoroughly like Roger to ignore the horse's thirst. "Roger, did thee have a purpose in coming here this morning?"

He glanced away from her to the barn again, and Damaris thought again of the hidden cave. "You're not going to invite me into the house?"

Damaris had a sudden, awful image of Roger striding into her kitchen and finding Jonathan. No matter what she told Roger, he'd never believe anything beyond the evidence of a half-naked man in her house, and by nightfall the story would be in the mouth of every gossip in Newport. She didn't doubt for a minute that Roger would do that to her, if for no other reason than that she was Eben's widow.

"I asked you, Damaris," he repeated testily, "if you were going to invite me inside or not?"

"Thee still hasn't told me why thee's here," she answered stubbornly.

His face rigid, Roger swung himself back up onto the horse, sharply jerking the animal's head back. "Perhaps I just wanted to see how you were faring," he said curtly. "Like it or not, your name is the same as mine, and I might have some small concern for you, alone out here on this miserable farm."

"I thank thee for thy concern, Roger," she said, hoping he didn't hear the little quiver in her words. *O God, guide my feet on this treacherous path!*

"Thanks in place of hospitality, Damaris? In my mother's time, no stranger was ever turned away from Nantasket, let alone kin." He dug his heels into the horse's sides and drove the stallion up over the stone wall instead of through the gate.

Damaris remained in the yard, uncertain whether to laugh or weep. She'd angered Roger, no mistake, and over what? Hospitality, or her lack of it. Because she'd welcomed one man into her home, she'd been forced to turn away another. She doubted Roger's mother could have sorted it out any better.

But at least Roger had given her another reason to go to Newport. She would have Daniel and Caleb load the wagon at the cave tonight, and they'd make their deliveries in the morning. She'd check again at the customs house to inquire of any ships reported lost that might have belonged to Jonathan, and see if any of her letters to Boston with the same question had been answered. And then, with the new bag of smuggler's coins heavy in her pocket, she would call on her sister-in-law Evelyn, and try to be as pleasant and agreeable as she could to repair the rift between Roger and herself.

Jonathan waited until the sounds of the wagon had finally faded and he was certain Damaris was well on her way to Newport. Then, tossing back the coverlet, he pushed himself upright and carefully began to unbind the wound on his leg. Damaris had been so blasted mysterious about the wound, and he'd had enough mysteries lately to last the rest of his days. It was his leg; he had a right to know. His fingers shaking slightly, he pulled back the dressing, and recognized the deep, angry wound that the ball and its removal had left in his thigh.

Instinctively Jonathan whirled about to meet the bearded man with the bloody knife charging across the deck toward him. The man ducked as Jonathan's cutlass sliced through the air over his head, but as he lunged forward with the knife, Jonathan's boot kicked him squarely in the side and he staggered back with arms thrown overhead. Swiftly Jonathan raised the cutlass, knowing he'd won to live, while the other man would die. The deck was already littered with the still, crumpled bodies of men and boys who hadn't been as lucky as Jonathan, and he reveled in it, feeling the fierce exhilaration of battle as he stared down at the stunned face of the man he meant to kill.

But as his blade slashed downward, Jonathan heard the pistol shot, smelled the acrid gunpowder beside him. The cutlass found its mark, slicing through the man's chest, at the same instant that Jonathan felt the ball tearing into his own thigh. Stupidly he stared down at the growing dark stain on his breeches, and at the pulpy patch of red that matched his scarlet coat. He groped for the support of the mainmast, willing himself not to falter, not to feel the white-hot pain radiating from his leg. The cutlass slipped unnoticed from his fingers, and Jonathan watched both it and the other man's body slide away across the deck.

Then, suddenly, Jonathan was sliding too, the entire deck canting nearly vertical beneath his feet. As men both living and dead tumbled past him, he barely caught himself on the hatch cover, his fingers already too weak to hang on for long. Damnation, he was going to go overboard with the others, and there wasn't a blessed thing he could do to save himself....

* * *

Damaris sat in her sister-in-law's oak-paneled parlor, perched uneasily on the edge of a caneback chair, with a delft saucer of chocolate and milk balanced on her knees. Three other women had also come to call, all friends of Evelyn's, and after they had made their greetings and condolences, they had promptly forgotten Damaris was in the room, launching into an animated discussion of the new silk lutestring just arrived that week from London.

Evelyn rolled her eyes and gave her embarrassed little shrugs, knowing she was failing as a hostess by not including her sister-in-law in the conversation, but Damaris only smiled shyly in return, content to let the others' chatter fill the room. In their bright clothing, the women seemed like the Caribbean birds that Eben had described to her, with Evelyn the most brilliant, in a bodice and skirt of emerald green looped over a darker green petticoat, and gold ribands threaded through her chestnut hair. She was plump and merry, with laughing eyes nearly the same color as her hair, and Damaris felt certain that Roger would have wedded her even without the fortune she'd brought to their marriage. Evelyn's tiny white hands fluttered around the porcelain chocolate pot, twirling the mill to mix a head onto the hot milk within, and self-consciously Damaris tucked her own hands, chapped and red from work, beneath the saucer and into her apron.

She let her gaze wander out the window, to the noisy traffic on Broad Street. Newport had grown so much in the six years since she'd left, and accustomed as she was to the solitude of Nantasket, Damaris found the perpetual ruckus of carts and horses, oxen and wagons, sailors and farmers and fishwives, almost unbearable. In another quarter hour she could look for Daniel and Caleb, and escape back to her farm. Perhaps they'd have news of Jonathan's people that she could tell him at supper.

Unconsciously she chewed on her lower lip, remembering how quiet Jonathan had become after Roger had left. He'd been polite but distant, so quiet that at first she'd worried that his fever had returned. His color had been good, and he'd eaten well, but there had been no more teasing, and no more talk of them both being castaways. He had, in fact, behaved exactly the way she'd thought she wanted him to, and yet, perversely, she now missed the familiarity he'd shown before.

With a start, Damaris realized the other women were leaving, and quickly she, too, rose, still clutching the cup of now-cold chocolate. But as the housemaid came to show the others to the door, Evelyn took Damaris's elbow to hold her back.

"Wait, sister, stay a while," she whispered excitedly. "Now that you're really here among us, I can't let you go so soon. Besides, I've something to tell I know you'll want to hear!"

Reluctantly Damaris returned to her chair, folding her hands in her apron. She hadn't missed the scornful look from the housemaid, any more than she had been able to ignore the condescending graciousness of the ladies, and she felt as out of place here as her own earthenware and pewter would have looked beside Evelyn's porcelain and sterling.

"Roger will be so pleased you've come!" exclaimed Evelyn as she hurried back, her silk skirts rustling across the floor. She drew her chair closer beside Damaris's, and smiled expectantly, arching the thin lines of her plucked eyebrows. "He said you wouldn't, but I said you would, if he only could promise to ask nicely, which, of course, being Roger, he probably didn't. He's scarce fit for genteel company, and spends entirely too much time in his blessed countinghouse, wishing after gold and silver. As if we wanted for anything more, la!"

She flicked her little hand at the wrist and laughed. "And just because he is such a scold, and because you've been kind enough to come today, I shall tell you a jewel of a secret! That's what Roger says, anyway, though I think you should know, struggling all alone on that dreadful farm."

"It's not dreadful," said Damaris plaintively. "I like it. I could no more trade places with thee here—"

"Oh, no matter, dear heart, no matter at all!" Evelyn swept away Damaris's objections with another airy wave of her hand. "I know you're a Quaker, and you have to say things like that, more's the pity. But let me tell you Roger's secret. He's discovered there's a whole ship full of wild rascals set to come marauding here to our very island, outlaws and pirates and smugglers and heaven only knows what other sort of very wicked men. He swears he's had enough of villains who cheat the Crown and rob honest people, and so he's going to order a special patrol to catch them all."

Damaris felt herself go very still. She'd have to get a message to Captain de Vere as soon as she could, and take everything from the cave. The little strongbox full of coins could be buried in the kitchen garden, and she'd have to pray, beg, and outright order Daniel Reed to stay out of the Newport rumshops, or at least to use his mouth only for drinking. She couldn't risk Daniel's bragging getting back to Roger.

Or perhaps Roger already knew. Perhaps that was why he'd come to Nantasket yesterday, and why he'd kept peering at her barn as if he could see straight through the siding. And perhaps, somehow, he already knew the truth, whatever it was, about Jonathan.

"Pray, Evelyn, why does thee tell me all this?" she managed to ask faintly. "And why doesn't Roger want me to know?"

"Well, *I'd* want to know, if there were pirates waiting to murder me in my bed." Evelyn shrugged, then dipped her little finger in the top of the chocolate pot and licked it clean. "But Roger doesn't want you to be frightened, no matter how bad it might be. He says that as long as you insist on staying out on Nantasket Point by yourself, there's no use in scaring you about outlaws that likely won't come near your place. That's partly why Roger's doing this, you know, to keep you from coming to harm."

Evelyn laid her hand on Damaris's, her eyes round with excitement. "And when they've caught the scoundrels, oh, my dear! La, what a holiday we'll make of it then! We'll have sailors and soldiers, all pretty in their uniforms, to see that justice is done, and we'll watch the villains dance at the end of the ropes. Just like Tyburn!''

''Aye, just like Tyburn,'' echoed Damaris, staring at the dark rings of dry chocolate on the empty cups before Evelyn. Like Tyburn, indeed. She didn't think she'd ever be able to drink chocolate again without being sick.

From the upstairs window, Roger watched Damaris climb up onto the wagon seat beside her tenant with the straw-colored hair—one of the Reeds, that's who he was—while the black man sat in the back among the barrels and bags of seed corn. Slowly the wagon headed down Broad Street for the long trip back to Nantasket.

Roger made a little tent of his spread fingers, tapping the tips together while he thought. Damaris Allyn was a pretty woman, prettier than he remembered. Widowhood seemed to agree with her, if such a thing was possible, and he supposed it was, considering she'd been married to Eben.

But if he'd undervalued her comeliness, he'd underestimated her spirit, too. He'd ridden out to Nantasket yesterday fully expecting to act the generous brother-in-law, ready to rescue the poor widow from the burden of her lonely existence, and instead she'd turned him off the property as if he were some beggar. *Her* property. Eben had made sure of that with a will that left every last pebble of the farm to her and away from him, his only brother. Only in Rhode Island would such a will stand; Roger knew because he'd seen three lawyers shake their heads over the careful wording and advise him not to bother contesting it, and each time he could almost hear Eben's raucous laughter mocking him.

He heard his wife's scurrying steps pause outside his door, then move on to her own room. He didn't expect her to join him; nor did he particularly care. Her constant chatter and gossip irritated him almost as much as the way she still clung to her father, visiting the old man every morning with a devotion that she'd never shown to Roger. If only she'd recognized that her duty now lay with her husband, she wouldn't have been so clumsy about asking the old miser for more money. A loan, of course, merely to help Roger cover a few investments that had gone sour in Jamaica, but her father had refused even to hear the details, while Evelyn had stood silently behind his chair, fussing with the ribbon on her fan.

But she had helped him today. The way she'd hurried off, away from him, was proof enough that her conscience was heavy, and Roger smiled to himself. His empty-headed little wife had doubtless told Damaris every word he'd carefully forbidden her to say, and added a few of her own, as well. With luck, tonight Damaris would be seeing cutthroats in every shadow, and she would soon come running back to Newport to stay.

None of it was true, of course, this talk of him chasing after criminals like some sort of crusading knight. Quite the opposite, for the last thing Roger wished was to end the liberal payments from all the captains who expected him to turn a blind eye to their undeclared cargoes. He had grander plans, too, plans for the future that wouldn't depend on greasy, smirking shipmasters, or his miserly father-in-law. His fortunes were changing; he could feel it. But he needed Nantasket, and the neat little harbor that nestled under the point, and he needed it without the curious eyes of Damaris Allyn.

Roger's smile widened, and he chuckled to himself. This time next year he would be keeping a carriage—London-built, of course. Perhaps he'd even journey there himself to oversee the work. And wallpaper for the parlor, in the best Chinese manner, instead of the old-fashioned, provincial paneling he'd been forced to make do with, and a gilt looking glass for over the mantel. All this, and the chance to take Nantasket back from Eben's widow. The future could not be better.

By the time the wagon reached the Turners' house, the sun had set and the moon had risen, a bright sliver hanging over the horizon. It was too late to unload the wagon now, and since most of its contents were for Caleb, Damaris decided to leave the wagon and horse with him until morning, and walk the rest of the way home.

Climbing over the last hill, she saw that her house was dark, without a candle or lantern in any window to greet her. Worried, she quickened her pace, hopping and sliding down the steep path. She had placed a flint and rushes within Jonathan's reach before she'd left this morning, and candles, too, along with food and cider. Quiet or not, he had seemed so much better that she hadn't bothered to ask Ruth to come.

What if he'd pushed himself too fast, and the fever had returned?

Suddenly, Damaris thought of what Evelyn had told her. She'd been concentrating so much on Roger's plan to catch smugglers like herself that she'd only half listened when Evelyn had spoken of pirates. Now, though, in the too-quiet yard, Damaris remembered her warnings, and Captain de Vere's, as well. She slowed her footsteps, trying to move silently across the yard. What if thieves had come by sea and robbed her house while she was gone? They wouldn't have expected to find anyone else at home. What would they have done to Jonathan? Even she knew that pirates were notorious for leaving no witnesses. Or, worse yet, the one possibility she'd refused to accept: What if Jonathan *was* one of them, and they'd come here to find him?

From the outside, her house looked the same as she'd left it. The door hadn't been forced open, and none of the windows were broken. Her heart thumping in her chest, and every nerve on edge, she peeked through one of the kitchen casements. The fire had died down to a scattered handful of embers, and she could make out nothing beyond the dark shapes and shadows of furniture. Maybe Jonathan was only asleep, and he hadn't even realized it was night.

Or maybe the thieves were still inside, waiting now for her...

"Stop thy fancies, Damaris!" she whispered sternly to herself. *"Thee's never been weakhearted before this, and thee's not about to start now!"*

Though she'd opened the door times beyond counting, now her shaking fingers fumbled with the latch, and she'd never heard anything as loud as the squeak of the hinges when she eased the door open just enough to slip inside. Then she waited another moment, her body rigid with expectation, hoping vainly that her eyes might grow more accustomed to the dark room. She took a deep breath, and with arms outstretched to feel her way, she stepped tentatively forward.

The man's hand was over her mouth before she could cry out, his fingers forced back against her lips. She twisted to try to pull away, but his other arm had circled like an iron band around her waist. Effortlessly the man tossed her to the floor, and as she kicked and fought in terror, he pinned her beneath his own body. She couldn't breathe beneath his weight, and though his face was nothing but shadows above hers, she saw the faint firelight flicker off polished metal, a knife's blade. He was so much bigger and stronger and, God preserve her soul, he was going to kill her.

"Fight me, lass," he said hoarsely, "and I swear you'll be the one to regret it."

Chapter Five

Damaris clamped her teeth together and bit his fingers. He yelped and swore and jerked his hand away from her mouth.

"What does thee mean by treating me like this, Jonathan Sparhawk?" Damaris demanded angrily. She wiggled her hands free and up under his chest and shoved, but he was like a boulder that wouldn't move. Once again she thought of how very different Jonathan was from Eben, hard and lean where her husband had been soft. He was breathing hard, his face so close over hers that she felt every word hot on her cheek.

But at least he was dressed. She felt the rough linen of his shirt and, farther down, the coarse wool of his breeches against her legs. Humiliated, she realized that her skirts had hiked up past her knees and above her stockings when he'd tossed her down, and that the scratchy wool fabric, and the large male body it covered, were pressed against the bare skin of her thighs. She wriggled beneath him, trying now to pull her skirts down. "This is my house, my kitchen! Let me go now!"

"That's my decision to make, Damaris, not yours."
The truth was that Jonathan wasn't sure he could let
her up. Hauling her down and holding her was taking
every bit of strength he had, and freeing her would
mean he would have to sit up, even stand, and he was
embarrassingly certain he wouldn't be able to, not just
yet. "If it's your kitchen, your house, then why did
you come skulking into it like some damned Mohican
brave?"

"Don't swear at me!"

"I'll swear all I damn well please until you start
giving me answers!" Why the devil was she wiggling
like that beneath him? Her height was a good match
for his own, and he'd already decided she wasn't one
of those wispy women who would get lost somewhere
around his chest. But right now he wasn't in the mood
to consider the possibilities, and he certainly didn't
welcome the way her body was moving against his.
"Lie still, damn you!"

Damaris froze, her face scarlet in the dark as she
realized how he'd misinterpreted her attempts to cover
her legs. "Since there were no lights, I guessed thee
was asleep," she said defensively. "I didn't want to
wake thee."

"Oh, aye, and I warrant you have snow in July and
daisies in December, too. The truth, Damaris."

"Truth! What does thee know of truth?" she cried.
"What was thee doing hiding in the shadows with a
knife—*my* knife—guilty as sin, and twice as wicked?"

His laugh was harsh. "Men with bullet wounds
should take care that their enemies don't return to
finish the task. Did you really think I wouldn't look

beneath your tidy little bandage? That's the work of a pistol, lass, and I'll carry the scar to my grave. So, who did it, Damaris?''

"I told thee already! Thee was injured when we found thee—"

"Damaris..." he said, turning her name into a warning.

"I can't tell thee, Jonathan, because I do not know!" She was on the edge of tears, and her voice was trembling with frustration and fear. "Maybe thee really is a pirate, as the others say. Maybe thee will kill me now for crossing thee, and think nothing of my blood on thy soul. But I can't tell thee what I don't know. Why, why, can't thee believe me?''

But now, for the first time, he did. In his mind's eye Jonathan saw the terrified face of a sailor the moment before he plunged his sword into the man's chest. He remembered the screams of the other dying men around him, and a trim merchant sloop careening without a master, and he saw himself, in a coat as red as the blood on the deck around him, striving to take the captain's empty place. He closed his eyes, trying now to forget what he'd wanted so much to recall. A pirate—a black-hearted villain who preyed on other sailors, without mercy or conscience. No wonder no friend or crew mate, no brother or sister, had come searching for him. What decent person would care what became of a scoundrel like him?

Damaris Allyn. She was the one decent person who did—God alone knew why—and look how he treated her. He groaned, and sent the knife sliding harmlessly across the bare floor. He wanted to cry out for her forgiveness, and he wanted to bury his face against the softness of her breasts and believe that goodness like hers mattered more than the wicked mess he'd made of himself. He wanted to hear her say his name again in her odd, breathy voice, to find the solace he'd found once before in her lips, and he wanted to forget, forget...

Instead, he rolled off her, onto his back, and stared up into the darkness. He heard her scramble to her feet, and her skirts brushed against his wrist as she moved to the fireplace. She poked at the embers to make them flare before she added more wood, and then noisily busied herself with the pots and kettles.

Slowly Jonathan pulled himself to his feet, using first a heavy bench and then the wall for support. The wounded muscles in his leg jumped in protest, but at least the pain was real, something he could accept and deal with. *A pirate, for God's sake!*

"I'll have supper for thee soon," Damaris was saying. "Nothing fancy, mind, but thee—"

"I'm not hungry," he said. "Who else knows I'm here, Damaris?"

Damaris paused in her work, but kept her back toward him. "Only my tenants, Daniel and Seth Reed, and the Turners. No one else."

"Another way, then, that I owe you thanks." He watched the way the firelight played across the long curve of her back and the swell of her hips. Tendrils of golden hair escaped from beneath her cap, now knocked endearingly askew on her head. "I know I've caused you trouble enough, but I'll be gone as soon as I'm able. You have my word, for what that's worth."

Now she spun around to face him. "Thee owes me nothing, Jonathan. Thee may leave or thee may stay, whatever thee wishes." Her expression troubled, she swallowed hard and licked her lip. "It was wrong of me not to call out to you, I know, but when the house was dark I was frightened."

He smiled wearily. "Frightened of me, sweetheart? God knows you'd have reason."

"I should never have said that about thee being a pirate," she said vehemently. "It was Daniel who said it first, nothing but another of his rum-born fancies, and then Ruth, who's as likely to believe ill of anyone as not, but I've never believed it myself of thee, not for a moment. What thee did tonight was as much my own fault as thine. Thee was wise to be careful."

"It doesn't matter, Damaris. It doesn't matter at all." He hobbled unsteadily to the trundle bed, cursing himself for being unable to walk straight with her watching. Wincing, he eased himself down on the low bed and lay facing the wall. He did not turn back.

When Damaris came downstairs the next morning, Jonathan was gone.

He had folded the coverlet across the foot of the bed and neatly smoothed the pillow before he left, but there was no other sign that he had been there at all. Damaris couldn't believe he'd leave like this, without at least saying goodbye, and again she blamed herself for repeating Daniel's nonsense about the pirates. She had known how vulnerable Jonathan was, yet she'd babbled on anyway, repeating gossip that he'd probably accepted as gospel.

Yet where could he go? She'd seen last night how much his leg still pained him, and that just from walking ten paces. Suddenly she thought of her pair of chestnut geldings in the barn, Royal and Puck, trained for saddles, as well as for hauling, and she grabbed her cloak and ran toward the barn. Halfway across the yard, she remembered that the horses were still with the wagon at the Turners' house, and as her steps slowed she realized, too, how little faith in Jonathan her suspicion demonstrated. Maybe he was right. Maybe she was frightened of him, not for anything he'd done, but for what she'd let other people tell her, and she shook her head in dismay. What had happened to her own instincts, her own trust in Jonathan?

She looked toward the water, watching the gulls wheel and dance overhead, and far down by the rocks on the point a patch of red caught her eye. She'd have recognized that scarlet coat anywhere. Even from here, she thought she could see the sunlight winking off the twin rows of polished buttons, and her heart leapt with foolish, giddy pleasure at the knowledge that he hadn't yet vanished from her life. With her skirts whipping around her legs, she walked swiftly down the beach to the point.

He was sprawled across the rocks, his wounded leg outstretched and a crude crutch beside it. She was pleased by how much better he looked this morning. The wind had blown the ruddiness back into his cheeks, and, untied, his long, black hair danced around his face. When he squinted into the sun, she saw that his eyes were greener than she'd ever noticed indoors, and she saw, too, that he'd shaved himself, the skin on his jaw scraped a shade pinker beneath the tan.

"I see thee found thy coat," she called, uncertain of his mood after last night.

"I'd have to be blind to miss a coat like this," answered Jonathan dryly, but he patted the rock beside his by way of an invitation. If she wasn't going to mention last night, then he wouldn't, either. Today he was determined to be cheerful, or at least civil.

Nimbly Damaris clambered up to join him, taking care to anchor her billowing skirts securely beneath her legs as she settled on the damp granite. Jonathan liked the way she moved, graceful and confident, without any mincing, ladylike airs, and it was easy, too easy, to remember how perfectly their bodies had fitted together last night. What he'd give to yank that foolish cap off her head and set all that glorious honey-colored hair free in the wind!

But, instead, he felt inside the coat and then held out his hand to her with six gold guineas in his palm. "You're an honest innkeeper, Mistress Allyn, to leave these in my pocket. Here, take it as your reward for all your good services."

Damaris shook her head and kept her hands linked around her knees, but still he held the coins out to her.

"What, no share in my pirate's plunder?" he asked lightly. In profile her face was very serious, her plump little chin resolutely set. "Too pure to be tainted by my ill-gotten gold?"

"Nay, Jonathan, it's not that. I told thee before, my hospitality has no price, but since I know 'tis often the way of others to expect payment, I don't begrudge thee the gesture.'' Her brow furrowed, and impatiently she swept a loose strand of hair back from her face. ''It's how thee keeps speaking of being a pirate, even if in jest. I don't believe it of thee, and I wish I'd never burdened thee with my foolish tales! I wish—''

''Shh, hush now, lass.'' Jonathan tapped one finger across his lips for silence, and then pressed the same finger gently across her own lips. ''I told you last night it didn't matter.''

The intimacy of his finger on her lips startled her, and, flustered, she quickly drew back. Jonathan smiled unevenly, the right side of his mouth cocking upward, and he let his hand drop back to the coins in his other palm. He hadn't intended to touch her, even that tiny bit, but God help him, she was tempting.

''The morning's too fine to spoil it with sad looks and regrets,'' he said lightly. ''No more pirate talk, I swear. But next time, Scheherazade, be careful of the truth behind the tales you spin for me.''

He separated one coin from the rest and dropped it in her apron. ''When one of your men goes to Newport, have him find me a coat that's less gaudy. I've no wish to be spotted ten leagues away, like some prize cardinal. A felt hat and a shirt or two, as well, and tobacco, Virginian, if there's any left over.''

Damaris stared down at the coin, which bore the stern profiles of old King William and Queen Mary. ''Does this mean that thee won't be leaving today?'' she asked in a tiny voice.

''I'll leave when I'm able, or when you toss me out, and neither today seems likely.'' He glanced at her sideways, the lopsided smile once again back in place. "Besides, I'd say winter's been hard on your barn's shingles, and if you don't mend the fences 'round your kitchen garden, you'll have every doe and cony in there waiting for the shoots."

She had the uncomfortable feeling that he was teasing her without her realizing it. "Caleb will get to the roof when he's finished with the spring sowing, and as for fences, there hasn't been a deer or a rabbit on Aquidneck for seventy-five years. On an island, thee only needs to rid thyself of such pests once, and there's an end to them. But what does it matter to thee?"

"Ah, Damaris, I'd hoped to earn my way in your estimable employ, but it seems you've no place for me."

"Thee?" she asked scornfully. "What does thee know of shingles and garden fences?"

"More than I'd care to admit to most men. Keep it a secret between us, lass, but I was born on a farm much like this one, and you'll find me quite tolerably useful splitting shingles and such."

"But thy leg—"

"My leg will benefit mightily from the work, Damaris." To demonstrate, he rose, and with the crutch made his way off the rocks to the beach, awkwardly but without mishap. "It's coddling and cosseting that make men cripples. When I broke this poor selfsame leg before, the surgeon begged to take it off, it was such a pitiful mess. But I proved him wrong, and I'll prove it to you, too."

Damaris scrambled down the rocks to join him. He was one of the few men she didn't meet eye-to-eye or, worse, look down upon, and she liked knowing she didn't have to round her shoulders to seem shorter when she walked beside him. "Then thee is remembering more?"

"More than I did." And more, he thought grimly to himself, than he wished he did. "But step lively, sweetheart. Rabbits or no, I mean to have your fences lashed back together before dinner."

For the next five days, Jonathan worked from sunrise to nightfall around the farm. To Damaris's surprise, he was every bit as skilled as he'd promised, and by the end of the week not only were the garden fences mended and new shingles split for the roof, but the hinge pins on every casement in the house had been oiled to keep them from sticking, a new rope for the well was threaded through the sweep, the guinea hens' house was set once again level on the ground, and the horses' harnesses were pieced and neatly mended. Damaris had to admit that in this brief time Jonathan had done more for Nantasket than Eben had done in six years.

He was unflaggingly cheerful, too, with no hints of moodiness or discontent; nor had he tried to kiss her or touch her again, or to behave in any way that wasn't entirely proper. And yet beneath his good humor she recognized a deep unhappiness, a frustration that all the hard work in the world couldn't ease. Too often she'd catch the desperation in his eyes and knew the images that haunted him as clearly as if he'd spoken, images of himself as a pirate, a murderer, and a thief.

She could see it when he split the shingles, all his energy and concentration focused on swinging the heavy wooden beetle through the air to strike the iron wedge. With his shirt clinging damply to his torso from perspiration, he saw nothing beyond that wedge and the piece of wood he meant to split, and felt none of the pain the effort must have brought to his leg. The beetle never once missed or glanced off the wedge. Every split had to be perfect, and it was that intensity that made her lie awake at night, upstairs, alone, in the big curtained bed she'd shared with Eben. Jonathan was as tightly coiled as overwound clockwork, with every day lived without knowledge of himself another twist of a straining key. It was obvious just to look at Jonathan that he was a physical man. What worried her was the thought that he might be a violent one, as well.

Downstairs in the kitchen, Jonathan's nights were no more restful. He had tried, honestly tried, by his actions to convince both her and himself that he wasn't the man he feared, but one glance at her wide blue eyes showed how wretchedly he was failing. Oh, she smiled shyly when he teased with her, and still treated him to her best cooking like a favored guest, but he saw the truth in how she watched him when she didn't think he noticed, and how she greeted her tenants with too much enthusiasm, urging them to remain with trumped-up excuses as if she needed a blasted chaperon.

He'd been right, of course. He, Jonathan Sparhawk, or whoever the devil he was, frightened her. All the fence-fixing in the world wouldn't convince her that he might not slit her throat some night, and deep down he wasn't convinced he wouldn't, either. Killing that sailor had been easy enough. And what about the friends he no doubt had, men as wicked as himself, who might come to Nantasket seeking him? What would become of her then?

He worked each day until he was barely able to stumble to his bed from exhaustion, but as soon as he lay in the dark, he began to think of Damaris, and instantly his body would be taut and awake, every weary muscle aching for her. The more time he spent in her company, the more he longed to find with her the pleasure that that first fever-bound kiss had promised. He wanted her with an intensity that stunned him. But most of all he yearned to claim a small moment of the peace she seemed always to carry with her, the chance to both find and lose himself in her embrace.

He had to leave. He had no honest reason for staying. In another fortnight, he'd be strong enough to find a berth on some vessel, even if it was only some wretched coaster. He had to leave Nantasket before he defiled and destroyed the one good thing in his life. He only prayed she would understand.

The sun had already dipped below the hill and taken the weak spring warmth with it. Ruth had left to begin supper for her family, and alone Damaris hurried to finish clearing the dead leaves and branches from around the apple trees before the sun truly set and First Day began. As her long-toothed rake scraped through the dry weeds, she thought of Jonathan re-

pairing the pasture fences with the Reeds, and hoped
that this once Daniel had been able to keep his rumshop prattle to himself. She bent to toss a fallen branch
aside, and didn't see the man until he called her name.

"You be Mistress Allyn, don't ye?" he demanded,
and swiftly Damaris straightened, the rake crossways
in her hands. Another stranger—for all love, must
every tide bring one this spring?—and from his
clothes, another sailor, though hardly of the same
rank as Jonathan. The man wore wide-legged trou-
sers of patched sail canvas, and a stained striped
waistcoat that hung like a petticoat beneath his short
jacket. A length of calico was tied loosely around his
throat, and where his graying hair had thinned, the top
of his head was as brown and leathery as the skin on
his face.

When she didn't answer immediately, he spat and
scratched the back of his neck, clearly annoyed. "Get
on wit' ye now, woman, an' tell yer man Sam Hull be
here t' see him."

"I'm sorry to tell thee that thee has traveled for
naught, Sam Hull," said Damaris uneasily, wishing
that Ruth were still here with her. She heard the crack
of a dry branch to her left, and saw then the second
man, smaller and younger than Sam Hull, but no
more respectable in a filthy calamico coat. Her fingers tightened on the rake in her hands. "My husband died last autumn."

"I told ye he weren't here, Sam," said the smaller
man. His front teeth were missing, and a faint whistle
punctuated his speech. "Else he wouldn't've left his
woman all alone."

"Sometimes I don't believe you've got a thimbleful o' wits 'tween yer ears, Elijah Barnum," declared Hull irritably. "If she be a widow-woman, her man can't be here, can he?"

Barnum whistled to himself, but showed neither grief nor surprise at Eben's death. No close friends, then, decided Damaris, or perhaps they'd already heard it elsewhere. But why pretend not to know?

"Eben Allyn owed me money," said Hull bluntly. "Ye bein' his widow, I 'spect ye shall want to settle his score all proper for him."

"Why would Eben have owed thee money?" asked Damaris, the old fear of Eben's debts haunting her again.

"He owed it t' nigh everyone else in Newport," said Elijah, and he sniggered until Hull glared at him.

"Your husband owed me twenty-five guineas for something he needed done in a business way. Well, now it be done, an' I 'spect to be paid what's owed me."

"I won't give thee a ha'penny without more proof than thy say-so," said Damaris, striving to be firm and to keep the tremor from her voice. She didn't believe these men at all, but she didn't have the twenty-five guineas she feared it would take to make them leave, either. "Not a ha'penny, Sam Hull."

Hull scowled and shook his head from side to side like a dog worrying a bone. "That won't do, mistress, won't do at all. Robbin' a man o' what be rightly his! What would yer old man say?"

"He'd say it was time thee was on thy way, the same as I'll tell thee now," said Damaris, determined to be brave. They were trespassing on her land, and she had every right to ask them to leave. "Thee had best hurry. The road to Newport can be a trial for travelers after dark."

Hull's scowl deepened. Before Damaris could stop him, he snatched the rake from her and grabbed her wrists, jerking her close to him. She gasped and tried to pull free, but Barnum shoved her back into Hull's chest. As Damaris struggled, she could hear his odd sibilant laughter behind her.

"I don't figure we be leaving yet, mistress," said Hull, his breath strong with rum and onions. "There be other ways t'settle your debt. Ye must get a mite lonely out here anyways, bein' a widow an' all."

"Let her go," thundered Jonathan from behind them. In his hands was a musket he'd found in the barn, the flint primed and the latch drawn back as he aimed at the sailor.

Instantly Hull obeyed, his hands held up and his eyes staring as he backed away. "I—I meant th' lady no harm," he stammered. "I only meant to startle her a bit. See fer yerself, she's come t' no ill!"

"What I want to see is you heading back to whatever rat's hole you crawled out of," said Jonathan. "And if I ever see any part of either of you on this land again, I'll nail your black hides to the masthead myself."

Hull didn't wait to answer, trotting and stumbling away through the apple trees, with Barnum at his heels. Jonathan watched them go, then lowered the gun from his shoulder, his hand shaking slightly from the rage he'd barely held in check. What if he hadn't seen the men first, far enough off on the road to let him fetch the musket from the house? When Jonathan thought of what could have happened if he hadn't, what that filthy, seafaring trash could have done to her, he was certain he could have killed both men outright.

He forced a smile to his face and turned toward Damaris, his arms outstretched. As much as he wanted to comfort her, he, too, needed reassurance that she was unharmed, that he'd rescued her in time.

But gratitude was very far from Damaris's mind. Angry patches of red showed bright on her cheeks as she marched up to Jonathan. Without a word, she wrested the musket from his hands, and with both hands tossed it end over end into the pile of leaves. Then she stared up at Jonathan's stunned face, her eyes flashing with fury.

''As long as thee is on my land, as my guest, thee must never, *ever* shame me like that again!''

Chapter Six

"What in high holy blazes are you talking about?" demanded Jonathan. "You could have shot us both dead, tossing a musket like that!" He limped toward the pile of sticks and old leaves where the gun had landed, but she raced there first and stood blocking his way with her hands on her hips.

"Nay, thee must leave the cursed thing there! Tomorrow I'll throw it in the ocean, and the world will be rid of one more piece of man's foolishness!" He tried again to retrieve the gun, but she stepped in front of him, glowering fiercely.

"Damaris, have you lost your wits?" he said in exasperation. "I'll grant it's not the best musket I've ever held, but to throw it in the ocean . . ."

"Where did thee get it? Did Daniel buy it for thee? If he did, the little rogue—"

"Don't blame him. I found it Tuesday in the barn, wrapped in an old trading blanket. Powder and bullets, too."

For a long moment, she studied him, her eyes slanted suspiciously. Then she turned and scrambled into the leaves, pulling the musket out by the barrel.

"God in heaven, Damaris, you'll blow your own head off!" This time Jonathan grabbed the gun from her hands and quickly disarmed the flint, while Damaris, heedless of his warning, peered at a carved mark on the stock.

"It *is* Eben's!" she cried, and made a little wordless cry. "He swore to me that he'd given up all firearms! He promised he'd never keep another one on Nantasket, and I believed him, and now it seems all the time we were wed he'd kept one hidden. He swore it to me, Jonathan, and he *lied!*"

Abruptly she turned away from Jonathan, unwilling to let him see the angry, unshed tears so perilously close to spilling over. She couldn't believe that Eben had treated his oath to her so lightly, and it hurt. Furiously she lashed out at the nearest tree, striking her open palm hard enough against the rough bark to scrape the skin raw. She yelped and shook her hand as if she could shake away the pain. *Here then, Damaris, is the swift reward for thy intemperance!*

Jonathan had considered offering a convenient shoulder to cry on, but thought better of it after she hit the tree. "Mayhap I'm just thicker than an old stump, sweetheart," he said tentatively, "but why the devil would you make a man swear off his musket?"

She spun around to face him again, clutching her scraped hand. "It's not me, Jonathan, it's the world," she said urgently. "Unless men can learn to put aside their differences and their weapons and trust in God, there will never be any sort of harmony."

"You mean, after all those fat Newport Quakers have done to you, you still believe their prattle?" he asked incredulously. "Oh, I'll grant you it makes for a pretty enough sermon from the parson on the Sabbath—"

"Friends don't have sermons or parsons," she said crossly, "or Sabbaths, either."

"Damaris, listen to me! You can't live out here alone without some way to protect yourself. Eben knew that. If he kept this musket, he did it to keep you safe."

"Safe! If muskets are to keep thee safe, then why does thee hobble about from the hole one left in thy leg?"

"The things don't fire themselves, Damaris," Jonathan explained with what he judged remarkable patience. "You can pitch every last musket and pistol into the ocean, and you won't stop men from trying to slaughter each other piecemeal. They'll just turn to knives, or hatchets, or whatever else lies handy. Fists work well enough."

"So thee simply refuses to understand." Damaris folded her arms across her chest with an unspoken resignation that infuriated Jonathan. "At least thee is honest, which is more than Eben was. But I cannot condone thy show of violence, not on my land."

"Who just hit the damned tree?" he thundered.

Damaris felt her cheeks redden, but she clung to her composure as she held out her hand. "Please, Jonathan, return the gun to me."

"Nay, I will not." He lifted the musket up over his head and held it there, out of her reach. "I'll wager I'm every bit as dishonest as your old husband, because as long as I'm here I'm not going to watch you play at being a meek little dove waiting for some fox like Hull to snatch you up. Why the devil would your Eben owe money to a rascal like that?''

Jonathan was surprised by her reaction—the dismay in the way her mouth popped open, and the quick, unexpected guilt that made her eyes look hurriedly away from his own. What could she possibly have to hide?

''I—I never questioned Eben's affairs,'' she stammered, and she knew from his half smile that Jonathan didn't believe her. She'd be lost altogether if he asked anything more, she'd grow flustered and babble out everything about Eben and the smuggling.

''Why would your husband have anything to do with a rascal like that?'' he asked again, watching her closely. ''What will you do if Hull comes back?''

''He won't,'' said Damaris, swallowing hard. ''On Second Day, I'll go to Newport and swear out a statement against him with Eben's brother. Thee can be certain that if Sam Hull's anywhere near Newport, Roger will see to it that he'll cause me no more trouble.''

Slowly Jonathan lowered the musket, resting the butt on the ground. Damaris seemed past fighting over it now, and besides, his arm had gotten tired holding the musket in the air. ''What makes this Roger such a power of goodness?''

''Because he's the magistrate in charge of the naval court.'' Damaris sighed, and nibbled impatiently on her lower lip. She didn't really want to go to Roger, but it seemed the only way to stop Jonathan from asking any more questions. ''Of course Roger's very worldly, and he shared no love with Eben—nor with me, either—but I think he has a conscience, and will tend to this if I ask him.''

Staring out into the deepening twilight, Jonathan didn't reply. What did it matter if her brother-in-law was the sailors' magistrate? Damaris hadn't sold him off for a reward yet, and he doubted she'd do it now. But the thought of being so close to the law made Jonathan uncomfortably aware of what might be at risk. He'd seen convicted men hanged, from public gibbets and from yardarms, and it wasn't a pleasant way to die.

He could be gone tonight once she was asleep. He could head for the docks, and any vessel that would take him. But where would that leave Damaris? He looked at her now, standing before him, her cap and her grubby apron ghostly pale in the twilight. She was frowning down at the scraped place on her hand, and with her head bowed she seemed achingly vulnerable. She had saved his life without question. How could he go off and leave her alone to risk her own?

"I'll come with you to Newport," he said before he could change his mind. "I don't want you alone until this is settled."

She glanced up at him sternly without lifting her head. "I don't need thee to protect me."

"Nay, lass, you're wrong," he said. "You do, and I will."

Roger leaned forward in his leather-backed chair, his hands clasped on the desk before him, as he listened to Damaris describe the sailor who'd threat-

ened her. Roger's expression was grave, and he nodded
and clicked his tongue and asked the appropriate
questions, but inwardly his satisfaction grew with
every word his sister-in-law earnestly told him. When
Hull hadn't returned to claim the other half of his
promised ten shillings, Roger had decided the sailor
had changed his mind and fled with the sure money in
his pocket. But now it seemed the man had done his
task, and done it well. Eben's little Quaker wife had
come running to Newport for reassurance. No real
harm had come to her, but she was nervous and she
was scared, and Roger could not have been more satisfied.

"And so you chased this villain off your property
yourself?" he asked, managing to sound properly
outraged. "The mere thought of a lady forced to defend herself as you have done is almost unbearable!"

Damaris hesitated and blushed, staring down at her
lap in confusion. Oh, aye, thought Roger with pleasure, the experience had been quite dreadful for her,
and he consciously softened his tone. "If it is too
painful for you to describe . . ."

"Thee is kindness itself, Roger," Damaris murmured, her hands twisting the edge of her apron. How
could she possibly finish her story without mention-
ing Jonathan? Already a half-dozen times before she'd
nearly said his name, and she felt drained and on edge
from the effort of weighing every word before she
spoke it. She thought she'd been clever enough, leaving Jonathan with the horses near Long Wharf and
walking the rest of the way alone, but she hadn't
counted on her own nervousness. Coming to Roger

had been a mistake from the first, and it was all Jonathan's fault anyway. If he hadn't made such a fuss over the musket, then she wouldn't have had to prove herself by swearing out a complaint. *He* had driven her to this! Nantasket would be overrun by Roger's revenue men, and it was all Jonathan's fault.

"No, my dear, you've told me enough," declared Roger. "I won't press you further." He drew a sheet of paper from the drawer and began to write quickly, the pen scratching across the page. With a relieved sigh, Damaris slumped back in her chair.

With an answering sigh of his own, Roger threw down the pen and shook his head. "My hands are tied, sister. To let this outrage go unpunished on Allyn land pains me no end, but I have no men, no resources at my disposal."

Damaris's eyes widened as she realized what he was saying. "But Evelyn said thee had a special patrol—"

Roger frowned, crossing his arms over his lace-frilled chest. "Then my lady wife has, I fear, spoken out of turn. I'd like to put an end to the outlaws who plunder our land and our seas, but the governor sees it differently." There, he thought with satisfaction, that should do it. Her eyes were as wide as a deer's caught in a lantern's light. "My hands are tied."

"Then thee will do nothing?" she asked incredulously, her voice squeaking, oddly high. Lord, she couldn't believe her good fortune! "Thee will send no one to Nantasket?"

Sorrowfully Roger shook his head, the long curls of his wig grazing the desk. "I cannot, Damaris, and it grieves me thoroughly to admit it. However, I can of-

fer you a haven here, in my home, a guaranteed ref-
uge, if you wish to honor Evelyn and myself—''

"Oh, nay, Roger that won't be necessary," said
Damaris, already standing and retying her cloak about
her shoulders. She couldn't wait to tell Jonathan,
though of course he couldn't appreciate how well everything had turned out. "I thank thee for thy concern, of course, but I won't burden thee any further.
Thee is generosity itself to open thy home to me, but
there is far too much that requires my presence at
Nantasket. Thee must give my respects to Evelyn. Nay,
stay where thee is, I can find my own way."

Instantly Roger was on his feet, chagrined that she'd
stood before him. "Damaris, please, reconsider. At
least stay tonight and dine with us, and think over the
danger you're courting by remaining alone at a lonely
farm!"

"Oh, nay, Roger, I can't, not tonight, not with—"
She broke off, barely before saying Jonathan's name,
and her cheeks scarlet as she lamely stumbled on.
"Not without notice to Evelyn, I mean. But next
week, on Second Day, I will come, if thee wishes."

Roger bowed graciously. "So it shall be, Damaris.
We will be honored."

But she was already out the door, and through the
window Roger could see her rushing down the street,
her cloak flapping out behind her. He could have
sworn she'd been on the edge of staying in Newport
with him, and yet at the last she'd decided to return to
the farm. He'd simply have to try again, that was all,
let slip a few more lurid tales to Evelyn before Damaris came to dinner, and make sure he left them

alone. Maybe he'd drop a word or two to some of the Quaker elders on her behalf, and try to lure her back to town that way. If that didn't work, he'd send some other man out to Nantasket again, and this time tell him to be rough, to do whatever was necessary to change her mind.

Roger glanced down at the nonsense he'd written as she had described Hull. With a grunt, he crumpled the paper in his fist and tossed it into the fire. Damaris Allyn was a strange, unpredictable creature, with none of the graces he prized in a woman, and scarcely a penny to her soul before Eben had been mad enough to wed her. But she was, after all, only a woman, and Roger had little doubt that she would at last bend to his wishes.

Jonathan sat in the farthest corner of the tavern, the dank wooden tankard still half-full on the table before him. It had perhaps been cowardly not to go with Damaris, but magistrates and swearing oaths against trespassers . . . No, that would have been pushing his luck. Instead, he had purposely chosen a tavern that catered to common seamen, and with two days' growth of beard to darken his jaw, and the well-worn clothing that Daniel had bought, he had hoped no one would recognize him, and no one had. From habit he had taken a bench with his back against the wall and a clear view of the doorway, ready to fight or flee, whichever seemed wiser. From habit, too, he would have welcomed the former course, even with a bad leg. Although Damaris had glowered and outright forbidden him to bring the musket, she would have savored his compliance less if she'd known about the knife tucked into the top of his boot.

Jonathan smiled wryly to himself, remembering how stiff and proud she'd been beside him on the wagon seat on the trip into town. For two days now, she had spoken to him only when she had to, and she'd made it very clear she didn't want him to come with her today. He'd scarcely let her out of his sight the whole time, and maybe that was what had made her so prickly. Despite her habitual reserve, he knew she watched him whenever she thought he didn't notice, watched him with a healthy interest that was anything but modest. She was, after all, a Quaker, not a nun. That first night, when they'd kissed, had proved that, and he liked the idea that she might be suffering as much as he.

But he was positive there was more to her silence than that Quakerly foolishness about the gun, and more, too, to Sam Hull's visit, than she wanted to admit. None of it made his decision to watch over her any easier.

He swirled the rum around his tongue, thinking. He'd realized, once he'd taken the time to notice, that Nantasket was full of riddles. Nearly everything in the house was imported, from the kettles in the kitchen to the caneback chairs in the parlor. Clearly, Eben Allyn had liked his comforts, regardless of the cost. But the farm itself was mostly fallow, the fields left to turn wild, and the pasture untouched for years. How, then, had Eben purchased all those new London goods?

And his death hadn't left Damaris wanting, either. Maybe she really did know as little of her husband's affairs as she claimed, but she certainly wasn't chary with the profits. When she had left the horses at the stable, Jonathan had seen the little pouch she'd pulled from her pocket, heavy from the coins inside it. Farmers traded or bartered for goods, not for hard money, and certainly not with nonexistent crops.

Across the room, a tall man with a voice too loud from liquor slammed his tankard on the bare planks of the table. "And I tell you, ye worthless cur, that Cap'n Graham treats his men right an' fair! You join up wit' us, an' in a fortnight you'll have all the fancy ladies dancin' on yer whim, yer pockets will be so weighed down wit' French an' Spanish gold!"

His companion only shrugged and tapped his pipe clean on the edge of the bench. "Ye can stow yer captains an' yer promises. Before I go fightin' any Spaniards, I mean t' know th' vessel. This sloop *Tiger,* now, she come sprung up from nowhere, wit' no man t' swear t' her worthiness. An' what of th' rest o' th' people, eh? I won't serve wit' no gold-hungry landsmen."

Jonathan had heard enough. With only a royal charter to mark the difference, privateering was close to pirating, and in his present mood Jonathan found his conscience already too burdened to listen to the sailors argue. Disgusted, he quickly downed the rest of his rum and tossed a coin to the pock-faced serving wench.

Damaris found him in the stable yard, listening to the hostler and absently scratching the muzzle of one of her chestnut geldings. Beneath the broad brim of his felt hat, his face was set, and his thoughts were clearly far away. It was, decided Damaris, almost as if the trip to Newport had switched their moods. Relief made her feel almost giddy, happier than she'd felt in weeks, while Jonathan seemed grimly withdrawn into himself. Perhaps it was the rum so evident on his breath. Spirits had often made Eben gloomy. Maybe Jonathan was like that, as well, and she couldn't resist a little self-righteous sniff as he passed near to her. Though she benefited by it, she never had understood why worldly men chose to poison themselves with strong drink.

Without a word, Jonathan boosted her up on to the seat of the cart, and climbed in beside her. He maneuvered the horses easily through the crowded streets, and once they had reached the rutted path that was the only road to Nantasket Point, he let Royal and Puck set their own pace, the harnesses jingling merrily. With both hands, Damaris clung purposefully to the bench seat instead of to Jonathan as the two-wheeled cart bounced and jostled over the uneven ground, far faster than Daniel or Caleb ever dared. If the axle cracked or they lost a wheel, Damaris felt certain, they'd be dead in an instant.

But with the wind in her face and the cloudless spring sky overhead, the Sound, to the south of them, a deep and sparkling blue, Damaris found it impossible to feel anything but the purest joy in being alive. Shyly she glanced up at Jonathan, wishing today he'd be more sociable.

"Something you'd like to say, Damaris?" he asked over the rumble of the cart wheels, his eyes remaining on the horses and the road. The April afternoon had lifted his spirits, as well, almost as much as having Damaris looking pleasingly contrite beside him.

Self-consciously Damaris ducked her head and chewed on her lower lip, wondering if he expected her to apologize. Because of that wretched gun of Eben's, she knew, she'd been a shrew toward Jonathan these last days, but she wasn't sure how to begin being civil again. "The day is very fair, isn't it?"

"Fair enough," he agreed. "Couldn't beg the Maker for one finer."

"Aye, that's true." Damaris took a deep breath, wishing she was more adept at conversation. Why was she never lost for words when he angered her?

"Anything else you'd like to tell me?" Jonathan half hoped she'd volunteer how the meeting with her brother-in-law had gone, but Damaris just shook her head, her cheeks a bright pink. Ah, well, he thought mildly, there was time enough to ask her outright.

"Lost in your own thoughts, then," he continued. "No harm to that, is there? Unless you're considering how close you came to sending me off to my reward with Eben's old musket. Now, those kinds of thoughts I couldn't countenance, not and enjoy this fine, fair day."

"Nay, Jonathan, thee must know I didn't mean thee any harm!" Damaris cried, turning toward him. But then she saw how his mouth twitched, the merriment crinkling his eyes as he tried not to laugh. Teasing meant he wasn't angry with her. Roger wasn't going to send soldiers to Nantasket, and Jonathan still liked her well enough to tease her. She glanced again at Jonathan, tipped back her head and laughed, the joyful, lighthearted peals of laughter rippling out across the fields around.

For a moment, Jonathan just stared at her. With surprise, he realized that this was the first time he'd heard her laugh, and he found the sound enchanting. She looked years younger, and impossibly pretty, her blue eyes snapping and her cheeks rosy from the wind, and he let his own deep, rich laughter mingle happily with hers. For her to put aside her seriousness like this for him was a special gift he hadn't expected, and he wondered if she, too, realized the sudden, subtle shift in their relationship.

They rode on in comfortable silence, neither one willing to break the mood by speaking. At the top of a small hill crowned by a cluster of wind-gnarled pines, Jonathan drew the horses to a halt, and Damaris turned toward him questioningly.

"Down with you, now," he ordered with mock seriousness. "Go on, I want you over by the bayberries."

"Why should I?" she answered, her chin high with defiance, but a smile still on her lips. "We're nowhere near home, and I can't fancy an honest reason why thee would set me out on the road like this."

"Damaris, please. If I haven't murdered you before this, I'm not likely to do so here, in the middle of the day, in plain view of the road," he said patiently. "Now go wait for me there, and either cover your eyes or turn your back."

Still she hesitated, more from curiosity than from coquettishness. "Why?"

"So I can surprise you, sweetheart," he said, a hint of irritation finally creeping into his tone. "High holy blazes, if all you women Friends are such a suspicious lot, it's a wonder the sect hasn't died out entirely."

That cut a bit too close to the truth for Damaris. She scrambled down over the wheel and to the ground with as much dignity as she could muster, and went to stand on the spot he indicated, beside the twisted trees. She covered her eyes gingerly, with just her fingertips, her elbows akimbo. Planned surprises like the one Jonathan had promised were outside her experience, and despite his assurances, she felt oddly vulnerable, her heart quickening.

She heard the wagon creak as he dismounted, and his uneven steps across the grass as he came to stand before her. There was the squeak of dry willow—a basket?—and the rattle of crockery, and Damaris's curiosity grew.

"All's well, sweetheart," said Jonathan at last. "Now open those pretty blue eyes of yours."

Damaris lowered her hands from her eyes and gasped. Spread before her on a cloth on the grass was the most lavish supper a Newport innkeeper could put up on short notice: a small roast goose stuffed with hard-cooked eggs, sweet onions pickled in vinegar, a wedge of Gloucester cheese, preserved cherries, a round loaf of fine-milled wheat flour, and a cake dark with Spanish raisins. Beside the empty basket that had carried the food sprawled Jonathan, leaning back on his elbows. He grinned happily, delighting in Damaris's obvious pleasure as she knelt down on the grass beside him.

"Thee can't know what this means to me," she began, then stopped, overwhelmed. She could only smile and shake her head in wonder, her eyes bright with unexpected tears.

"I know all you've done for me, lass," said Jonathan gruffly, touched by her response. It hadn't been easy to think of a gift she'd accept—the usual ribbons and gewgaws wouldn't suit Damaris—but her genuine pleasure in the simple meal made him feel more like a king than if he'd showered her with pearls. "You've treated me right well when you'd neither reason nor need, and this trifle's but a small way to show my thanks."

"'Tis I who owe thee now, Jonathan. A feast like this—I cannot recall when another cooked for me last, and not I for others. Not since my mother came ill, and that when I was ten."

She felt herself babbling, and broke off again, staring down into her apron before she slowly raised her gaze to meet his. He was smiling, squinting in the bright afternoon light, all the little lines radiating from his impossibly green eyes. To the left of his upper lip was a tiny crescent scar, pale against his ruddy tan, and she wondered that she'd never noticed it before. How many other things about him would she miss when he left her?

"Ah, Jonathan," she said softly. "Thee can't know how much thee has given me already." As carefully as if she feared he might shatter beneath her touch, she reached out to place her hand on Jonathan's arm, her fingers resting on the rough wool frieze of his coat. She was being very bold, very forward, and part of her conscience warned of the consequences. But somehow, today, beneath this springtime sun, consequences didn't seem to matter much, and she watched the grin fade from Jonathan's face.

What the devil was happening? wondered Jonathan. He had meant to thank her, not seduce her, and yet he had the unnerving feeling that she'd decided otherwise. He stared into her wide, serious eyes, and told himself he must be mistaken. He tried to think of how he—they—shouldn't be doing this. But, almost imperceptibly, she was coming closer, leaning into him. Her lower lip quivered uncertainly as her mouth neared his, and already the fragance of her skin filled his senses. He tried to think—

Hell, he was tired of thinking. Instead, he caught her around the waist and pulled her down on the grass beside him.

Chapter Seven

Last summer's dry grass rustled beneath Damaris's cloak as she sank back onto the ground, with Jonathan's arm curled possessively around her waist. As he bent over her, she tentatively reached up to touch his jaw, feeling the stubble of his beard rough beneath her fingertips as his long hair fell forward to graze the back of her hand. A faint hint of rum still clung to him, now blended inextricably for her with the dark, masculine scent—oiled leather and salt spray and tobacco—that was his alone. His eyes were half-closed, their expression shadowed by his lashes, and beneath his scrutiny Damaris felt excitement tightening in her chest.

In her bed alone, sleepless, she had imagined this moment times beyond counting, and yet the reality of it, of Jonathan himself, made her feel suddenly shy and awkward. She was a widow, not some skittish, callow maid, and she was here beside Jonathan by her own choice. But her husband had only desired her in their bed, by night and with the curtains drawn tight around them, and he would never have tumbled her in a meadow by the sea in the golden light of day. But neither had Eben made her blood quicken in her veins and her breath grow short, the way Jonathan could just by looking at her with his green cat's eyes, looking at her as he was now. She'd never forgotten what it had been like to kiss him that one time before, and breathlessly she longed to learn if it could be like that again.

"Relax, lass, I'm not about to gobble you up in one great bite, you know," he said lightly, tracing the bow of her lips with his forefinger. "You're really far too lovely to waste that way."

She felt her cheeks grow warm at his teasing. "Thee speaks foolishness, Jonathan." She meant to chide him, but her shy smile betrayed the unexpected pleasure she'd found in his compliment. "Stuff and nonsense, that's all it is."

"Truth, Damaris, it's only the truth." Gently he untied the laces of her little cap, and as he tugged it off, her hairpins came with it. Freed, the thick coil of her hair unwound and tumbled loose like captured sunlight around her face and shoulders, and he buried his fingers deep in the silken mass. With her hair unbound, she was once again the woman he'd kissed in his fever-bound dreams, the passionate woman who had ever since hidden herself from him behind a wall of ritual modesty. He saw how her blue eyes were clouded with desire, darkening like the sky before a storm. Realizing she wanted him was like a stimulant—not that he needed one, not with his own body already tense and demanding with anticipation.

"Ah, my sweet Scheherazade," he murmured, his voice dark and low. "What tales shall we write together, eh?"

With a small shudder of anticipation, Damaris closed her eyes and lifted her pursed mouth expectantly toward his. Jonathan smiled to himself at the eager inexperience of the gesture. Old Eben might have been her husband, but clearly the man had never wooed her like a lover, never showed her the intricacies of pleasure between men and women. Jonathan would not be so selfish. Ignoring her mouth, his lips instead swept across her cheeks, her chin, the throbbing pulse at her throat, feather-light and teasing, until she moaned at the unexpected sensations. At last he sought her lips, savoring their softness for the breath of a moment before his mouth crushed down on hers.

Damaris arched into the hard line of his body, striving to keep pace with the desire that now seemed bent on sweeping her away. She slid her hands up his arms, and her fingers clutched at his shoulders as she melted against him, molding her body to fit more completely against his.

In return, he shifted closer, the hard, muscled length of his thigh tangling in her skirts as he pressed between her legs. She shivered as his hand caressed the column of her throat, his fingers spreading across her shoulder and beneath her linen kerchief. Deftly he loosened the lacings of her bodice and eased the fabric lower. Her lips broke free from his, and she gasped as he cupped one breast, deliberately working his work-hardened palm across her nipple in lazy, tantalizing circles. Slowly his lips traced the same path, pausing only to mark the wild pounding of her life-blood at her throat. There was for Damaris a moment when only the cool spring breeze caressed the tenderness of her breast. Then Jonathan's mouth found her, and she cried out as pleasure rippled through her, her fingers twining tightly in his hair as she cradled his head close to her.

Jonathan doubted he'd ever desired a woman more than he wanted Damaris now. He suckled hungrily at her breast, the taste of her unbelievably sweet. What little hold he had managed to keep on his own need was rapidly unraveling, and he didn't care. He couldn't. All thought and feeling and desire centered on her and her alone.

Damaris clung to him desperately, yearning for what only he could give. Every kiss, every caress, increased the strange tension growing tighter and tighter within her body, the sweet agony of a pleasure she had never known before. Jonathan had already carried her far beyond what she'd shared with Eben, and instinctively she knew that only Jonathan could bring her back. She would trust him because she had to, because she had no choice and didn't want one. Only Jonathan.

"Love me, Jonathan," she whispered raggedly. "Oh, love me!"

Love me.

The simple words pierced Jonathan as surely as polished steel. His heart pounding with unfulfilled desire, he laid his cheek on the silky pillow of her breasts and closed his eyes, trying to deny what he knew to be true. *Love me.* A woman like Damaris wouldn't say that carelessly, not even in passion. For her it would mean more than the act alone, endlessly more. *Love me.* Too well he knew what she was asking, and that he couldn't begin to give it to her. How could he offer her the future she deserved, when he still had no past to begin it? An afternoon's seductive pleasure between a woman and a man, a common coupling in a meadow—that was all he had to offer Damaris Allyn, and it could never begin to be enough. He had killed and he had stolen, but if he took her now, like this, knowing he would be gone from Nantasket as soon as he was able—that would be the worst thing he'd ever done.

Oh, love me...

His breathing still labored, he rolled away from her and willed himself to stand. "Get up," he said abruptly, frustration turning his voice harsh. She lay frozen at his feet, her mouth full and her breasts swollen from his kisses, her eyes wide with confusion. How had he let this happen at all? Her simple dark clothing in disarray was more erotic to him than a whole London brothel's worth of lace and satin, and he raked his shaking hands back through his hair, trying to drive the image from his mind. "Get up, damn it!"

"Thee—thee must not swear at me," Damaris whispered as she found her voice at last. Unsteadily she rose to her knees, pulling her clothing back into place. She felt almost ill from unfulfillment, the unrelieved tension making her fingers shake. Jonathan's face was rigid with disgust, and he couldn't even bear to meet her eyes. What had she done to make him turn on her like this? she wondered desperately. Why had everything gone so hideously wrong between them?

It was the clumsiness with which she tried to redress her hair that finally touched Jonathan, the lumpy, lopsided knot in place of the sleek twist beneath the simple cap. He had meant to save her, not hurt her, not like this.

"Forgive me, Damaris," he said wearily. "God knows I didn't want this to happen between us. But to have you there waiting, so full of love and passion... I couldn't do it, Damaris."

Mutely Damaris nodded, the color draining from her face. Now she understood. He didn't—no, *couldn't*—love her. How much clearer could it be?

Belatedly Jonathan held out his hand to help her to her feet, but she ignored him, concentrating instead on repacking the forgotten goose in the basket. If she kept her hands busy, perhaps she could overcome this sick feeling of shame and humiliation, and the awful pain that went with it.

Miserably Jonathan watched her piling the food blindly into the basket, all her customary careful order gone. "Damaris, please, listen to me—"

"Nay, don't, thee's said enough already!" she cried. She scrambled to her feet, her hands clenched around the basket's willow handle, her knuckles white. "I have been the most foolish woman under God's heaven, and I have none to blame but myself. No man save my husband has ever desired me before. Why should thee be any different? I'm not fair like Evelyn, nor can I say clever things to make thee laugh, and I'm tall and graceless as a stork.''

"Nay, Damaris, never that." Why was it that nothing he ever planned with her turned out as it should? He stepped forward to catch her in his arms, to hold her again and show her how wrong she was, but she darted back, the heavy basket swinging awkwardly from her hand.

"Thee must not pity me, Jonathan. That I couldn't bear." Her voice cracked with anguish but her eyes stayed dry, and she gave a little shrug of her shoulders, as if to shed her misery. "I mistook thy kindness for something else, and that is all thee need ever know. That, and that I am sorry.''

"I'm sorry, too," he said softly. Although she wouldn't trust anything he said now, he hated letting so much misunderstanding hang between them. Yet maybe it was better this way. This way she wouldn't believe him to be something he wasn't, and she wouldn't miss him when he finally left. Better, cleaner. So why did he feel as if he'd just been kicked in the stomach?

He reached for the basket, and she let him take it, staring resolutely past him, as if he weren't there. "Come along now, Damaris," he said, surprising himself with his own impassivity. "High time we headed home.''

With a thump, Ruth dropped the heavy basket of fresh-washed laundry on the kitchen floor. "So yer prize bull's taken himself off, then?" she asked, cocking her head to indicate the empty place where Jonathan's trundle bed had been.

"I'll thank thee not to be so common, Ruth," answered Damaris tartly, even as she blushed, remembering the awful afternoon before in the meadow. "If thee means Jonathan, he's moved his things to the loft in the barn, that's all. With his leg almost healed, there's no reason for him to remain in here."

But Ruth only laughed, easing Eli from the sling on her back where she had carried him Indian-style. "So all his brawn an' pretty face were naught but show, eh? More's the pity fer ye, mistress. He had the look o' a woman-pleasing rogue, but ye can't always trust th' truth o' yer eyes to judge yer livestock, can ye?"

"Ruth!"

The older woman chuckled knowingly as she sat on the bench and unlaced her bodice to feed the wriggling baby in her lap. "Whatever th' reason, it's good he's gone from yer hearth, mistress. Word come t' Daniel through his cousin this morning that yer Dutchman's due at the Point tonight."

"Tonight!" Dismayed, Damaris sank down on the bench beside Ruth. "I'd written to Captain de Vere not to come at all this month, let alone this soon. Why, he's scarce had the time to sail to New York and back. And tonight, of all nights! I'm pledged to dine with Roger and Evelyn in town, and of course I must go, but I must be there for Captain de Vere, as well. Oh, Ruth, why tonight?"

"'Tis not so bad, mistress. You go on to yer brother's house. If de Vere comes—ye know half the time he don't, leastways not when he says—then I'll send one o' my lads to fetch ye an' Caleb home.''

Damaris rubbed the back of her hand, considering. ''I can tell Roger the lambing's begun. Roger's so much bound up by town living now, he wouldn't question that. And if I'm in his house, he won't suspect me.''

Ruth nodded wisely. ''Ye can go straight t' the beach or t' the cave, without comin' back here, and without that Jonathan man seein' what yer about.'' Her golden eyes narrowed with suspicion. ''Oh, he's been cheerful enough, workin' like any other man in yer hire, but there be something about him that still rings false t' my mind.''

''He is not, I think, a man at peace with himself,'' said Damaris carefully, ''but I don't believe him to be as wicked as thee suspects.''

''Ye be too kind by half, mistress, always lookin' fer the good, even if none be there t' find. The sooner that one's gone from here, an' not just t' the barn, the better fer us all.'' She rocked gently back and forth as she nursed the baby, the hammered brass hoops at her ears catching the sunlight from the windows. She grinned suddenly at Damaris. ''Ye know well I wouldn't've said those things about ye an' him if I believed true you'd lain together. Empty-headed foolishness, that was.''

Damaris forced herself to smile in return, and reached out to stroke a finger across the baby's velvety cheek. ''Empty-headed foolishness,'' she repeated softly. ''Aye, that's all any of it was.''

* * *

Damaris stared down at the porcelain plate set before her, and at the elegant arrangement of sliced roast veal and new peas in cream. From the moment Roger had escorted her into the candlelit room reserved for dining only, Damaris had dreaded this moment, praying that one of the Turner boys would appear to rescue her. But the turtle soup had come and gone, and now, with the second remove on the table, she couldn't avoid the problem anymore. She would simply have to follow Evelyn's lead, and watch how she used the odd, short forks with the three stubby tines.

"Is there something amiss with your veal, Damaris?" asked Roger solicitously, noting how she still sat with her hands in her lap. "I can have another dish prepared, if you prefer."

Quickly Damaris shook her head. "Thank thee, no, Roger, this is perfect." She glanced across to Evelyn, who was listening raptly to the conversation of the gentleman beside her. Without drawing her gaze for even a moment from the gentleman's, Evelyn pierced a bite of the meat before her with her fork, crooked her wrist elegantly, and lifted the fork and the veal to her mouth. Damaris watched, aghast. Her mother had taught her that forks were to hold meat for cutting only. No genteel person would ever use one for eating.

"'Tis all the fashion at court, my dear," whispered Roger, recognizing her reluctance. "From Italy, of course, where all such frippery begins, but once you practice a bit, these little forks make good sense. Much neater than stabbing away like a savage. Here, please, allow me to show you."

As he came to stand behind her chair, Roger leaned around Damaris to place the fork properly in her hand. She stiffened as he bent over her shoulder, the long curls of his periwig brushing across the back of her neck and his breath warm with wine on her cheek. "Thank thee, Roger," she murmured uneasily, "but I can manage well enough from here."

"Oh, no, dear sister," he said with a smile. "These Italian ways can prove more difficult than they look."

To Damaris's embarrassment, he guided the fork to her lips as if she were a clumsy child, leaving her no choice but to smile and nod stupidly as she chewed. To make it worse, he took his own napkin and dabbed at her lips, smiling triumphantly, as if he'd just granted her all the secrets of the world.

"Roger," said Evelyn with icy calm. "Are you quite done guiding your backward sister in the art of feeding herself, that you may address your other guests, as well?"

"I am not backward, Evelyn," answered Damaris. Carefully she laid the fork across her plate, all too aware that every eye around the table was watching her, and every ear waiting for her reply. She fought against the anger rising within her, anger aimed not so much at Evelyn as at Roger, for touching her, using her, in a fashion that could only wound his wife. "My ways are plain by choice, and being a daughter of this colony, I fear I have no experience with forks made for Romish Italian gentlemen."

"Evelyn, need I remind you that Damaris is both our guest and my brother's widow?" Roger settled his hands on Damaris's shoulders, the weight of his palms burning through the heavy gray silk of her one good gown. "I myself find a little plainness refreshing in this house."

"Plainness!" Evelyn practically spat the word, and Damaris was horrified to see the tears that brightened the younger woman's eyes. "What would you know of plainness? Who always wants more and more and *more,* who can't let a single ship arrive from London but that he must have whatever is the fashion at the court? And who must pay for it all, as if my poor father spins gold from straw?"

Damaris felt Roger's fingers unconsciously tighten on her shoulders. "You forget yourself, Evelyn. If you are unwell, I'm certain our guests shall understand if you choose to withdraw."

But Evelyn didn't seem to hear him. "If it's plainness you want, then I shall be as plain as our plain Quaker Damaris." She rose so quickly, she tipped her chair back, and it crashed on the carpet behind her. Awkwardly the three other men at the table stood also, holding their napkins as they stared down at their half-eaten veal and away from Evelyn.

"You'll have your plain, sirrah, oh, you'll have it," she continued, more to herself now than to Roger. With trembling fingers, she thrust her napkin into her water goblet, her rings clicking against the crystal, and then scrubbed the sodden damask across her painted cheeks. The red and white came off in streaks like piebald patchwork, until, boldly, Evelyn held her face up for scrutiny as her tears at last spilled down her bare cheeks. "There now, Master Allyn," she cried, "there's the plain face you'd have me show the world!"

Damaris gasped, and so did the others at the table. With the mask of white lead gone, Evelyn's pretty face was mottled with bruises, some bright purple and new, others faded to pale yellow.

No one noticed the serving girl come gliding into the room and dip a negligible curtsey to Damaris. "If you please, Mistress Allyn, there's a boy here for you says you're wanted urgent at home."

Never was Damaris so thankful for an excuse to flee.

Jonathan sat in the inky shadow of the barn, only the ember of his pipe a glowing spot of light in the blackness. Overhead, clouds hid the sliver of the waning moon. A perfect night for mischief, decided Jonathan uneasily, and he turned again toward the empty road to Nantasket, hoping to hear the rattle of the wagon that would bring Damaris home. Ruth had been the one to tell him she'd gone off to Newport for supper, with Caleb to drive. Caleb was a good man, loyal and strong, but Jonathan still wished he'd been there in his place. At least he would have had the sense to ignore Damaris's foolishness about guns. Lord, but he hated thinking of her out there on that long road this late at night!

He sighed, poking holes in the dirt with his make-shift cane. He couldn't blame her for not asking him, not after what had happened in the meadow. He was amazed she'd even speak to him at all. Moving out to the barn hadn't improved things, either, since she'd interpreted that as one more mark of rejection, rather than an overdue attempt to salvage her reputation. He should have left her house days ago. Hell, he should just leave the blasted farm entirely, and be done with it, and with her.

Why the devil was he being so bloody honorable all of a sudden, anyway? His memory regarding women seemed clear enough, and he'd never before been so damned scrupulous about where he took his pleasure, or why. He'd certainly never before trimmed his own sails with a willing fair creature panting beneath him.

But then, that was the problem right there. As much as he desired her, Damaris wasn't just another tavern wench. Until he could remember who or what he was, she was the one truth, the single fragment of goodness left in his life, and he was almost afraid of the power he'd unwittingly given her over him. He'd almost think he was half in love with the woman.

He tipped his head back against the barn's pine deals and smiled wryly at his own superstition. Lord, next he'd believe in whistling for the wind, or refusing to sail on Fridays. Damaris was a woman of flesh and blood—very real, very tempting flesh and blood—not some lucky talisman to keep in his pocket. She had saved his life, and he owed it to her to protect hers in return. That, he thought, was a more reasonable explanation, something akin to a debt of honor. An eye for an eye, and all that sort of thing.

In the barn, one of the horses stirred, and the other nickered sleepily in reply. With the stars hidden overhead, Jonathan had no way of knowing how much of the night had already slipped away, but he felt certain it was late, far too late for Damaris to be lingering over supper. Where the hell was she, anyway?

"Set me down here, Caleb," said Damaris impatiently as the cart came into sight of the farm. "I must go to the cave first, and there's no need for thee and Asa to come, too. I'll meet thee at the point with the others."

Even as he slowed the horse, Caleb shook his head. "It don't be right, mistress," he said. "Ye runnin' off like that alone. Asa an' I best come wi' ye."

From the bed of the cart, behind them, came Asa's voice, cracking abruptly with adolescence. "'Course we'll come wit' ye, Mistress Allyn. Mam would boil our hides fer breakfast if'n we didn't."

Caleb snorted, but didn't deny it, and in the dark Damaris smiled to herself. "Nay, thee two go for the wagon. I'll warrant it will take thee both to convince poor weary Royal here that he must go out again beside Puck. I'll be safe enough on my own land."

The wagon slowed and finally stopped, and Damaris climbed down. She pulled her cloak around her body and waved her hand at father and son. "Go on, take thyselves away. I'll come to no harm. Go now, and I vow I won't tell Ruth."

Although the night was dark, she moved confidently across the familiar meadow, holding her silk skirts high against the heavy dew that already clung to the tall grass. It was Eben who had insisted on her having this one gown made of silk, and it was she who had insisted it be dark and untrimmed, not at all the frivolous creation he'd longed to see her wear. She remembered how much he had loved to give her gifts—spoiling her, he called it—and remembered, too, her own pleas for frugality. She thought again of Evelyn's accusations, and realized sadly that perhaps the two half brothers had been more alike than either of them had realized.

But she and Eben had never come to blows over his spending, or anything else, and Damaris shuddered at the memory of Evelyn's battered face. Although she didn't want to believe that Roger had done that to his wife, what other explanation could there be?

Yet Eben had told Damaris that, while Evelyn Stoddard was an heiress, his brother's marriage three years earlier had been considered a love match. Perhaps there was more behind Evelyn's troubled outburst, and her bruises, too, than a quarrel about money. Who ever knew what truly passed between man and wife?

Still thinking of Roger and Evelyn, Damaris hurried down the sandy slope to the entrance of the cave. She twisted past the clump of bayberries that hid the narrow entrance, tugging her cloak free where it snagged on the wiry branches, and felt along the high ledge of rock for the little tin box that hid the flint for the lantern. With her fingers guiding her along the rough stone wall, she made her way deeper into the cave, counting her footsteps in the dark until she blindly reached the niche that held the lantern. The tiny flame did little to light the cave's winding passage, and familiar though it was, she shivered. The rush of the ocean on the beach echoed oddly through the passage, lonely and faraway. Trying not to listen,

Damaris hurried back to the largest part of the cave, where the smuggled wine and liquor were stored.

Since Roger's visit to Nantasket, she had secretly moved the small chest of gold coins to the cave, burying it in the sand in a place where not even Caleb or the Reed brothers would know to look. Setting the lantern on the floor of the cave, she kicked at the spot with her shoe until she struck the chest's ironbound lid. Quickly she crouched down to sweep the rest of the sand clear, unwrapped the rag she had tied around the padlock, and slipped the key from her pocket into the lock. With the grinding sound of sand in the hinges, she opened the chest, and rapidly began to count out the coins she would need, plus a few to spare. With de Vere, she never knew exactly what the price would be.

The sand had muffled the footsteps behind her, and her first realization that she was no longer alone came with the long, low whistle that echoed eerily through the passage. She grabbed the lantern and scrambled to her feet, clutching the gold to her chest.

"Oh, Scheherazade," said Jonathan softly as he gazed around at the neat stacks of hogsheads and then back to Damaris. The coins were spilling from her fingers. "This is the one tale I wouldn't have believed of you."

Chapter Eight

"How did thee get here?" demanded Damaris sharply, drawing herself up very straight. "No one knows about this place!"

"Anyone would that took the time to follow you, Damaris," said Jonathan. "You don't exactly hide your trail. I was waiting for you outside the barn when I saw the wagon pull up, and you climb out."

Now that his initial surprise at the cave's contents was fading, Jonathan began to realize exactly how much danger Damaris was in. She couldn't possibly comprehend the risk she was running, smuggling like this, but he did, and he didn't like it. He came forward into the main chamber of the cave, running his hand along the rows of barrels as he bent closer to read the marks stenciled on the oaken heads. "Teneriffe, Lorient, Amsterdam. You've quite a pretty assortment here, sweetheart, and I'd wager my life not a drop of it's burdened with tariffs. But how does an upstanding Quaker lass justify smuggling liquor? Seems to me your faith doesn't take much to spirits."

"I don't drink them, Jonathan," explained Damaris tartly. The conflict had never sat well on her own conscience—not that she'd admit it to Jonathan—but there had been no other way. "I merely sell them to others, and if they choose to drink strong waters, that is their decision, not mine."

"The fact that it's also the most profitable trade you could come upon has nothing to do with it, of course. What's that old saying about you Quakers? 'One foot in the meeting house and one in the counting-house'?"

"Thee is unkind to repeat such things about Friends!"

"And you're being a witless little fool!" snapped Jonathan, his bantering tone gone, as he slowly came toward her. By the lantern's flickering light, he seemed much larger, and the strong lines of his face harsher, and for the first time Damaris felt herself shrink away from him. "Don't you know how dangerous smuggling is? Breaking the law is the least of it. You've probably fixed that already with that magistrate brother-in-law of yours. But when you move outside the law, you move outside the law's protection, as well. If word of this cave and what it holds ever reached the wrong ears, you'd be dead in your bed without so much as a by-your-leave."

"No one knows," she said, clinging to stubbornness for courage. "No one but Caleb and Daniel and Seth."

"My, my, but that sets my worries all to rest," he said sarcastically. "A lady who doesn't believe in guns and three farmers guarding, what, three or four hundred guineas' worth of illegal spirits?"

"No one knows," she repeated, her false courage beginning to falter. She really didn't know him at all, not the way he looked now.

He was inches away from her, his height forcing her to look up at him, his voice hammering at her relentlessly. "No one save those bastards Hull and Barnum, and likely every other sot they've tipped a dram with. No one save whoever brings this stuff in, and his whole crew. And no one, of course, save the man who murdered your husband. Smugglers don't die in their beds, Damaris, leastways not of apoplexy."

She closed her eyes, trying to blot out the truth of what he said.

It was the voices in the kitchen below that had awakened her that night, Caleb's and Seth's and not Eben's, and instantly she had known something was wrong. She had rushed downstairs in time to see them gently lay her husband on the table, and when they had noticed her there on the step, the men had shuffled back, their heads bowed, uncertain of her response.

With the floor cold beneath her bare feet, she came forward, slowly, to where her husband lay. By the candlelight she saw that his shirt was changed from white to an uneven red, the fabric already stiffening around the small, ragged hole in the linen over his breast. His face was a pale gray, his eyes still open wide with stunned surprise. She knew she should close his eyes this last time, but she couldn't bring herself to touch him, not like this. To feel the chill of death beneath her fingers would make it real.

"He died at once, Mistress Allyn," said a blond man with ruddy cheeks whom she guessed must be Captain de Vere. *"He didn't suffer. In the fog we didn't see the other boat until it was too late, and when we fired back on them, they fled, the cowardly bastards!"*

Damaris nodded, accepting his explanation and nothing else. "Was anyone else...anyone else..."

"We're all unhurt, mistress," said Caleb miserably. *"Only Master Eben was taken."*

She clutched her shawl more tightly around her shoulders, staring down at her husband's body. His long, sandy hair had been tangled by the wind, and carefully she reached out to smooth it back to cover the balding patch on the crown, the wispy place that she had always pretended not to see when he asked her if it had worsened. She thought of him frowning anxiously into the looking glass, trying to see for himself. And then, finally, too late to help Eben, her tears had come.

"What does thee want from me?" she whispered hoarsely to Jonathan, her eyes still closed. "How much will it take to buy thy silence?"

"Hell, Damaris, what I want is for you to stop this foolishness now, before you get yourself killed!" He grabbed her face in both his hands and shook it. He wanted her to accept the hard reality of her actions, not hide from him like a petulant child. "Look at me, lass! Look at me, and swear you'll give this up!"

Damaris's eyes flew open, and she wrenched free. His touch was more than she could bear. "I owe thee nothing, Jonathan Sparhawk, no swearing and no promises!'' she cried at him bitterly. "Does thee truly believe I would continue in this trade if I had a choice? If I give it up now, I'll lose Nantasket, and I'll become like my mother, a poor, plain widow dependent on the charity of others. What kind of choice is that? And what of Caleb and Ruth and their children? There are too many in the colony who hold to slavery, and few would welcome a freed African and his family. Would thee have me cast them out simply because thee asks me to?''

Impatiently Jonathan swept his long hair back off his forehead, longing to take her in his arms again. "Then let me help you, sweetheart, and keep you from harm's way.''

"Help me! Help thyself would be more to the truth.'' She felt cornered, trapped, in a game whose rules only he knew. He had rejected her once, and the shame and hurt were still too fresh for her to make herself vulnerable again. Instead she wrapped her pain in anger, sharp words masking her loneliness. "Thee speaks of lawless ways with great familiarity. The only one I rob is the king of his taxes, and he will never mark the difference. All others I pay in hard money. Can thee say as much? Help me, for all love! Why would thee help me?''

"Because I care for you, Damaris,'' he said, catching her by the wrists. All around her dark skirts the gold coins dropped from her hands, flashing briefly in the lantern's light. Furious, she twisted and plunged back, trying to break free as the coins scattered around her in the dark. But he effortlessly pulled her against his chest, his grip on her wrists pinning her tightly against him.

"Thee doesn't care for me, not one whit!" she gasped, her breath short with desperation. There had been a time when she had wanted to hear that from him, and would have believed it. But not now, not here, not this way. "Thee has made thy feelings for me clear enough, hasn't thee? Faith, I doubt thee would even know *how* to care for another!"

"What, like your honest Master Eben?" Jonathan countered angrily. "Now there's a man who knew how to look after his woman. Ignored a perfectly good piece of land for a trade that got him killed, and left you without the money to keep you and your people from starving. Didn't even bother to teach you the first thing about kissing, either."

"Meaning he didn't teach me ways best left to a brothel!"

"More's the pity for you, sweetheart, for you've all the makings of a first-rate learner." Again she tried to twist free, and again he pulled her back. Her eyes were bright with outrage as she fought him. With her there against his chest, her lips so near to his, Jonathan knew that the line between passion and anger would be an easy one to cross.

"I hate thee," she said vehemently, her fists pounding on the hard barrier of his chest. "I hate thee! Ruth is right! Thee is a dangerous man, with thy handsome face and thy honey-sweet words and thy bold promises that thee has no intention of keeping!"

He turned his head quickly toward the cave's entrance, hearing the faint voices from the beach before she did. "Hearken, Damaris, they're coming for you. Tell them I'm with you now, that I know everything. You tell them so they believe you, and I swear by all that's holy that I'll help you get free of all this. I can, sweetheart, and I will, but you have to let me."

She glared at him, feeling trapped. She had no choice, and he knew it. "Thee is the most villainous, deceitful, dishonorable man I have ever known."

"Aye, likely I am," he said roughly, "and you would never want me otherwise."

He crushed her to his chest, trapping her hands between their bodies as his mouth swept down on hers. He kissed her without gentleness, without tenderness, forcing her mouth to open for his. She felt the roughness of his beard scrape across her lips, and the wet warmth on her cheek where his mouth slashed across hers. With her palms she pressed back against his chest, struggling more against herself than against him as she felt her anger melting into desire. Beneath her fingers she could feel the powerful, quick beating of his heart beneath the linen of his shirt.

Possessively Jonathan pulled her closer, releasing her hands as his own spread and slid down her length, his palms open and his fingers splayed as he learned her body. He moved lower, across the stiff, tabbed edge of her stays, to find the soft swell of her hips and buttocks, and he lifted her against his thigh with a low animal groan. Damaris clung to him, not trusting her legs to support her now, and her own cries were lost in the union of their mouths.

But from the corner of her eye she caught the re-flected light of a second lantern bobbing along the passage. She heard her name called, echoing, a question. Caleb. And another voice, his son's. With a little gasp, she pulled herself free of Jonathan, smoothing the rumpled silk of her skirts with trembling fingers as she tried to compose herself. Faith, would her heart never slow again?

"Whatever else you believe of me, Damaris," whispered Jonathan hoarsely behind her, his breath so hot on her ear that she felt herself melting all over again, "don't tell yourself I didn't want you."

Caleb held the lantern high before him, confused by the sight of them there together. "Mistress Allyn," he began uncertainly, and then he cleared his throat. "Mistress Allyn, we thought ye might have come t' harm. We didn't know ye weren't alone."

"It's all right, Caleb. Thee did well to be concerned." She swallowed and took a breath, a breath so deep as to be almost a sigh. "Jonathan knows of our trading, and he will be joining us tonight."

She paused, waiting for a protest that did not come. Both men merely nodded. "Are the others waiting?"

"Aye, mistress. Boat's unloaded, an' th' wagon's full. That's why we come lookin' fer ye."

"Then, pray, let's not keep the captain any longer."

Caleb hesitated, gazing pointedly at her feet. "Beggin' yer pardon, mistress, but he won't care when we come if we don't bring him th' money."

Her cheeks pink, Damaris sank down on her knees, sifting through the sand for the scattered coins. Beside her, Jonathan knelt, too, and carelessly let his fingers brush against hers in the sand. "You need me,

Damaris," he whispered for her ears only, "and I promise you won't be sorry that you admitted it."

"Does this captain have a name?" asked Jonathan as the four of them walked down the beach.

"Johannes de Vere." Damaris pulled her cloak tighter around her body. The wind had shifted, coming from the northeast now, cold and sharp for this time of year, and the silk gown offered little warmth. The storm the clouds and wind promised would surely come by dawn.

"A Dutchman," said Jonathan, and shook his head. "I don't trust Dutchmen. Never have."

"That's just as well, since he likely won't trust thee, either." She had a bad feeling about tonight, and not only from the weather. She glanced at Jonathan, beside her. To watch him walk, he seemed scarcely to lean upon the stick for support, and yet his footprints in the stand were uneven, the scarred leg still not bearing his full weight. She shivered in the wind, wondering if tonight he felt he'd won as surely as she felt she'd lost.

De Vere and his men were waiting up above the beach and the rocks, beside the loaded wagon, joking among themselves in Dutch. Daniel and Seth stood apart from them, their shoulders hunched dejectedly against the wind.

"I'm sorry to have kept thee, Captain de Vere," said Damaris breathlessly. "I was in Newport when I learned you'd arrived."

But de Vere was staring past her at Jonathan, not even hearing her apologies, and all the laughing and the joking of the other Dutchmen had abruptly halted, as well. Levelly Jonathan returned their scrutiny. It could be no more than that Jonathan was a stranger, interrupting their lawbreaking, or that he presented such a daunting figure, half a head taller than the rest of them, his long black hair blowing in the wind and his expression severe.

But what Jonathan suspected was that they recognized him, and that somewhere, sometime that he couldn't remember, he'd personally brought these men to grief. Perhaps one of them was responsible for putting that ball in his leg, and if he wasn't careful, they might be tempted to finish the job here tonight.

Oblivious to the undercurrents among the men, Damaris plunged on. "This is Jonathan Sparhawk, Captain de Vere. He's helping me here at Nantasket, with my... my accounts." Damaris grimaced to herself at the awkward explanation, but faith, how could she explain it any better when she wasn't sure herself what Jonathan meant to do?

"You should take care who you share your secrets with, little widow, especially in these times." De Vere let his glance shift for a moment towards Jonathan. "You could be playing partners with the devil himself and not even know until it was too late."

"To be sure, Captain, Jonathan is a Massachusetts man, but that doesn't merit thee ranking him with the devil," answered Damaris testily, ignoring the choking noise de Vere was making in the back of his throat. She was sick to death of men warning her about each other. "If I have chosen to trust him, then thee can do so, too. Now, has thee brought everything I asked for last time? More of the canary, and more—''

"Nay, Mistress Allyn, I told you, these be hard times for sailors, hard times for trading. No canary at all to be had for love or money, on account of those bastards that take for free." This time he didn't dare look at Jonathan, but the pause was emphasis enough. "All I could bring for you this run was Madeira, and you'd best be thankful for that."

"Madeira!" exclaimed Damaris. "Thee knows I've no custom here for Madeira!"

"I told you before, there's nothing else to be had," insisted de Vere doggedly. Over and over he smoothed the ends of his yellow mustache with his fingers. "You'll have to tell your gentlemen that it's Madeira, or plain rum and beer like the rest of us. Now let's move along to what you owe me. Seeing as it is first-quality Madeira, that's sixty-five guineas."

"Sixty-five guineas for something I didn't ask thee for!"

"Sixty-five guineas is a fair enough price, and you know it. Now come, mistress, show the good sense your Maker gave you. Everything's stowed tidy in your wagon, and I've no wish to tarry ashore, with the wind what it is. Sixty-five guineas."

"Forty, de Vere," said Jonathan. "Forty, and consider yourself damned fortunate to get that."

"Forty!" cried de Vere furiously. "What do you get out of this, you black cur, sticking your nose where it don't belong? Or maybe that's it, maybe you already got your nose sniffing between the pretty widow's thighs, eh?" He slipped his hand inside his doublet.

From the corner of her eye Damaris caught the swift, sweeping motion of the thick stick Jonathan used for walking as he caught de Vere cleanly in the belly. The man doubled over the stick and flew backward, his men scattering as he dropped onto the sandy ground with a dull thud. He rolled over on his side, clutching his belly and groaning, as Jonathan leaned over him to pull out the small pistol from beneath the man's doublet.

"You know Mistress Allyn's both a lady and a Friend, de Vere." Jonathan held the pistol gingerly between thumb and forefinger, swinging it gently. Since none of the other Dutchmen had come to their captain's defense, he was gambling that de Vere had been the only one armed. "She don't take kindly to firearms on her land. As for the other—I think your price just dropped to thirty guineas for speaking lies about a decent woman."

With her head bent and her heart pounding, Damaris counted out thirty coins in her palm and handed them to Jonathan. She had never liked de Vere, but she had never suspected him of really wishing her harm, either, and the sight of his hidden pistol had chilled her in a way that the wind couldn't. She didn't like to imagine what might have happened if Jonathan hadn't insisted on coming with her, or if he hadn't been so quick to react. Perhaps this was how it had been when Eben had died. She tried to blot out the sudden picture of Jonathan, too, lying stiff and cold.

Jonathan prodded de Vere with the toe of his boot, and the man groaned. Shaking his head in disgust, Jonathan bent over and tucked the heavy handful of gold coins in de Vere's pocket. "Next time you'll bring what the lady asks, and not someone else's leavings. And next time you'll keep your slander and lies to yourself, and mind your manners around this lady, or you'll answer again to me."

As soon as Jonathan stepped back to Damaris's side, two of the sailors rushed over to de Vere, dragging him, groaning, to his feet and then hauling him back to the ketch's boat. As Jonathan watched their stumbling departure, he continued to swing de Vere's pistol in his hand, softly whistling a military retreat.

"How'd ye know th' cap'n had a gun, Master Sparhawk?" asked Daniel, his voice full of admiration, and Damaris noticed how in ten minutes, Jonathan had been elevated to a full-fledged "master" in the eyes of her tenants. "How'd ye know it wouldn't be loaded, an' that he wouldn't try t' shoot ye?"

"I didn't," said Jonathan simply. He looked to make certain that the boat was more than a gunshot away, then flipped the pistol up into his palm, settling his fingers around the polished butt. Spanish-made, he guessed, with a good balance and a rifled bore. De Vere would miss a gun like this. In one fluid gesture, Jonathan raised and straightened his arm, aimed at the branch of a pine tree fifty paces away, and fired. The branch cracked and split and dropped to the ground, as out in the water the four sailors pulled harder at the oars, fearing the shot was for them, and the two horses lurched in the wagon's traces with much the same concern. Jonathan couldn't help grinning at the three Nantasket men, who were regarding him with something close to worship. But his smile faded when he saw the stiff set of Damaris's expression, saw the way her arms were folded tightly across her chest.

"If thee is quite done, Jonathan," she said, "I should like to unload the wagon and go home."

To Jonathan's surprise, she decided not to sit on the bench up front with Caleb and Asa, but chose instead to ride with him in the back, her knees bent up under her skirts and her back pressed against the wagon's rough sides. In a way, Jonathan wished she hadn't. Now that the excitement of facing down de Vere had passed, he was tired, dead tired, and his leg ached painfully as they jostled over the rutted road. One look at Damaris's straight back told him that whatever she wanted to say he wouldn't be in the mood to hear.

"Jonathan," she began at last, more softly than he'd expected. She had pulled her hood up, and all of her face except her mouth was in shadow. "I would speak to thee about the gun."

He let out his breath in one long, low gust. "Hell, Damaris, what do you want me to say? I'm too tired to argue Quaker this and that with you tonight. If I hadn't taken de Vere's pistol from him, he would have shot me, and maybe you, too, and that's an end to it, as far as I can see. Maybe I shouldn't have fired it afterward, but it's the easiest way to unload a gun I know."

"Nay, it's not that." She hesitated, wrapping her hands tightly around her knees. "Thee might have been killed."

"Would you have cared if I had?"

"Oh, Jonathan, how could I not?" she answered, her voice hardly more than a tremulous whisper. "Thee was right about Eben. They told me he was dead the moment the bullet struck him, but when they brought him home to me there was still so much blood, and the startled look would not leave his eyes, even when I closed them myself."

He saw her bite her lower lip to keep from crying, the little white teeth digging into the plump red flesh. "I never knew there was so much blood within any man. I couldn't live through that again, not with thee, too. Thee tried to warn me about Captain de Vere, and I wouldn't listen, just as I thought I was right to forbid thee keeping Eben's musket. Faith, what a foolish woman thee must judge me to be!"

He saw the single tear slide down her cheek to hang for a moment on her jaw. "Nay, sweetheart, never foolish," he said gruffly, covering her clasped hands with one of his own. "Too trusting by half, but I wouldn't change that."

She sniffed loudly. "Thee knows, then, that I don't truly hate thee?"

"I'm not sure it's in you to hate anyone, Damaris," he said softly.

She merely shook her head, the shadow of her hood moving across her face. How could she ever tell him how frightened she had been of losing him? He was like Eben that way, never believing in his own mortality, or perhaps it was like that with all men. Yet she let her fingers turn and twine into his, taking comfort in the strength of his touch.

"Thee was so sure of thyself with Captain de Vere. Thee has done that before, hasn't thee?"

"What, call a man out when he's of a mind to cheat me?" said Jonathan, striving to keep his tone light. "Aye, I'll warrant I have."

"But thee still doesn't know for sure, does thee?" she asked sadly. "I have not asked, but I guessed that if thy memory had returned, thee would have left Nantasket by now."

His fingers tightened on hers, and now it was he who drew comfort from the contact. "Strange things come back to me—the name of the horse I had as a boy, a song my mother sang as she churned butter— but nothing to tell me who I am now, as a man. Oh, I could sail a full-rigged ship to Bermuda and back and cite every landfall along the way, but I can't tell you the name of my last vessel, or how I came to land on your beach. And it's hell not knowing, Damaris," he said in despair. "It's hell. I'm still as much adrift as a newborn babe."

The wagon lurched to a halt before the barn as the first cold drops of rain came, blown nearly sideways by the wind. Stiffly Jonathan rose to his feet, and Damaris followed, her fingers still tangled in his. Despite what had passed between them in the cave, she knew he would return to the loft in the barn to sleep, and she was reluctant to let him go just yet. The wind whipped back her hood as she turned her face up toward Jonathan's.

"Thee said I needed thee, and already thee has been proven right," she said. "But I think thee needs me, too." She reached up and kissed him swiftly, so swiftly that her lips barely grazed his, and then hopped off the wagon before he could stop her.

Jonathan watched her run toward the house, her white stockings pale beneath the flurry of her dark skirts. He still could feel the feathery touch of her kiss on his lips, and he wondered if she expected him to follow her. She was right, he did need her, more than he'd ever needed a woman before, and the certainty of it frightened him more than any gun could have. God in heaven, what were they going to do to each other?

The rain on his face was cold, and tasted salty from the sea. Turning the collar of his coat up against the wind, he climbed awkwardly down from the wagon, and began to help Caleb and Asa with the horses.

Roger walked slowly down the length of King's Wharf, measuring his steps to match those of old Simon Willet beside him. Not that Roger minded; by the time they reached the end of the wharf, he expected to have a good deal of Willet's gold in his own pocket.

"So you say your *Wisdom* will be ready to sail for Surinam on Friday," continued Roger amiably. "Fourteen horses and mares, oats, corn, and hay, all bound for the sugar plantations. A good cargo, that one, Willet. Your profits should be handsome."

Willet grunted and resettled his hat. The wide brim was rolled, after the fashion favored by elder Friends. "Thee knows to a shilling what I'll see, Allyn. What will it cost me this time to change thy knowledge?"

"Four percent would make me most forgetful," said Roger with a smile. After three days of rain, this morning had dawned fair and warm, as April should be, and the sun felt pleasantly warm on his back.

"That's half a point higher than last voyage," grumbled Willet. "Thee grows greedier than the heathen agents in Saint Christopher."

"And you'll triple the difference when your horses come to market," said Roger. He was long accustomed to the complaints of the Newport merchants. If they expected him to make certain adjustments in their captain's papers and manifests, then he expected them to share in return. But he understood their reluctance, and was willing to grant a few allowances of his own to keep in their good graces. He patted Willet on the shoulder. "To make your shipmaster's journey a mite easier, I'll see to it that the charges against the *Wisdom*'s three hands are dropped in time for sailing."

Willet grunted with disapproval. "All three are wastrels and drunkards. They'd be better served in thy gaol than in my vessel."

"They're all three prime hands, prime young seamen, and you know as well as I do that your captain's been at my gate each day this week, begging for them back."

Willet grunted again, and smiled as best he could with the half-dozen teeth that remained. "There's no secrets kept from thee, is there, Allyn? Well, so it must be. Come with me to the house now, and Elisabeth will give thee a dish of tea while I find thy, ah, share."

"I must send my regrets to your kind lady, Willet, for I fear I've other business to attend." Any business at all, thought Roger, that could keep him out of the grasp of Elisabeth Willet's pious nattering and twice-strained tea. "Have the *Wisdom*'s master come around this evening, and I'll have everything waiting in order for him."

Willet nodded and turned to go, but Roger caught his arm. "Pray, Willet, there is one other favor I would ask of you."

The older man scowled sourly, his white brows bristling. "How much will thy favor cost me, Allyn?"

"Not a penny from your pocketbook, I swear. It's a more personal request that I ask." Intrigued, Willet waited, both hands on his cane as he leaned closer to listen. "You are, I believe, acquainted with my brother's widow?"

"Damaris Allyn. Oh, aye, I know of her," said Willet, his tone contemptuous. "Her mother Sarah Clarke was a good woman, dear to my wife, but the daughter married out of meeting, as thee well knows. A willful girl, a shame to her friends and a sorrow to her mother. The pretty ones so often are. Her contrariness has barred her from being received back into unity."

"She is all those things, Willet," said Roger, letting a note of sadness creep into his words, "but she is also my only brother's relict, and I worry for her. She lives alone at Nantasket, and I fear that she will come to some grave harm. I would have her come back here, to Newport, so that I can relieve her of the burden of the farm."

"What would thee have me do, Allyn? If the woman's unwilling to condemn her own waywardness, thee can't expect the meeting to receive her back unrepentant.''

''Perhaps if your wife could go to her, speak to her of her mother's wishes, she might bend,'' said Roger persuasively. ''If she knew the comfort of her faith was waiting here for her again, she might be convinced to return. You can't mean to abandon her completely, can you, Willet?''

''I'll present the case before my wife, and if she agrees with thee, she'll visit Damaris herself.'' Impatiently he thumped his cane on the wooden dock. ''Beyond that, Allyn, I can promise thee no more.''

But Roger was content enough as he looked out over the harbor full of sails. Elisabeth Willet wouldn't be able to resist the challenge of bringing Damaris back to the meeting, and back to Newport, as well. Then Nantasket would be his, and the sheltered cove with it, and finally he could begin his new venture, the venture that would at last make him wealthy.

He tipped a small patch of snuff onto the back of his hand and inhaled, relishing the sharp fragrance of the tobacco as it filled his head. He'd begun taking snuff instead of a pipe while courting Evelyn, back when it had mattered to him what gentlemanly affectations pleased her, and the habit had long outlasted his affection for his wife.

Inwardly he grimaced, remembering how she'd tried to humiliate him before their friends, and Damaris, too, with that trumped-up show of a bruise. He had but used his hand on her, and then only when her petulant ill humor had provoked him beyond all bearing. How many other husbands would be so tolerant?

No matter how winsome Evelyn had been as a maid, thought Roger bitterly, no matter how much he'd desired her body and her fortune, he should have turned his back on both until her father had died and her money was her own. The old man had poisoned his daughter against him, and Roger's own love had gone with it. Perhaps if Evelyn had borne him a child, she would have ceased being a little girl herself, and their marriage might have been different. Strange to think how both he and Eben had wed barren women.

But he wouldn't let it bother him today, not with the future so nearly in his grasp. He flicked a crumb of snuff from the lace of his cravat, and headed back to dictate the revised papers for Willet's Surinam venture.

Chapter Nine

"Look, lass, there she is," said Jonathan proudly as he pointed over Damaris's shoulder to the cove. "There lies the answer to your greatest question."

"My greatest question?" Beside him on the hill-side, Damaris squinted out at the little sloop bobbing at anchor, and then up at Jonathan again. "Then thee means to tell me that thee's kept thyself on that boat these last three days?"

"Nay, Damaris, though that is part of it. I meant the Madeira," he explained. Wherever he had gone, decided Damaris, he'd enjoyed himself; she'd seldom seen him look so happy as he did now, grinning into the wind with his waistcoat unbuttoned and his turned-back shirtsleeves billowing like sails from his arms, and a three-days' growth of beard darkening his jaw. "You've twenty casks of the stuff, and no market here in Newport for it. It's piss-poor wine, Damaris—de Vere played you false enough there—and you wouldn't want to sell it to anyone you knew, anyway. So we'll do what any reasonable trader does. We'll take our wares to another market."

"Thee makes no sense, Jonathan," she said, rubbing her bare forearms. He had found her with Ruth at the stream, scrubbing the Nantasket sheep before they would be shorn of their winter fleeces next week. Despite the sun, she was chilly up here in the breeze from the water. Her oldest woolen skirt was still soaked from wading and splashing in the stream, the fabric clinging heavily to her legs, while her feet were bare in wooden clogs. "The only persons I trust to sell to live in Newport, and thee certainly doesn't need a boat to go there."

"A sloop, sweetheart, not a boat. A sloop." Her hair was simply plaited, like a thick braid of dark gold, and Jonathan couldn't resist stroking his hand lightly down the back of her head. To his delight, she arched against his hand like a cat, then shyly drew away, her chin ducked but her eyes still following him through the veil of her lashes. Three days he'd been away from her, and it had felt like an eternity.

"A sloop, then," she said, wishing she dared to touch his hair as he had hers. "Why do we need a sloop?"

"Because tonight, my innocent lass, you and I, with the Reeds as our crew, are sailing up the bay to Providence, to sell that wretched Madeira."

Damaris gasped. "Providence! Thee is a man, a mariner who has seen the world, but faith, Jonathan, I've never journeyed beyond Newport, or even thought to leave Aquidneck!"

"Truth to tell, Damaris, I doubt I've ever sailed before with a woman, either, so this'll be a first time for us both."

"But Providence is miles and miles away, and we know no one there," she protested, hardly reassured. "How can thee possibly hope to sell the wine?"

"'Tis but thirty miles by the river from Nantasket, Damaris. We'll be up and back in three days, or so we should be, if I'm to return the sloop to her owner by Saturday as promised." His eyes sparkled suspiciously. "And as for the rest, I fancied you'd peddle your wine from house to house like a milkmaid, a yoke across your shoulders and a keg dangling at either arm."

"Thee is teasing me again!" said Damaris indignantly, and shoved him so hard he stumbled backward, laughing. "I did but ask thee a reasonable question, and instead of answering, thee must go off making merry at my expense."

Jonathan made a great effort to be serious, but the corners of his mouth still twitched and tugged with a willfulness that Damaris found at once appealing and annoying. "Providence isn't so grand a place as Newport, and I warrant we'll find a taker without much trouble. Most likely a tavernkeeper who's not too particular and will take the whole lot. But beyond that, you'll have to trust me, sweeting, just as you've trusted me this far."

Damaris sighed and pulled her braid over one shoulder, pretending to study the ends. "As I've trusted thee these past three days?" she asked in a small voice. She knew she had no right at all to ask where he'd been, but curiosity had overcome her best intentions. "Thee left with the rain, and returned with the sun."

"Oh, Damaris," said Jonathan softly. Jealous or worried, either one meant she'd missed him. "I've spent the past three days in Newport, in the kind of rumshop you don't even know exists, praying the dice would tumble my way often enough to lay down the money to borrow that little sloop. Ask Daniel and Seth, if you've any doubts. They'll swear the only female I cried out for was Dame Fortune."

"Thee tossed dice for money?" asked Damaris with dismay. "Oh Jonathan, thee should have asked me instead. First guns, now gaming!"

"And smuggling, and strong spirits, and a wicked man come to eat supper at your hearth," he teased. Instead of a bodice or stays, she wore only faded quilted jumps without sleeves, and where the wide neckline of her shift had slipped down her arm was a triangle of soft, rounded shoulder that Jonathan now began to trace with his thumb. "You do mean to give me supper, don't you?"

"I should give thee what thee deserves, Jonathan Sparhawk," she said, but with none of the tartness she'd intended. Far from it, she thought guiltily; she was beginning to sound as coquettish as Evelyn. And from the way Jonathan was caressing her shoulder, she realized he would try to kiss her soon, too, here on this hilltop, in plain sight of Ruth and likely Daniel and Seth. Jonathan's hand had strayed up her throat to her chin, and gently he was turning her face, lifting it up toward his. This time she knew she didn't want him to stop, but the thought of what Ruth would say gave her the strength she needed. She lowered her chin, put both hands on his chest, and shoved.

The openmouthed surprise on Jonathan's face made her laugh out loud, and she turned and ran, her skirts in her hands as she skipped and slid down the hill toward the house. With his wounded leg, she was sure he wouldn't catch her, but after she'd paused long enough to kick off the heavy clogs, they reached the back door almost at the same time, both laughing and out of breath.

"So you'll give me what I deserve, will you, sweetheart?" demanded Jonathan with mock seriousness as he grabbed her, shrieking and squirming with laughter, around the waist. "Who'll be the one to decide that, eh? Will you be my judge and jury and executioner, too?"

"Damaris Clarke." Elisabeth Willet's voice was icy with disapproval. It was a voice that Damaris hadn't heard for six years, but would have recognized anywhere. She pushed herself free of Jonathan and ran her hands over her windblown hair, feeling her courage plummet.

There were three of them standing in the doorway of her front room, Elisabeth Willet, Hannah Hoxie, and Mary Cort, stern and immaculate in their starched caps and dark green aprons, all three acquaintances of her mother's, all three Friends who had not spoken to Damaris since her wedding. In their shocked expressions, Damaris could see herself reflected all too clearly—her skirts, without petticoats, hiked high over bare legs and bare feet, no stays, her hair carelessly braided, without a cap, laughing wantonly in the arms of a man far too handsome to be a Friend, a man who decidedly looked as if he'd spent the past three days and nights gaming in a dockside rumshop.

"Damaris Clarke," said Elisabeth again. "Thee surprises me."

"And thee me, Elisabeth," Damaris managed to say. She saw Hannah sniff, her gaze sweeping around the kitchen to fault her housekeeping. "Welcome to my home, all of thee. May I offer thee tea or cider, or a bite of an orange cake I made this morning?"

"Nay, Damaris Clarke," said Mary, "we won't be here long."

Damaris lifted her head high, trying to face them down. "Three times now thee have called me by my father's name," she said quietly. "Perhaps thee has forgotten that I wed Ebenezer Allyn, and as his wife took his name."

Elisabeth sighed, irritated that the obvious must be explained. "Because thee married out of meeting, Damaris, to us thee remains no more than Thomas Clarke's daughter. But we thought that with Ebenezer Allyn's death, thee might wish to return to the comfort of thy Friends."

Hannah sniffed again. "From what I see," she said, staring pointedly at Jonathan, "Damaris has quite a sufficiency of comfort to help bear her grief."

That was too much for Jonathan. "And what the devil's wrong with her finding it wherever she can?" he said sharply as he came to stand behind Damaris, his hands resting protectively on her shoulders. "It's nigh on eight months since her husband died, and this is the first time you old cats could bother to come see her!"

"Jonathan, please, they are guests in my home," said Damaris. Much as she longed to shrink back and let him defend her, this was her battle to fight, one begun long before she'd met him.

"Pray, Damaris, do not distress thyself," said Hannah, "for we shall leave you now to thy—thy comforts. Good day to thee." With a little twitch of her head, she swept purposefully out the front door to the open carriage waiting with a driver in the yard. Mary followed, with a nod that was only slightly more gracious, leaving Damaris facing Elisabeth, each of them standing with her hands folded across her apron.

Alone, Elisabeth's plump face softened as she studied the younger woman before her. "Damaris, would thee please ask this man to leave us?" she asked gently. "I would speak to thee alone."

Jonathan's fingers tightened on her shoulders. "Nay, madam, I've no wish to leave her to be chewed up and spat out by your—"

"I'll be well enough, Jonathan." Damaris turned to look up at him, her eyes beseeching. "Please. I'll find thee when Elisabeth has left."

He swept a loose wisp of hair back from her brow, glanced fiercely back at Elisabeth, and then, reluctantly, he headed for the barn.

"That young man loves thee, Damaris," said Elisabeth sadly. "Does thee share the same affections for him?"

Damaris blushed, and stared down at the floor in her confusion. "He is not one of us, Elisabeth, so what does it matter to thee?"

"One of us? So thee has not entirely cast thyself away from the Friends," said Elisabeth, musing. "I thought as much. Thee has kept thy plain speech, and despite what Hannah may say to the women's committee, thy household is in order, and I believe that in thy heart thee still keeps to our ways."

Troubled, Damaris could only shake her head, thinking of guns and gambling and a cave filled with spirits, of men fighting on her beach and moonlit sailings to Providence, and of the wanton quickening she felt in her blood every time Jonathan kissed her. Elisabeth thought he loved her; faith, if it were only as simple as that!

"Come back to us, Damaris," the older woman urged warmly. "Come back to Newport, where thee belongs. If thee would but read a paper admitting thy missteps and stating thy desire to return to the meeting, thee would be welcome again."

"But thee would have me tell the meeting that I am sorry I wed Eben, that my marriage was no more than a willful transgression," said Damaris slowly, her hands now clenched so tightly that the knuckles showed white. "I would rather be cast off by thy meeting a hundred times than be taken back on terms such as those."

"Damaris, think of thy mother! Think of the sorrow this refusal would have caused her!"

"My mother would have wished me to be happy, Elisabeth," said Damaris, remembering her mother's wasted, pain-ravaged face, and how little happiness she had found in her own life. "And here at Nantasket I believe I am."

"With that black-haired rogue to share thy misdeeds?"

Damaris lifted her head and nodded slowly.

"Thee is certain of this, Damaris?"

This time her nod was more determined. There would, she knew, be no turning back now. In the eyes of the Newport Friends, what she had just admitted to Elisabeth Willet would be as irrevocable as her wedding to Eben. Jonathan had never spoken of love, or marriage, or any future that included her, yet with that nod of her head Damaris had joined herself to him.

Elisabeth's cheeks quivered with anger, and whatever sentiment she had felt for the daughter of her old friend vanished. "Thee will learn someday, child, that happiness in this life is but a brief and empty pleasure, and thee will wish then that thee had not been so stubborn. May the Lord watch over thee, Damaris Clarke, and preserve thee through whatever wickedness thee may wrongfully choose."

Damaris watched her leave, watched the carriage circle the yard and take the road back to Newport, then sank to her knees, with her face buried in her hands. She had always tried so hard to do what was right, yet Elisabeth's words echoed over and over in her head.

May the Lord preserve thee through whatever wickedness thee may wrongfully choose.

Once, she had chosen Eben, and in return for the loss of her friends she had found happiness and a home and companionship that had ended sharply in sorrow. But she had never regretted her decision, and she did not regret it now. And now she had chosen

Jonathan. In another six years' time, would she still be
as certain she'd done the right thing?

"I don't believe there was ever a more perfect
night," said Damaris dreamily as she sat on the deck
of the little sloop, staring up at the stars and the moon
as they made their way upriver with the tide, toward
Providence. Once she had adjusted to the motion of
the sloop under sail, she'd felt her cares drop from her
shoulders like a weight. The sloop seemed almost like
a living creature, twisting and turning in time with the
wind and the water, and Damaris had never felt as
much a part of the elements as she did this night. She
sighed contentedly, snuggling further against the
bundle of cordage and spare sails, where she had
dozed off and on all night.

With his body braced against the tiller, Jonathan
chuckled at how much pleasure was contained in that
single sigh. A full moon, enough wind to fill his sails,
a sweet little sloop that danced to his whim, and an
even sweeter woman for company—he was contented
enough himself. Her hair looked like the moonlight
itself, silver-gold and glistening, and in her voice was
that same promise he'd heard this afternoon, before
those women had descended like a trio of Quaker
witches. Damaris wouldn't tell him what the tall one
had said, but it had been enough to make her quiet
and withdrawn until he'd rowed her out to the sloop.
As far as he was concerned, all that blasted Madeira
could wind up in the bay, and this run would still be
worth the trouble, if only for making her smile again.

"Most men will tell you a woman aboard brings naught but ill luck, but we're making better time than I'd dare reckon," he said, instead of giving voice to all the nonsense about moonbeams in her hair that was filling his head. There'd be time enough for that when Daniel Reed wasn't within earshot. "We'll clear Namquit Point before daybreak, and Providence before noon."

"I don't care if we never get there!" declared Damaris fervently. "I'd rather thee sailed wherever thee pleased, and I could lie here forever with nothing more to do than look at the stars."

"Ye couldn't pick a finer sailor than Cap'n Sparhawk," said Daniel Reed staunchly, and Damaris smiled at him sheepishly for having forgotten he was even there. "Cap'n Sparhawk could take us anywhere ye please, mistress."

"Ah, now, Daniel, I told you none of that captain talk," said Jonathan, and Damaris heard the unspoken warning that Daniel evidently didn't. "A little pleasure cruise like this one doesn't make a man a captain."

"Nay, but th' others at Claggert's said otherwise," said Daniel, his yellow head bobbing up and down with excitement. "They said t' me ye had th' look of a fightin' man for certain, an' they was all set an' ready t' sign ye to a ship t' go privateerin' an' make your fortune!"

Damaris sat upright. "Privateering?" she asked apprehensively. "And how would they know if thee were a fighting man, Jonathan?"

"They don't, sweetheart," he said, a little too quickly to satisfy Damaris. "It was only stuff and nonsense, born of rum and thick heads and the sight of my game leg."

"But Cap'n Sparhawk, them men said—"

"Daniel, shut your trap," ordered Jonathan, "or I'll do it for you. And no more captain, mind?"

Daniel's shoulders drooped dejectedly. "Aye, Master Sparhawk."

But the words had been said, and Jonathan could have throttled Daniel. Damaris had enough to worry about without adding rumshop tattle to the mix. And yet the three men who'd tried to hire him had been serious, and Jonathan had had the uneasy feeling that they'd recognized him. He hadn't liked the sound of that "fighting man" nonsense, either, any more than he'd welcomed the wary respect he'd sensed the moment he'd stepped into Claggert's, how half the men had stepped away from him as if he had the plague.

Carefully Damaris felt her way aft to join him, steadying herself with both hands on the sloop's low taffrail. "The men knew who thee was, didn't they?" she asked.

"I told you, Damaris, it was nothing," said Jonathan curtly. "You of all people should know better than to listen to Daniel."

"Thee won't tell me?" she asked wistfully.

Resolutely he stared away from her and out over the water, to the black tip of Patience Island, to the west. If he met those blue eyes now, he'd confess everything. "When you can tell me what that old Quaker crone said to you, I'll tell you what happened at Claggert's. Fair's fair, sweetheart.''

"Aye, fair's fair," she echoed, with a sad attempt at petulance. "And neither of us will ever know."

"Oh, Damaris, lass." He hated holding anything back from her, but he wouldn't burden her with empty speculation. Yet why was it, the harder he tried not to hurt her, the more he did? With his free arm, he reached out and drew her close, and with a little sigh she settled against him, her back curving into his chest as her skirts billowed and tangled around his widespread legs. He wanted so much to be able to give her the world, but all he had this night was a sky filled with stars, and the beating of his own heart. Gently he let his lips play over the soft place beneath her ear. They were both of them castaways, and they were both of them adrift. But he would find them a safe harbor. He would find it for them both.

"Tell me, Damaris, how are you at stretching the truth an inch or two at the market?" asked Jonathan as he and Daniel tied the sloop to the common mooring. "Do you ever say there's eighteen pippins in your basket when you know you've twenty, or swear your butter's fresh when it's only extra salt that's kept it from stinking?"

Damaris looked at him closely. "Thee is asking me if I lie, isn't thee?" she said suspiciously. "Well, I don't, Jonathan, and proud I am of it."

He grinned at her, and Damaris steeled herself to be royally teased, at the very least. "You don't lie, or you can't?"

She opened her mouth to answer, then stopped, realizing at the last moment how large a trap he'd laid for her. "I do not tell untruths," she said carefully. "Neither would I be able to tell them, even if I so wished to do."

"Aha, sweeting, the very answer I expected!" His grin widened as he unrolled his shirtsleeves and buttoned the cuffs before shrugging on his coat. "You remember that, now, no matter what else may happen. I'm counting on you to remain the most honest creature I've ever had the pleasure to know."

"Jonathan, what is thee planning?" This was going to be something a good deal worse than teasing. His grin was warning enough.

"I'm going to find us a customer for our Dutchman's folly," he said, lifting his hat long enough to smooth back his hair and resettling it squarely on his head. "I want you to stay here with the Reeds, where I know you'll be safe. You're too pretty by half to be left to roam any docks without a guard."

"Jonathan, wait—"

He bent down to kiss her swiftly on the forehead. "I'll be back as soon as I can, Damaris. And, mind, I'm counting on you to be truthful!"

She watched him walk whistling down the dock, as full of himself as if he owned the entire town. "Daniel, does thee know what Jonathan is going to do?" she asked, but the man shook his head.

"I wouldn't tell ye if I did know, Mistress Allyn," he said glumly. "Not after last night. I thought he'd wallop me good for speakin' out like I did, after I'd sworn I wouldn't an' all."

"Even though I'm the one whose land thee works, and who sees that thee and thy brother have a roof over thy head?" asked Damaris. "Or has thee forgotten that Jonathan's not thy master?"

"Nay, mistress, I know full well he's not." Daniel rubbed his hands on the seat of his breeches, clearly considering what to say next. "But, meaning no disrespect to ye, mistress, there be some things that haven't been th' same since Master Allyn died. Ye do your best, but some things need a man t' do them proper. Master Sparhawk, he knows."

And Damaris knew, too, more than she'd ever admit to Daniel. She turned back to the rail and tried to interest herself in the town before her. Like Newport, Providence began low near the water, then rose high along a hillside, but there, as far as Damaris was concerned, the similarity ended. To her eye, Providence seemed small and mean, nothing but rude warehouses and shops and raw, new houses, none that she could see as fine as her own at Nantasket, and certainly none like the grand houses, like Roger's, that lined Broad Street in Newport. The harbor seemed well enough, but why should any merchant come this far to trade, when Newport lay so near to the mouth of the bay?

No, there wasn't enough to interest her here, at least not enough to make her stop wondering where Jonathan had disappeared to. It hardly seemed fair that men could wander off wherever they chose, while women were expected to stay in one place all their lives. She had been so excited about sailing clear to Providence, and yet here she was again, bound to one spot as if she were a tree with roots. She sighed and twisted the ribands on the wide, flat straw hat she wore against the sun, wishing Jonathan would come back.

She did not have long to wait. She rose excitedly as soon as she spotted him, coming toward her with his head bent, in deep conversation with a man in a striped apron and an ill-fitting wig. As he talked, Jonathan gestured, grandly even for him, laughing merrily, and once again Damaris began to wonder what he was planning.

"Damaris, lass, this is Master Samuel Collins, proprietor of the Green Turtle," Jonathan called as they walked toward the sloop. "Master Collins, this is Damaris Allyn, the lovely little Friend I've been speaking of."

Reluctantly Damaris extended her hand to Collins as he shuffled toward her. His shoes were worn down at the back, and looked more like slippers. He was very pale, and his eyes watered behind his spectacles, as if he seldom ventured out from behind his bar into daylight.

"No ceremony, mistress, I beg you," he said with a thin-lipped smile. "Master Sparhawk here has explained it all to me. Let me say you're a brave lady, a powerful brave lady. To steal away the wine under the very nose of that wretched brother of yours, just so you might save his soul for holy redemption—'tis the stuff of epics, ma'am!"

"Forgive me, Samuel Collins, but thee seems to know more of this than do I." Certain now that she was being made the center of some awful jest, Damaris swung her gaze over to Jonathan, who smiled at her innocently. "Jonathan, perhaps thee would like to tell me thy farfetched tale?"

But Jonathan only laughed and shrugged his shoulders as he looked at Collins. "There now, sir, what did I tell you? There's none that can touch her for modesty and virtue, and she'll dismiss any praise as worldly frippery."

"A paragon, Master Sparhawk!" gushed Collins, but there was no mistaking the greedy gleam in his watery eyes.

Damaris glowered at Jonathan. "I'll warn thee, Master Sparhawk, unless thee begins explaining, thee will feel my very worldly anger."

Collins shuffled forward to place a restraining hand on her arm. "Now, now, mistress, don't you be hasty. As a rule, I don't take custom from traders I don't know—the tax men are something fierce in this colony, what with every second rascal fitting himself up for smuggling—but in your case, I'm willing to help you out. Oh, aye, what would a proper little Quakeress know of ill-got wines?"

As both Jonathan and Collins again laughed heartily, Damaris finally began to realize what Jonathan had done, and to confirm her suspicions, Jonathan winked broadly at her from behind Collins. He'd lied his handsome head off to interest Collins, but then again, Collins was likely only dealing with them because he thought he could cheat her. She drew herself up straighter, her hands automatically smoothing her apron. Samuel Collins would learn soon enough what a Friend knew about ill-got wines.

"Thee is most kind, Samuel Collins," she said softly, her smile grateful, and the innkeeper smiled stupidly back at her. Inwardly she groaned, for here was yet another foolish man who mistook her plain speech for familiarity. "Thee will, I believe, be most surprised by the quality of the Madeira."

She heard Jonathan cough peculiarly, but didn't dare look his way. "Because Friends do not take strong spirits, I fear I must trust thee to place a fair value on the wine," she continued, noting how Collins could barely contain his excitement. "But I also must insist that thee pay me in hard money."

"Oh, mistress, I was misled," said Collins, crestfallen, as he looked in appeal to Jonathan. "Master Sparhawk told me you'd be willing to barter for goods."

Sadly Damaris shook her head. "Gold or silver, or—"

"As Master Collins said himself, don't be hasty, Damaris," interrupted Jonathan. "Master Collins here has himself a farm down near Tiverton, and the goods he's willing to trade are things you might have use for—flax and barley and Indian corn for planting, plus a parcel of indigo. I've seen it all myself."

Collins nodded eagerly, scratching his head up under his wig. "I'd meant it all for market tomorrow, but seeing as you're here today, you might as well have it instead. Won't be no Madeira to be had at market tomorrow, oh, no, and I've a sight more use for Madeira than Indian corn!"

Damaris pressed her clasped hands to her lips, pretending to hesitate as now she hid her own glee. Flax and barley and Indian corn could all be planted and harvested this year—three more crops to help make Nantasket self-sufficient. She could scarcely believe their good fortune.

"The whole lot of it's yours, miss," urged Collins. "Worth fifty guineas if it's worth a shilling."

Damaris could contain her smile no longer. "Then I believe we have an agreement, Samuel Collins."

"Ah, mistress, I knew you'd come 'round!" He was nearly dancing with excitement in his worn-out shoes. "I'll have my boys fetch the wagon directly. What a delight it is to trade with an honest person, mistress, a delight!"

As he hurried back to his tavern, Jonathan caught Damaris by her arm. "Pretty work, that," he said, chuckling. "You left me sitting on my backside in the dust, didn't you?"

Damaris smiled up at him impishly from beneath her broad hat. She still wasn't sure if being with Jonathan brought out her best or her worst, but faith, how much fun it was! "That man hoped to cheat me, and I didn't wish to let him. But I did as thee bid me, Jonathan. I never told an untruth."

Jonathan threw back his head and roared with laughter. "Like hell you didn't," he said. "And thee is the queen of England, too."

They were laughing still as they climbed, arm in arm, up the narrow path from the beach to the house at Nantasket. It was very late, closer to dawn than to midnight, the depth of the night marked only by the unceasing sound of the waves behind them and the soft cries of the night birds in the tall grass and the bayberry thickets.

"God in heaven, but I'd love to be there when one of Collins's regulars takes a swig of that Madeira!" began Jonathan again as Damaris bent to light the fire in the kitchen.

With its two stone walls, the house was always cold—even now, in May—but, strangely, tonight Damaris didn't notice it, not with Jonathan here with her. The tinder caught, and then the kindling, and slowly Damaris rose to face him.

He stood beside the open door, rubbing his fingers over the brim of the hat in his hands. Somehow the humor at Samuel Collins's expense had evaporated, and Jonathan's expression as he watched her had become serious, almost severe. His eyes were black in the fragile firelight as he gently shut the door and leaned his walking stick beside it. After a day and two nights spent mostly in an open boat, there were lines from the sun and from weariness etched into his face, his clothes were grimy and salt-stained and his hair was flattened by the hat, yet to Damaris he had never looked more handsome, because he had spent that time with her. She wondered, if she kissed him, whether his lips would taste salty, too.

"It's a little late to start a fire, isn't it?" he asked.

"I thought perhaps thee might like something to eat." She walked purposefully to the broad table, as if she meant to begin a meal, then stopped, her back to him and her palms flat on the table. "If I make thee supper, then I'll be able to spin out this night a little longer, won't I?''

He wanted to touch her, that was all. He wanted to touch her and love her and make her his. That was all, and that was everything, and he didn't give a damn about the consequences.

"If this night doesn't end," he said, his voice dark and low, "then there'll be no tomorrow."

"I'm not certain there will be, anyway," she said softly. She felt him lift her heavy plait from her back, felt him tug the riband from the end and begin to draw his fingers through her hair, unraveling the braid, and she let her head drop back, her eyes closed. "I'm not certain of much these days."

He gathered the weight of her hair in his hand and swept it to one side of her neck. He reached around and untied her cloak, the heavy wool sliding away and to the floor as he plucked away the kerchief that hid her chest. With his lips he traced the slender line of her now-bare throat, down across the long curve of her shoulder, until he found the little triangle at the edge of her gown where the sun off the water had burned her pink. Gently he kissed the flushed patch, as he'd wanted to do all day, and she moaned as his tongue licked across her fevered skin.

"You surprised me in Providence, Damaris," he whispered hoarsely. "Are you going to surprise me again now?"

Abruptly she twisted back toward him, into his chest, her hands braced behind her on the edge of the

table, gripping it so tightly she wondered if she'd split
the wood.

"I can't tell thee, Jonathan," she answered, in a
voice that hardly seemed her own. "I suppose thee
must stay and learn for thyself."

Chapter Ten

"Sweet Jesus, Damaris, you speak of my leaving as if I had a choice," Jonathan murmured incredulously. She was watching him through her lashes, her chin tucked low and her honey-colored hair loose around her face, the white edge of her shift above her bodice only faintly paler than her skin. For him her very guilessness was impossibly seductive. "There's no will in this world or the next that could carry me away from you tonight."

He took her face in both his hands, and his fingers spread as he tipped her head back up toward his, one rough thumb stroking her lower lip gently, teasing her lips apart, before his mouth lowered to hers. He kissed her hard, as if he wished to devour her, drawing her tongue against his own while his hands slid back into her hair, tangling deep in those silken waves. He felt the first tremor of desire sweep through her, and then her sigh of pleasure was lost within his mouth.

"How could you not know how lovely you are, sweetheart?" he murmured, the words warm on her ear. "Your skin is so soft, your hair like silk, and God,

the sweet taste of you. You're so beautiful, sweetheart, so very beautiful."

She wanted to tell him that he was wrong, that he
was the beautiful one, but she couldn't begin to find
the words. She would have to show him, instead, the
same way he was making her feel so special. Her lips
parted, and she trailed her tongue across the bristled
roughness of his unshaven cheeks. And oh, faith, he
did taste of salt, and the sea and the wind and everything that for her was male, and everything that was
Jonathan. Gently his teeth tugged at the tender nub of
her earlobe, and she gasped, feeling an odd fluttering
beginning low in her belly.

His hands slid down the length of her body and
back again in one long caress, learning the narrow-
ness of her waist and the swell of her hips beneath her
petticoats. Unconsciously she swayed her body toward him, exhaling her pleasure.

She wanted to touch him as he touched her, but uncertainty kept her hands locked on the table's edge,
uncertainty and the memory of that day in the
meadow, when she had tried to return his caresses, and
he had rebuffed her.

And yet now she needed to answer the way he was
touching her. Tentatively she reached out to tug his
shirt free from his breeches, sliding her hands under-
neath the linen, across the wide planes of muscle and
through the whorls of curling hair. To her great surprise, he groaned, so deep in his chest that she felt the
vibrations beneath her fingertips.

"Thee does not mind that I touch thee like this?"
she asked shyly. Her hands continued roaming be-

neath his shirt, around to his back, and when he moved his arms to pull her closer, she could feel the muscles working, shifting beneath his skin. "Eben said to do so was wanton and unwifely, but with thee it doesn't seem wrong at all."

"Then Eben was a fool, sweetheart." He hooked one finger in the bow at the top of her bodice to untie it, and slowly began to draw the lacings through the eyelets. "Please yourself, and you'll please me."

He slid her open bodice down over her shoulders and pressed his hands beneath her breasts, raising the soft flesh higher above the top of her stays as he lifted her breasts free of the stiff whalebone. Gently he caught each nipple between his thumb and forefinger, and Damaris cried out with startled delight. The fluttering in her belly was growing, tightening, in a way that made her heart race and her breath fall short. Her head arched back as his mouth moved along her throat, his tongue wet and hot as he teased her taut flesh, and involuntarily her fingers curled into his chest, her nails raking into his skin.

He felt his own urgency growing as his hands swept along the length of her back to her buttocks, kneading her curves through the skirt. She wore fewer petticoats than most women, but there was still too much fabric between them, and effortlessly he lifted her back onto the edge of the table. Her legs fell open on either side of his body, and he slid his hand beneath the petticoats and along her stockings until he found the soft, bare skin above her garter, above her knee. With his fingertips he traced little circles along the inside of her thigh, and now she was the one who sought his mouth, her kiss like a flame in the rising fever of his desire.

Desperately she clung to his shoulders as she pulled him closer. Her whole being ached for something she couldn't have named. Her breasts were heavy, and her body was tensed so tightly she could hardly bear it. She had never felt this way when Eben had loved her, and she struggled to understand what was happening, why it all was so different with Jonathan. Instinctively she circled her legs around his waist, and his fingers dug into the bare flesh of her hips.

Damnation, he thought as his control shredded, she wasn't some tavern wench to be tossed back on the table after closing time! He wanted to take her to her bed, to undress her and make love to her with the tenderness she deserved, yet the sight of her, there in the moonlight, her lovely body still half-clothed, her hair tousled and her eyes cloudy with arousal, and her legs, God, her legs were so impossibly long and wrapped around him and she was open and there for him. When he touched her with his fingers, she was slick and soft and ready, and when he drew back, she whimpered in frustration, her head thrown back and her legs stiffening.

She couldn't wait, and neither could he. He tore at the buttons on his breeches, his arousal almost painful. He lifted her legs high over his arms and thrust into her. She was so tight around him, so incredibly hot and tight.

She moaned and rocked her hips against him, matching the rhythm of his movements as she drew him deeper within her body. She could not believe the way he filled her so completely, and with each thrust from him she cried out. They were soft little cries in the beginning, cries that grew wilder and harsher as her passion scaled, until at last she reached the crest, hovering there for a lifetime and more before tumbling over the edge. From far away she heard him call her name, and trembling with the force of her release, she collapsed against him.

He held her there against his chest as their passion faded, her cheek nestled into the hollow of his shoulder. Now his hands played idly along her spine, gentling her, and she sighed with contentment. She shifted her body against his where they still were joined, the last tremors of her pleasure quivering in her belly.

"I never knew, Jonathan," she whispered. She felt languid and light-headed, and she couldn't have thought even if she'd wanted to. Her whole world had narrowed to this moment, and to Jonathan. To have shared such joy with her must mean he loved her; she could not imagine it otherwise. "I never knew any of this until now."

Jonathan drew her closer, unwilling to surrender even for a second the sensation of her body so soft and relaxed around him. Blast that old bastard of a husband for keeping her such an innocent! She was quiet enough in his arms now, but earlier she'd been so full of passion that she'd made him shake with a desire he couldn't contain. And she'd come with him, answering him, wanting him as much as he wanted her. Ah, Damaris, his pretty Quaker widow, his love, his world. He twisted his fist in the silk of her hair and pressed it to his lips. She burrowed closer into his shoulder, her sigh shattering into little shudders against his skin.

She was still too dazed to hear the horse galloping into the yard, the footsteps running up to the house, but Jonathan heard, and his arms tightened protectively around Damaris's waist. Automatically he glanced over her head to the musket, loaded and primed, that now always leaned in the corner, by the tall chest. With the door bolted, they would be safe enough from the single rider, but uneasily Jonathan wondered who would come here at his hour, so close to dawn, and in such a hurry.

Reluctantly he unthreaded her arms from around his neck. "Damaris, sweeting, there's someone here."

She chuckled and kissed the salty hollow at his throat. "There's thee and there's me, and no one else."

"Nay, lass, there's another in the yard." He pulled apart from her, quickly buttoning his breeches, and she gasped at the emptiness he left behind. Her skin felt chilled without his touch, and she drew her knees together and up onto the table, tugging her skirts down over her legs as she curled up into herself, trying to hold on to the last of his warmth.

The pounding at the door startled her, and she twisted around as if she could see through the oak itself. Clumsily she began to rethread the laces of her bodice, hurrying to cover herself.

"Mistress Allyn, I beg ye, come at once!" shouted the unknown man up toward the bedchamber, where he plainly believed Damaris to be sleeping. "It's Ned Carr from Master Roger Allyn's household, mistress, and I've grave news to tell ye! For God's sake, Mistress Allyn, please come!''

"You stay here, Damaris," said Jonathan firmly, "and I'll send him on his way."

But Damaris shook her head. "Nay, Jonathan, I know the man, and he wouldn't be here without reason." She eased herself off the table, her legs as shaky as a new foal's. How could they be speaking so calmly, as if nothing had changed, as if she couldn't still feel his wetness on her thighs? "I must answer."

Jonathan caught her by the arm, steadying her. "You don't have to open that door to anyone, Damaris. Whatever he has to say will keep until morning."

"I must, Jonathan," she said numbly, shoving her hair back from her face with both hands. "I must. It's my house, and it's right that I should open my door."

As she gazed up at him, seeing his face so severe in the moonlight, she felt oddly close to tears. She touched her hand lightly to his jaw, and he turned his mouth into it, kissing her palm. She closed her eyes against the sensations that so simple a touch could rouse in her again.

"Mistress Allyn!" the man shouted again, more urgently this time. "Will ye come, Mistress Allyn?"

Reluctantly she withdrew her hand from Jonathan's lips, and hurried to the door. As she unfastened the bolt, she was aware of Jonathan stepping back into the shadows, where he would not be seen, back to where the musket waited. She hesitated, her hand on the door frame, wishing he didn't feel the need for the gun. She'd come to accept the reasons behind his warnings, but she still hated having the musket in her house, and she hated even more the violence it represented.

Ned Carr stood twisting his knit cap in his hands, his face shiny with sweat even in the cool early morning. He ducked his head awkwardly in a kind of half bow, and thrust a letter into her hands.

"Terrible news, mistress, terrible news," he blurted out as Damaris cracked the wax seal. "Our mistress dead, an' our master gone mad wit' grief!"

Damaris froze, the letter remaining unread in her fingers, and Ned took her silence for encouragement.

"Fell down th' front stairs, she did, an' broke her neck, our poor lady! Master Allyn found her all tumbled an' bent, an' wept like his heart was broke. 'Twas all we could do t' pull him away so she could be laid out proper. What a sad, sorry night, mistress!"

Damaris nodded mutely, trying to accept what he said. She remembered the steep front stairs rising straight to the second floor in the Newport house, the first stairway she'd ever seen without a twist and a landing that might have broken Evelyn's fall. She remembered, too, the high, curving heels on Evelyn's little shoes, and how her skirts had swept grandly along the ground. It would have been so dreadfully easy for her to catch her heel and pitch down that long flight of stairs, just the way Ned said.

Yet she also remembered the bruises on Evelyn's face that she'd blamed on Roger, and the chilly bitterness that Damaris had seen between them. *No!* She was wrong even to consider it. Eben had called his half brother many names, but *murderer* hadn't been among them. Faith, what was she thinking?

Dawn had faded the night sky to a pale gray, and she held the letter up to read in the faint light. The words were slashed across the page, speckled with ink where the pen had sputtered under pressure.

Damaris—What Ned tells you of my Evelyn is true. I am lost, lost! I beg you come to me with him if you can. Sister you are my only kin. R.A.

Neatly she refolded the paper, pressing the broken seal back together with her fingers. She sensed Jonathan's presence behind her even before Ned swallowed audibly and ducked his head again at the tall stranger behind Mistress Allyn.

"Evelyn has died in an accident, and Roger asks that I come to him," she said softly, handing him the letter to read. "Of course I shall go."

Rapidly Jonathan scanned Roger's note, swearing under his breath. She couldn't leave him now, not with so much still hanging unsaid between them. "Why the devil should you? Did he come to you when Eben died?"

"Nay," she said, so quietly he nearly missed her words. "No one from Newport did. But can't thee see that's why I must go to him?"

"What I see, Damaris, is you being too damnably trusting for your own good," he said sharply. Lord, if it weren't for that gaping idiot at the door, he'd take her in his arms and show her why she shouldn't go.

"What I see is a man whose wife has turned up dead, a wife you've said yourself he'd struck before."

Ned gasped at Jonathan's insinuation but Damaris merely shook her head. "Roger didn't do this, Jonathan, and I won't have thee implying that he did."

Jonathan seized her arm. "Don't go, Damaris."

"Thee gives me orders?" she asked, more in sadness than in anger. Gently she disengaged her arm from his grasp. "If I truly believed he had killed Evelyn, I would not go. I would never speak with anyone who had taken another's life. Doesn't thee know me well enough to understand that?"

Oh, aye, he understood well enough, thought Jonathan bitterly, and he saw for the thousandth time the sailor's twisted face as the sword tore deep into his chest. He understood too well. If Damaris ever learned the truth, she would be gone from him forever.

With his arms hanging empty at his sides, he let her go now, and prayed she would come back. She had to. How else could he tell her how much he loved her?

Roger was pacing again, crossing the polished floor of the front room over and over as the yellow silk of his banyon billowed out behind him. He realized it and stopped abruptly, took a deep breath, and forced himself to relax. It was one thing to be distracted by grief—no one would fault him for that—but to stalk about like a nervous cat smacked of an uneasy conscience, and of guilt that he had no business feeling.

It was not his fault that his wife was dead. That was the truth, plain and simple. They had quarreled and she had run away from him, but it was her own clumsiness that had sent her toppling down the stairs, her hands flailing wildly and her petticoats swirling like a sea of lace and holland linen. He hadn't touched her, and it wasn't his fault. He thought he'd heard the sound of her neck cracking, of death claiming her, when she finally struck the floor, but more likely he'd imagined it. Dr. Clifton had said she might have died as easily on the first step as on the last. But still in his head Roger heard the odd little crack, and he could not put aside the image of Evelyn's body, as crumpled and motionless as a discarded doll. But it wasn't his fault, and no one could say otherwise.

And he had loved her once.

Though the candles on the tea table had guttered out, he didn't bother to send for more. The sky was lightening in the windows to the east, the rising sun gilding the long blades of the windmills on the hill above town, and he wondered how many people already knew of Evelyn's death. Sad news always traveled quickly. He guessed he could put off callers until afternoon, or even tomorrow, if he ordered the shutters bolted, but the longer he avoided his acquaintances, and their questions carefully masked by condolences, the more curious they would become. Absently he plucked at the lace at his cuff as he heard the tall clock in the hall chime seven times. His sister-in-law should be here soon.

It had been Dr. Clifton's idea to summon Damaris from Nantasket, but even as Roger had written to her he'd begun to see the advantages of having her here now. She was calmness itself, and her quiet presence would help settle the servants, and, he hoped, silence their gossip, too. She would see to the details of Evelyn's burial, and the gathering at the house afterward. Although she'd fallen out with her own sect, her reputation as a decent woman was still impeccable, and with her by his side as his brother's widow, Roger knew, he would be a model of bereavement that would stop even the sharpest tongues. And best of all, once she was here, living in his house, he might be able to coax her to remain, and the cove at Nantasket would be his.

She came into the room without waiting to be announced, her eyes bright with unshed tears as she held her hands out to Roger. "I am so sorry for thee, Roger," she said. "How well I understand what thee is feeling, to lose thy life's partner like this! When I think of Evelyn, so young and full of laughter, I can't believe she's gone."

"You're kind to come to me, Damaris," murmured Roger as he took both her hands in his and kissed her lightly on the cheek. Although her hair was sleek as always beneath her little cap, her skirt and apron were wrinkled and creased, and her cheeks were as coarsely sunburned as any common goodwife's. Which was, Roger reminded himself, exactly what she was, without any of the style or coquettishness he loved so much in women. Yet there was something different about her this morning, something elusive about her face and manner that had changed, something he couldn't quite determine.

"Tell me how I can help thee, Roger," she was saying, "whatever thee wishes me to do for thee."

"Merely having you here is help enough, Damaris," he said, and he meant it. Already her soft voice was helping him forget Evelyn's last frightened shrieks, and for the first time since his wife's fall, he found himself able to think clearly. He had of course sent word to Evelyn's father of her death, and Roger knew he should go to the old man today. It didn't seem fair that Evelyn had died before her father, and that the Stoddard fortune would now go somewhere other than Roger's own pockets. In fact, Roger would have staked his own life that he'd never see another Stoddard penny, and at a time when he needed every coin he could lay his hands on. He couldn't have imagined worse luck. If he were to be honest, he knew, he'd overcome the loss of Evelyn herself long before he stopped missing her income.

"Roger?" asked Damaris with concern. "Is thee ill? It is the shock, I know. Here, I beg thee, sit, for thy own good."

He let her lead him to a chair, and watched her as she poured him a glass of water and brought it to him, her movements more graceful than he'd ever noticed before. Perhaps his luck had not abandoned him after all. As a woman, Damaris was not to his taste, but she would bring Nantasket as her dower, and with the right buyer, the farmland would be worth a king's ransom.

Damaris handed him the tumbler and waited uneasily, her hands folded over her apron. She knew that grief took many faces, but Roger's odd half smile and distant eyes were disconcerting, and the implied intimacy of his dressing gown and his shaved head, bare

without its customary wig, made her uncomfortable.
But far worse was the way she would look at Roger
and see Jonathan instead, and how her mind kept returning over and over to what they had done together
in her kitchen only hours before. How much she
longed to be back at Nantasket with him, to be able to
tell him all the secrets of her heart, and learn if the joy
she'd discovered in his arms was more than the dream
it seemed now.

To her embarrassment, she felt herself begin to
blush, and she ducked her head, praying that Roger
wouldn't notice. At least, thankfully, he couldn't read
her thoughts. Faith, here she'd come to help in a house
in mourning, and all she could think of was her own
wantonness!

"Tell me what thee would have me do," she said
again.

Roger tapped his fingers against the rim of the
tumbler. "Stay here with me," he said, without looking at her. "Stay here, Damaris, as my guest and as my
guide. There are so many things about a household
that need a woman's hand, affairs that I always left to
Evelyn."

"Oh, Roger, I couldn't," she blurted out awkwardly before she saw the wounded look on his face.
"It isn't that I wouldn't wish to help thee, but I can't
leave Nantasket, not with the spring plantings and the
lambing."

And not with Jonathan waiting for me. For me!

Roger gazed up at her, beseeching, his eyes red-
rimmed. "Then may I ask you to stay until she is buried? Will you see me through that much? Surely Nan-

tasket can spare you for three days.'' Three days now, and then he meant to beg three days after that, and three more, until she would stay. He found her insistence on returning to that dismal farm irritating. She had been born in Newport; surely she could be made to see once again the advantages of life in town.

''Three days?'' She had promised Jonathan she'd be home by nightfall. Three days away from him would seem like an eternity, but her conscience reminded her that what Roger asked was little enough. She would stay, and Jonathan would understand. She sighed, accepting. ''Very well, Roger, I'll stay with thee through the gathering after the burial. But then, truly, I must be gone.''

Roger nodded and smiled sadly. He reached out to take her hand and lifted it briefly to his lips. ''I knew you wouldn't fail me, sister Damaris,'' he said softly, careful to keep the triumph he felt from his voice. ''I knew I could trust you now, when I need you most.''

It took all of Damaris's will not to pull her hand away.

On the day they buried Evelyn, Damaris stood beside Roger as she had promised, the two of them alone beside the grave. Evelyn's father, her only other relative, had been too ill and distraught to come, and the other mourners stood respectfully at a distance as the minister droned the solemn words from memory, never once turning the pages of the prayer book in his hands.

Damaris stared at the small mahogany casket with Evelyn's initials picked out in brass nail heads; in

death as in life, Roger had spared no expense. In
cheerful defiance of the ceremony, robins chirped and
sang among the pink apple blossoms in the tree across
from the burial ground, and in the distance Damaris
could hear children playing, and the raucous calls of
the men at the docks. That was life, that was real, not
her standing here at the grave of a woman she'd
scarcely known. From habit, her fingers began to
smooth her apron, or where her apron would have
been if she'd been wearing her own clothes. Instead,
Roger had insisted she wear a gown he'd had made for
her, black silk farandine that was so unlike her idea of
mourning that she felt miserably conspicuous and ill
at ease.

From the corner of her eye, she could see Roger,
head bent over the the small bouquet of white hyacinths he would lay on his wife's casket. He looked
very solemn, very sad, the very picture of a grieving
widower. But in these last days Damaris had come to
realize that his grief was as false as the long auburn
curls of his wig. Oh, Roger missed Evelyn, that was
clear enough, much as he'd miss any one of his other
possessions, but he'd seemed to spend far more time
considering the phrase to be engraved on the mourning rings and who to invite to the funeral than actu-
ally remembering his wife. Frivolous as she'd been,
Evelyn had deserved better, decided Damaris sadly,
and she wondered if there had ever been any love at all
between them.

But how in heaven had she become such an expert
on love? Again she thought of Jonathan, praying he'd
understood why she'd stayed away longer than she'd

promised. With Roger's household in turmoil, she hadn't been able to send a servant to Nantasket with a message, and even if she had, she wouldn't have known what to say.

Away from the power of Jonathan's physical attraction, she had tried to sort through her feelings. She loved him, she was certain enough of that, though the intensity and the newness of this love almost frightened her. But did he love her? He had protected her and cared for her and worked on her farm, he had held her and kissed her and made her tremble with joy beyond comprehension, but he had never said he loved her. When she had given herself to him, she had willingly sinned against her faith and broken the common law of her colony. She had been raised in a seaport, and she knew well what women were called who did what she had done. She knew she should feel shame and guilt for her own wanton frailty, but against all that her woman's heart rebelled. How could something as wondrous and fiercely beautiful as what she had shared with Jonathan be wicked? How could she repent of a sin she didn't feel was a sin?

She did not know. Soundlessly, wretchedly, she began to cry, hot tears sliding down her cheeks. *God help her, she did not know.*

Roger noted her tears with approval, and passed her his own black-bordered handkerchief. She had done well, his Quaker sister-in-law, seeing to his needs and comforts these last days in a way Evelyn never had, and he'd come to respect Eben's choice. He realized the minister had finished, and the two gravediggers were waiting expectantly for him. Gently Roger tossed

the hyacinths onto his wife's coffin as the first shov-
elfuls of dark, damp soil struck the polished mahogany. A tiny part of him ached at the finality of this
goodbye, a corner of his heart he had thought was
beyond caring. But quickly he shook the feeling off,
and turned to greet the mourners who now ap-
proached him.

First came the minister—which was as it should
be—then the governor, and afterward his fellow magistrates and merchants, all the most powerful and
wealthiest men of the town, and their wives. Their
numbers were far beyond what Roger had hoped,
given the rumors he knew were being whispered about
the circumstances of Evelyn's death, and eagerly he
looked forward to playing the host at the funeral feast
Damaris had arranged at his house.

"I thank you for coming, Simon," said Roger,
grasping Willet's hand warmly in his. "Your presence
is a comfort to me. I trust you and your good wife will
honor me by attending me at my home?"

To Roger's surprise, Willet only grunted and looked
uncomfortably down at his buckled shoes as his wife
stood toe-to-toe with Damaris, staring in stern silence
at the younger woman. Yet Damaris held her ground,
even daring to raise her chin bravely to meet the full
force of Elisabeth's disapproval.

"Thee has no shame, does thee, Damaris Clarke?"
said Elisabeth, letting each word ring out like a pro-
nouncement. "Nor decency, nor sense of seemliness,
nor any other quality of a virtuous woman. Isn't it bad
enough for thee to bring thyself and thy sin to this holy

place on this sad day, without summoning the partner in thy wickedness here, as well?''

Pointedly Elisabeth stared past Damaris. With a questioning look at his sister-in-law, Roger turned to follow the older woman's glance, as did every other mourner within earshot. With her cheeks flaming and her heartbeat throbbing in her ears, Damaris did not need to look to know who was there. She could feel him there, sensing his presence as surely as if he had laid his hands upon her shoulders. Slowly she turned with the others, toward the stone wall of the burial ground, and Jonathan, on horseback, watching her, only her.

Chapter Eleven

If Damaris had given him one sign of recognition, a wave or a nod, anything to show she welcomed him, Jonathan would have taken the horse over the stone wall in an instant to steal her away. Anger had brought him here to find her, anger and resentment that she could abandon him so readily. But the anger had vanished as soon as he'd seen her again, straight and severe and achingly beautiful in her black gown, and all that he felt now was a longing so raw that it threatened to tear him apart. Three days, that was all. How could he have missed her so much?

He watched, and he waited, the horse dancing nervously beneath him. She'd been crying, he could see that even from here, but that was natural at a burying. A quick smile through the tears was what he longed for. A smile from her would be more than enough.

But, surrounded by her people, she did not move, her golden head still turned toward him and her expression unchanging, and although the flush that stained her cheeks deepened beneath his scrutiny, she met and held his gaze without flinching. Was that all he meant to her, he thought as his hopes crumbled with despair, an embarrassment that merited a blush and nothing else?

At the edges of his vision he was aware of men breaking away from the gathering to come toward him, shouting at him and shaking their fists. They needn't bother. He wouldn't shame Damaris Allyn any longer with his public attentions. Roughly he pulled the horse's head around and dug his heels into the animal's sides. He would find a tavern and drink as much rum as it would take to tear her lovely face from his heart.

But, though the liquor seared his throat, her image stayed clear and sharp, haunting him still: how she'd watch him shyly from beneath her lashes, her chin tipped to one side; the silkiness of her honey gold hair as it slipped through his fingers; her sharp, sweet little cries when he'd brought her to pleasure.

His fingers tightened around the tankard, and he swore softly to himself. Had he really believed she'd choose him over her family and friends? What *had* he expected today, anyway? To carry her away across his saddle like the hero of some ancient ballad? His story was fit for a ballad, aye, but one more bawdy than gallant, the amorous young widow and the roving sailor, the kind of song he'd laughed at himself, maybe even contributed a lewd verse or two of his own to. But he wasn't laughing now, God help him. Damaris could prattle on all she wanted about needing him, but he was the one who'd fallen in love.

"Cap'n Sparhawk?" asked the young man uncertainly from the far side of the table, his eyes round as coins as he stared at Jonathan through the tavern's smoky gloom.

"Depends on who's asking, greenhorn," growled Jonathan. He was in no mood for company, and particularly not the company of this timid little whelp. Though Jonathan guessed the man to be past twenty, old enough to sprout a beard and a sparse cluster of hair on his chest above his shirt, he still had the gawkiness of a boy, and no notion at all of what to do with his oversize hands.

"It *is* ye, Cap'n, sir!" he exclaimed, too excited to notice the lack of welcome in Jonathan's manner. Hastily he whipped off the battered hat he wore, with a turkey feather through the cocked side. "I wouldn't warrant it 'cept with my own eyes, but here ye be, bold as life!"

Jonathan reached across the table and grabbed the man by his short sailor's jacket, jerking him down so their faces were level. "Hold your braying tongue, you young jackass! You may know my name, but that don't mean you have to go crying it about for the whole town to hear."

Silently the man nodded, slipping down onto the opposite bench as his eyes grew even larger. Muttering an oath under his breath, Jonathan released him and leaned back against the wall. Better to be recognized by this puppy than by the magistrate, but better still not to be recognized at all.

"So you know who I am, do you."

"'Course I do, same as I know my own name's Tom Cooke," he answered indignantly.

Bless the man for telling his name, thought Jonathan, or Tom would know for sure his captain hadn't the slightest idea who he was.

"Seein' as I've sailed for ye since I was a lad, nigh seven years now," Tom continued. "Never sailed for no one else. 'Ceptin' these last weeks, an' then only on account I thought you was dead, like th' others."

Jonathan motioned for the tavernkeeper to bring a tankard for Tom. Though outwardly he'd managed to keep his surly facade, his heart was pounding and his mouth was dry. If he wanted, he could learn the answers to every question that had plagued him these last weeks, but oddly, as he watched Tom gulp his rum, he wasn't sure anymore that he wanted to know. "How many of the crew are left?" he asked carefully.

Tom wiped his mouth with the back of his hand, thinking. "There's me an' Will an' old Henry an' Jeremy an' th' Wilton brothers. Seven, all told, wit' ye, an' that's a wonder right there. Ye remember how th' fightin' went against us, Cap'n Sparhawk?"

"I remember, Tom," said Jonathan quietly, and he did. It was the one thing he couldn't forget.

Tom looked down at his hat on the table, and slowly stroked the barbs of the turkey feather. "Ye lost a dozen good men wit' that day's work, an' both boys, too, God rest 'em all. Georgie, y'know, he was my sister's lad, an' I ain't gone home from fear o' havin' t' tell her to her face he's dead."

Jonathan could put no faces to either Georgie or the other boy, or to the twelve dead crewmen, either, but the pain in Tom's voice was vivid enough. Fourteen deaths on his head, thought Jonathan grimly, and that was only his own people. How many others had he killed himself? Everything he'd feared was true, and worse than he suspected.

And Damaris... Damaris would never forgive him if she learned of it. Not that she would now, least-ways not from him. Hearing the truth from Tom had left him no choice. He would disappear tonight, sail under another name on the next vessel that would take him, and Damaris could go on with her life without him. He remembered how coolly she'd stared at him in the churchyard. Perhaps, for her, his leaving wouldn't be unwelcome.

"Do you know what became of the sloop, Tom?" he asked, trying to shift to easier topics. "Did she go down in deep water, or break up on the rocks?"

"Neither, Cap'n Sparhawk," said Tom smugly, pleased for once to know more than his master. "She ran up on a shore with a sandy bottom, an' though she was stove in a bit aft on a snag o' rocks, she come through snug. 'Course, she lost her foremast an' most o' her lines with it, but nothing that couldn't be fixed. Most already be set t' rights."

Jonathan leaned forward with excitement. "Where is she, Tom? Who's got her?"

Tom slumped back dejectedly. "Ah, ye don't want t' know, indeed ye don't," he said, shaking his head sadly. "Them bastards that took us claimed protection o' th' Crown or some such foolishness, an' now yer poor *Leopard*'s put out to let by some fat-arse from th' admiralty. They lost all yer papers by accident on purpose, an' carried off all yer goods in th' bargain. Gave us that was left th' choice o' signin' on

fer privateerin', goin' after Spaniards fer some fine
Newport gentleman, or t' be hung fer pirates on
Gravelly Point.''

They wouldn't have given a pirate captain a choice,
thought Jonathan bitterly. If he'd been taken with the
rest of them, he'd be long dead and rotting on the
gibbet. The admiralty courts didn't linger over matters of piracy. He thought of Damaris again, and her
magistrate brother-in-law, and guessed she'd never
mentioned to him the castaway she'd found on her
beach. Unwittingly, she'd once again saved his life.
Either that, or the authorities were so convinced that
Captain Jonathan Sparhawk was already dead that
they hadn't bothered investigating.

At least they had been until he'd set himself up fine
as a lord for them to gawk at today in the churchyard.
One more reason to leave Newport, and tonight.

Tom looked up at him wistfully. ''Ye could take th'
Leopard back, Cap'n Sparhawk. Ye could count on
th' lot o' us that was her people t' fight behind ye
again. She's hardly guarded at all, 'specially at night.
Ye could take her back easy an' nice as kiss yer hand.''

But Jonathan shook his head. ''Nay, I doubt there's
fight enough left in me these days to take a shallop, let
alone an armed sloop. Besides, I've no wish to see
myself stretched at this Gravelly Point just yet.''

''Aye, sir, if that's how ye feel.'' Tom winked slyly.
''Though I warrant ye could even sign on proper if ye
were of a mind. A different name, o' course, but who
would know? Would be like ol' times t' have ye wit'
us.''

"A dangerous game, that one, Tom, though tempting." He had so little left of his old life that the idea of taking a new name seemed oddly appealing. Besides, it would be one more way to separate himself from Damaris, for in his mind he'd always hear his name the way she pronounced it in her soft, breathy voice. "Nay, I'll sign on with people who don't know me, and make my way from there."

"Aye, sir, though we'd all wish otherwise." Tom sighed so sadly that Jonathan signaled for his tankard to be refilled. "Ye been back home yerself, Cap'n Sparhawk?"

"I doubt my family wants any more to do with me these days than that sister of yours." Jonathan shook his head and stared down into his now-empty tankard. Part of him longed to ask after sisters he himself might have, to ask even as simple a question as where his home might be, but he decided against it. What decent family would claim a thieving murderer, anyway? "I've been keeping low with the people that fished me out of the water. Saved my life, they did, so I've been helping them out with their farm and such, by way of payment."

There, he thought, that sounded vague enough to keep Damaris out of his troubles. He'd been on Aquidneck long enough to see that the island was nothing but farms, and every one of them bordered the water.

Tom laughed uproariously, both his good humor and his familiarity helped a good deal by the additional rum. "Farmin', ye say? Ah, what th' folks at

Plumstead would give t' see Cap'n Jonathan Sparhawk turn his seafarin' hand t' a plow!"

Plumstead, Plumstead... The name hung just out of reach, so tantalizingly close in his consciousness that Jonathan closed his eyes with concentration, struggling to bring it back. He only half listened as Tom rambled on, until suddenly his attention jerked back to the other man's words.

"'Tis a pity ye didn't wind up wit' some o' th' smugglin' folks. This whole colony's so full o' people cheatin' th' Crown, I heard they don't even bother keepin' a customs house. Why, a man be here th' other night, Yorker Dutch, tellin' us all about some lady tradin' spirits. 'Course, we called him a drunken liar, an' sent him along." He guffawed again, and slapped the table. "Can ye fancy that in Massachusetts, now? A lady smugglin' spirits!"

With an effort, Jonathan kept his tone as light as Tom's. He wished he could rip Johannes de Vere's tongue right out of his rum-sodden head for bandying Damaris's good name and secrets about in a tavern. "Can you fancy a Massachusetts husband letting his woman go traipsing about with smugglers?"

"Ah, but Cap'n, she's a widow-lady, y'see, wit' no man t' answer to. Likely old as sin, an' twice as ugly, too, or I'd be of a mind t' go out there an' learn her a woman's place myself." He winked broadly and leered. "Sample her wares, too, an' I don't be meanin' only th' spirits. Widows is always th' most grateful o' God's female creatures."

As Tom laughed, Jonathan ordered himself not to care. Damaris Allyn wasn't his responsibility, and never had been. She was kind and generous, true, and she'd shared that with him when he'd needed it, but then he'd paid her back, working her farm and trading the Madeira for her. And that night in her kitchen he'd answered her questions about what she'd missed with that half-gelded husband of hers. Curiosity, that was all that had been, or else she wouldn't have been so quick to leave afterward.

Aye, anyone would say that he and Damaris were even now. He'd been fool enough to fall in love with her, but he'd get over that, as soon as he took himself out of her life and began again living his own.

As soon as the paneled front door of Roger's house had closed behind the last of the mourners from the funeral, Damaris gathered her skirts and rushed up the stairs toward the chamber where she'd slept. Close on her heels came Roger, covering two steps at a time to catch her, the thin veneer of civility he had managed throughout the day gone with the mourners.

"Don't you dare run from me now, Damaris!" he shouted as he reached up to grab her by the arm. "God's blood, madam, after how you've shamed my wife's memory this day, I deserve answers!"

"And thee mustn't dare touch me, Roger!" said Damaris as she jerked her arm free. "Newport may forgive thee one Allyn wife dead on these stairs, but not two!"

"Where's your meek Quaker tongue now? Gone with all your sham modesty, I'll wager! I wonder if poor Eben had any notion of the slut you were when he wed you!"

"Thee never cared a fig about thy brother, Roger, nor thy wife, from what I've seen in this house," Damaris said sharply, her own temper rising in response to his. "Thee cares only for thyself, and thee is welcome to thy own companionship!"

She tried to shut the door to her room between them, but he forced his way in behind her. Ignoring him, she began pulling the clothes she'd worn from Nantasket from the chest at the end of the bed, and quickly bundled them together. She didn't want the black farandine gown she was wearing now, but she refused to stay in Roger's house any longer, not even the few extra minutes it would take her to change.

With both hands, Roger slammed the lid of the chest shut and jerked her around to face him. "Who was that man in the churchyard, Damaris?"

She clutched the bundle of clothing in her arms, remembering. She had seen beyond that fierce, wild look of Jonathan's that had alarmed the others, beyond the way his long black hair had blown around his unshaven face, his shirt open at the throat and a red kerchief around his neck. She had seen instead the loneliness etched deep in his face, the pain and uncertainty that had told her at once that he hadn't understood why she had stayed away. No matter how shocked she had been to see him there—and she had been, so much so that she still half believed that she had imagined it all—she should have gone to him then and told him she loved him.

"I told thee who he is when thee asked me earlier," she said uneasily. Roger's grip on her shoulders hurt, his nails digging into her skin, and this time she found she couldn't shake herself free. "He's a seaman from Massachusetts who has been working for me at Nantasket."

"Aye, you told me that tale, but I didn't believe you then and I don't believe you now." With both hands, Roger shoved her away from him in disgust, and she stumbled backward. He was breathing heavily, his face deep red with rage, and though he and Damaris were close in size, she realized suddenly that she was right to be afraid of him. She saw how his fists were clenched at his sides, and she thought of Evelyn, and the bruises on Evelyn's face.

"Who is he, Damaris? Did you think I didn't notice how he looked at you? Not the way a servant looks at his mistress, but the way a rogue eyes a trollop he has possessed already, and hopes to possess again. Nay, madam, don't deny it! I was convinced of it even before Elisabeth Willet told me what she'd witnessed at Nantasket. Nantasket, for God's sake, in my mother's house!"

For a long moment, Damaris said nothing, letting the heat of Roger's fury roll over her. Some inward sense told her that to argue any further with him would be wrong, and that defensiveness was what he wanted. Instead she drew upon years of habitual calmness and bowed her head with a quiet resignation she was far from feeling.

"I'm a grown woman, Roger, thy brother's widow," she said carefully. "I don't answer to thee, nor do I answer to Elisabeth Willet."

As confidently as she could, Damaris turned her back on Roger long enough to take her cloak from the peg and walk to the door. She felt herself shaking, every nerve on edge, as she expected him to lash out at her at any moment. At the doorway, she paused, her head still bent, unable to meet the fury she knew she would find in Roger's eyes. "For thy mother's sake, I am sorry if thee believes I have dishonored her home. But for what thee has said to me this day, thee shall never be welcome there again."

She had nearly reached the end of town when a neat curricle rattled to a halt beside her, and Ned Carr hopped down over the near wheel, the whip tucked under his arm. "I'm sorry, mistress. A lady like ye shouldn't have had t' walk at all," he said, his hand outstretched to help her into the curricle. "But ye would leave in such a blessed hurry, wit'out any notice t' anyone."

Damaris looked down at the dust that already clung to the hem of her black gown. She had never thought of herself as a lady, and she doubted she would pass for one now, to anyone except Ned.

"I'm not going back, Ned," she said. "Thee can tell Master Allyn I said so, if he didn't understand me well enough before."

"Oh, nay, mistress, he understood well enough," said Ned uncomfortably. "He said I was t' take ye back t' Nantasket, if that was where ye wished t' go."

"More likely he doesn't want his neighbors whispering that he'd let me walk home," said Damaris as she climbed up into the curricle without Ned's help. "But I thank thee regardless, Ned."

She had Ned leave her by the long stone wall that marked the beginning of her property, and watched

the carriage disappear down the road back to Newport. Absently she bent to pluck one of the violets that
grew in the shadow of the wall, twirling the stem between her fingers as she walked toward the house. The
walls had been built long ago for the first Allyns by
obliging Narragansett Indians who hadn't realized the
Englishmen meant to stay and claim the land for
themselves. Forty years later, it had been the Allyns
who didn't understand when the Indians returned to
burn the farm and slaughter them and their livestock
in King Philip's war. Now Damaris felt she was the
one confused by a stranger on her land, and uneasily
she wondered what, if anything, lay ahead between
Jonathan and herself.

As she climbed the last rise she heard the sharp
thump of an axe biting into wood echoing between the
barn and the house. From the crest she watched Jonathan splitting the short chunks of logs for shingles.
The late-afternoon sun was still warm, and he worked
without a shirt, the sweat glistening on the broad, hard
muscles of his back and shoulders as over and over he
swung the axe in the same overhead arc. As she
watched, she felt something tighten inside her chest,
and she realized how much she had missed him, and
how much she loved him. What, she wondered, did he
feel in return? With a little sigh, she looped the bundle of clothing over her arm and headed down toward
the yard.

From the corner of his eye, Jonathan caught the
movement on the hillside beside him. In an instant he
had dropped the axe and grabbed the musket from the

fence beside him, and spun 'round to face whoever dared creep into the yard.

"So you've come back," he said without emotion when he saw it was Damaris. He lowered the gun from his shoulder, but gave her no warmer sign of a welcome. The ship he'd joined would leave with the tide after midnight for Bermuda. He'd come back to Nantasket only to return the horse and gather his belongings, and with time on his hands, he'd begun splitting the shingles to try to sweat the cheap rum out of his head. If he'd guessed he'd have to see Damaris again, he wouldn't have returned. He had never been any good at farewells, and this one, this one he knew would hurt.

"Of course I came back. Thee might recall, this is my home." None of the vulnerability that she'd seen earlier was left in his face now, and her heart sank. Maybe she'd imagined it was there after all. Maybe, if she was lucky, none of this whole awful day was real, and she'd wake up to find it all a dream. "Thee shouldn't wonder that I returned to it."

"Mighty fancy burial for that sister-in-law of yours," he said as he set the gun down beside the axe. She looked so tired and worn that it took all his resolve not to reach out to her. Earlier he had tied the red kerchief around his head to keep his hair from his eyes, and now he pulled it off and used it to wipe his face, thankful for something to do that did not involve touching her. "I'd wager the whole town came."

"Evelyn had many friends, and Roger has a wide acquaintance through trade." Damaris told herself she should go into the house and end this cold, remote conversation, but instead she held her ground, hoping against hope that he would warm to her and become again the man she loved.

"Precious lot of Quakers," he said bluntly, and hated himself for the way the pain flickered across her face. What was he doing, anyway? He'd meant merely to keep his distance, not to flail her alive. "What did they make of you being there?"

Her laugh was short and brittle. "Not as much as they made of thee, Jonathan. Mine was a scandal grown old and stale, but thee has managed to revive it quite wonderfully with thy appearance today."

"I don't do anything by halves. You must know that much about me by now."

"*Jonathan.*" She stared past his shoulder to the barn, concentrating on keeping the quaver from her voice. "If I have given thee even a hundredth of the pain that thee is giving me at this moment, I am sorry, so sorry, and I beg thee to forgive me if thee can. I didn't mean to stay away so long, but I believed I was needed, that it was proper for me to stay. But... but... oh, Jonathan, how right thee was about Roger!"

Still she didn't cry, but he heard the strain and fear in her voice, and automatically he slipped his arms around her shoulders and drew her close. With a broken sigh, she rested her cheek against his bare shoulder and let him hold her, his broad hands resting on her waist. It was strange, she thought, how much a part of home he had come to be for her. "After we left the burying ground, he—"

"I'm leaving," he said abruptly. He didn't want to hear about Roger, or how sad the funeral had been. He was done with getting himself tangled in her affairs. "Tonight. I'll clear Newport with the tide before dawn."

"Oh." Slowly she stepped away from him, letting his arms slip from her waist as the single syllable hung in the air between them. Now, strangely, her eyes were dry, as she searched his face for the answer she already knew. This, then, was what he had been trying to tell her earlier, in Newport. From the night she'd found him on the beach, she had known he would leave her. It had only been a matter of when. *"Oh."*

"You don't want me to stay, Damaris," he said roughly, even though she hadn't asked him to. He caught himself studying her black gown, cut much more fashionably than what she usually wore. French farandine—from Lyons, if he wasn't mistaken, silk and wool, woven with a muted figure—*Jesus, why was he pricing the clothes on her back now?* "We don't belong together, and you know why as well as I do."

She swallowed hard. "What I know, or what I want, doesn't really matter much to thee, does it?"

"Hell, Damaris, I don't know what the devil—"

"Don't swear at me, Jonathan," she said with an edge that he hadn't expected. "I've asked thee before not to speak thus in my presence, and thee never has heeded my request."

"Don't turn righteous with me, Damaris," he said sharply, raking his hand back through his hair. Damnation, she didn't even fight like other women! "We're long past the point when you can lecture me like a parson."

She lifted her chin a little higher. She didn't wish to be guilty of pridefulness, but she refused to beg him to stay. "Thee has always been free to leave whenever thee chose. Thee owes me no excuses. If thee sails to-night, thee goes with my blessings and my good wishes, and nothing else. May God be with thee on thy journey, Jonathan, and keep thee from harm."

She turned away, toward the house, each step of her dusty shoes another step away from him. He had left the door open, and she gently closed it behind her before she headed up the winding stairs to her chamber. Now the tears blurred her eyes, and she pressed her palm across her mouth to keep from sobbing out loud. She paused in her doorway, fighting against her misery. So she'd managed to keep her composure before him, and she hadn't humbled herself by begging. But what did she have to show for it? With a frustrated wail she hurled the bundle of clothing against the wall.

With the setting sun still slanting through the windows, the room was stuffy and hot, and the mourning gown that Roger had insisted upon clung heavily to her body. Evelyn's maid had helped her dress this morning, and now Damaris struggled to untie the back lacings of the bodice by herself. Over and over a bumblebee thumped angrily against the closed casement, as frustrated with his lot, thought Damaris unhappily, as she was herself. Still tugging at the gown, she swung open the casement, and the bee sailed out. Tentatively Damaris let herself glance down into the yard. There was the axe, and the pile of new shingles, but there was no sign of Jonathan. So he had left, exactly as he had promised. She leaned her head back against the window frame, her arms wrapped tightly over her chest, and closed her eyes against fresh tears.

The door to her chamber exploded open, and suddenly Jonathan seemed to fill the room. Quickly Damaris drew herself upright, clutching her unlaced bodice over her petticoat, stays, and shift.

"I won't let you have the last word in this, Damaris!" He was so angry he could not stand still, but instead paced unevenly back and forth before her, his hands slashing though the air. "I don't want your blasted permission, or blessing, or whatever other kind of Quaker foolishness that was supposed to be. I'm leaving, aye, but not before I make you understand why."

Damaris snuffled back the last of her tears. "I told thee that's not important."

"And I say it is." At least, he thought with small satisfaction, she cried the same as other women. Her nose was red and shiny, and her hair was trailing down around her cheeks, and red-rimmed though her eyes were, he'd never seen them look so blue, her lashes black and spiky with tears. "Remember when you called me a pirate, Damaris? You didn't mean to, but you did, because in your heart you believed it. And you were right, Damaris, because that *is* what I am, a pirate, a murderer, a thief that's wanted by the hangman."

She ducked her chin uncertainly. "Thee remembers this?"

"Nay, not all of it, but enough," he said heavily. There, he'd told her the truth. "Today I met a man in Newport who knew me, and knew what I've done, and asked me to do it again, and God help me, I almost agreed."

Her brows drawn together, Damaris shook the stray hair back from her forehead. "I don't believe thee, Jonathan."

He stopped his pacing, staring at her. "Damaris, it's not a question of whether you believe me or not. It's the truth. This man was one of my crew. He sailed and fought with me for seven years!"

"Then he's lying," she said quickly, her eyes troubled. "Jonathan, I can't believe these things of thee. Thee is not a wicked man, not like this."

He groaned and shook his head. "Damaris, sweeting, I don't remember it all, but I remember enough for it to be true." He looked away from her, unwilling to see the trust in her face, trust that he didn't deserve. "I remember the *Leopard,* a sloop with clean, fast lines I'd watched built myself. And I remember the last vessel we tried to take, and the fighting, and how we lost."

His face grew hard and his shoulders tensed and bunched as he relived that last fragment of his forgotten life, and again he felt the power of the blood lust taking hold of him. "I fought and I killed other men, Damaris, killed them with no more thought than you would pull a weed. You ask what I remember. I remember how good it felt to watch a man's lifeblood run down my sword, knowing that he died while I still lived. It felt *good,* Damaris."

Savagely his hand sliced through the air, as if he still held the sword. "Twelve of my own crew died that day, because I asked them to. God only knows how many of the others I sent to their graves, as well. Twelve men, and two boys. Boys I'd taken from their mothers to learn my trade, and all I did was teach them to steal and die. I can't forget that, Damaris, and neither should you."

Silently Damaris listened, her turmoil growing. From his anguish, she knew he believed what he said about himself, but deep inside, she didn't. She couldn't. There was no way she could reconcile what he was telling her now with the man she had come to know and love these last weeks. Yet there were the old scars on his chest, and the new one on his leg, his easy familiarity with guns and knives for fighting, and the practiced way he'd dealt with de Vere on the beach. And why should this man in the tavern lie?

Nay, it could not be true! Desperately she fought with her doubts. If he was what he said, then why would he have come back? A man as wicked as he claimed to be would have robbed her long ago, raped her if he'd wanted, perhaps even murdered her. He wouldn't have split shingles for her roof, or protected her, or made love to her until she cried with joy.

At last he swung around to face her. "I can't stay here with you any longer, sweeting," he said bleakly. "You don't deserve the trouble I'm bound to bring you. I can't save your life when I've made such a wreck of my own, and I can't replace Eben. I'm not the hero you want me to be, Damaris. I'm not even a particularly good man.''

''Oh, aye, Jonathan, I believe thee is,'' said Damaris softly. ''And thee is the man I love.''

Chapter Twelve

Jonathan winced as if he'd been struck, his dark brows drawn sharply together. "It's always been like that between us, hasn't it?" he demanded grimly. "You're always so damned honorable and giving, while I'm supposed to stand here and take it like some pathetic, grateful beggar."

Damaris gasped. "That isn't true, Jonathan! I've never done that to thee! Thee isn't being fair—"

"Fair?" His green eyes glittered, hard as glass. "Don't waste your sorry Quaker right and wrong on me. There's precious little in this world that's fair, Damaris, and that includes me."

But what was most unfair of all was the way she was standing there, so near to him that he could smell her warm fragrance, how she was quarreling with him in little more than her petticoats, clutching her gown to her breasts in that ridiculous, tempting manner that didn't hide a thing, the skin of her shoulders pale gold above the white shift. Jesus, he could make out the dusky circles of her nipples through the sheer linen. He wanted her—oh, aye, he couldn't deny that—but his desire went far deeper than her body alone, deeper than either of them realized.

She saw how he was looking at her, his gaze as intimate as any caress, and she blushed now, not in modesty or anticipation, but in shame. With his anger, he had forfeited his right to look at her like that. "Then what does thee want me to say, Jonathan? Must I lie like thee, and swear that I don't give a fig if thee stays or leaves? For thee *is* lying about that, isn't thee? I don't any more believe that thee truly wants to leave Nantasket tonight than I believe that thee is some great bloodthirsty pirate come to slit my throat!"

He took one step closer to her, his voice dropping to a low rumble. "Then why the devil are you making this so blessed hard for both of us?"

"Because I love thee, Jonathan Sparhawk." She was trembling, both with anger and with a kind of sick anticipation of his departure. She looked down from his face to his chest, to the pale slashes of scars beneath the dark, curling hair. She'd never dreamed she'd speak so boldly to a man, especially a man like this, but too much was at stake for her to keep silent. "If thee stays, I'll love thee, and if thee leaves with the night tide, I'll love thee, too. There's no help for it. Thee can judge better than I whether that's fair in your wicked world or not."

He stared at her, unable to trust what she was saying, but wanting desperately to believe he could. If she could ignore what he had been, perhaps he could, too. He was clutching at straws in a hurricane, and he knew it, but how could a berth as mate on a dingy Bermuda-bound coaster compare with the bright promise of love she held out before him? She had healed his wounded leg. Did he dare to find out if she had the power to mend his broken spirit, as well?

"Is it fair or not, Jonathan?" she said again. "Thee must tell—"

"The devil take your fairness!" He grabbed the crumpled gown from her, tossing it to one side as he linked his fingers with hers and pulled her hard against his chest. She began to protest, but his open mouth enveloped hers. Her eyes fluttered shut, and she felt almost dizzy from the intensity of his kiss, her fingers clutching at the hard, smooth muscles of his shoulders as he bent her backward over his arm. Her first thought was of relief, at knowing now he would not go from her tonight. It was her first thought, and her last, for as his mouth claimed hers and their kiss deepened, she soon forgot everything beyond the sensations he was rousing in her willing flesh.

His long fingers tore impatiently at the lacings on her stays until she heard the cord snap, and she shrugged her shoulders back, helping him free her of the buckram and whalebone. The petticoats came next, Damaris herself awkwardly untying each of the waistbands, letting them slide over her hips to puddle around her ankles in a tangle of linen. Warm and insistent, his lips moved along her throat, finding the velvety hollow of her shoulder, and with a little shudder she caught his face in her hands and lifted his mouth back to hers.

His hands settled on her waist, kneading the fullness of her hips and buttocks as he lifted her against him. As she arched into his chest, her breasts strained

against the sheer linen of her shift. With one swift
motion, he grabbed the hem of her shift and swept it
up and over her arms and head. Wide-eyed, she
gasped softly in surprise. Eben had always left her her
shift, and she had never before been naked with a
man. But there were many things she'd never done
before that she was doing now with Jonathan, and she
let him draw her back into his embrace, shivering at
this new feeling of her bare breasts against the rough
hair on his chest. She closed her eyes and rubbed her
cheek against his shoulder. Her tongue tasted the salt-
iness of his skin, and she heard him groan, his arms
tightening around her.

He carried her the two steps to her bed. Damaris
heard the scraping of the horn rings along the rod
overhead as he jerked back the curtains. She sank
down into the feather bed, the calico counterpane cool
beneath her fevered skin, and then he was there above
her, kissing her deeply, his tongue thrusting far into
her mouth, as he longed to do with her body.

"You're like a fire in my blood, lass," he whispered hoarsely, his hands stroking her breasts until
they ached, until she ached. "Your touch burns me,
but I can't leave. God help me, *I can't leave you.*"

"Jonathan," she murmured, his name all she could
manage coherently. "Oh, Jonathan!"

It was his turn now to give, and hers to take. She felt
unbelievably wanton, her body twisting wildly beneath him, seeking his, and she reached for his shoulders as for an anchor. But instead he slid away, down
the length of her body, his tongue wet and hot across
her skin as he kissed the quivering undersides of her

breasts, her belly, and lower, lower. He lifted her legs over his arms, nipping at the soft skin inside her knees as he parted her.

She lurched upward when his mouth found her, stunned by the realization of what he was doing, but he held her fast, pressing her gently back into the coverlet as his fingers gripped her hips. How did he know to do this? she wondered, and prayed he wouldn't stop. She felt the tension coiling in her body again the way it had with him that time in the kitchen, felt her thighs stiffen and tremble as she arched her hips against him. Her hands clutched fistfuls of the counterpane as her head thrashed frantically from side to side, her cries rising with her passion, until finally the tension exploded, and her release came with a force that left her panting and limp.

Jonathan had waited until he was certain she'd found her pleasure, but his own desire was beyond waiting now. His heart pounding and his breath ragged, he covered her body with his own, fitting himself between her legs, sliding into her. She was so slick and hot that he dared not move at first, struggling to find some last bit of control as he felt the final shudders of her pleasure tighten around him. Jesus, he didn't want this to end so soon, but he hadn't bargained for the intensity of his need for her. If it had been lust alone, he could have mastered it, but what he wanted was that and more, something elusive and intangible that only she could give. Over and over he whispered her name, like a chant, as slowly he began to move within her. She made a soft sound of contentment deep in her throat, rocking her hips up to seat him more deeply, and all his resolve shattered.

Damaris closed her eyes, reveling in the fullness of him within her, and traced her fingers across the breadth of his sweat-filmed shoulders. She could never have imagined that such glory could come from loving. His urgency rippled through her fingertips, and her hands tightened over the smooth, taut curves of his flanks as she felt the muscles tense and release with his movements. Without thinking, she began to match his rhythm, arching beneath him as she met his thrusts. When he kissed her, she could taste herself on his lips, and, unbelievably, she felt the magic deep within her belly beginning again. She crossed her legs over his back, taking him deeper, welcoming him, loving him, until at last they came together as one, bound together in one glorious moment of union.

Afterward they lay together without stirring, his head still pillowed on her breasts and her legs tangled around his. The sun had dropped below the hillside, and with evening the wind had swung round to blow from the water. The air was heavy with the sea, and the sound of the endless rush and hiss of the waves on the beach. Gently Damaris stroked Jonathan's head, running her fingers through the dark waves of his hair. So soft and silky, she thought drowsily as a curl twisted around her finger. Sometimes it seemed his hair was the only thing soft or yielding about him.

With a sigh, he shifted his weight to his elbows, raising his face over hers. "You don't lie, do you, Damaris Allyn?" he whispered roughly as he traced his thumb across her lower lip. "For all that you've been my Scheherazade, you've never yet told me a tale, have you?''

Confused, Damaris looked up at him, searching his green cat's eyes for his meaning. ''Thee knows what the truth means to me,'' she said uncertainly, ''and thee should know that I've never lied to thee, either.''

She saw how his mouth twisted as he tried to smile, ready to make light of what he asked if the answer she gave wasn't what he hoped, and her heart sank.

''So you do love me, Damaris?''

''Does thee doubt me, then?'' she asked sorrowfully, her arms sliding away from his neck. ''After what has just passed between us, thee still cannot trust me?''

He shook his head, his long hair brushing over her cheek. ''Nay, sweeting, never that,'' he answered with despair. '''Tis myself I don't trust. I love you, Damaris, I love you more than I could ever say or show you. Yet, given what I am, how can my love ever be enough for a woman like you?''

''Oh, but it is, Jonathan,'' she whispered unsteadily as she pulled his face down to kiss him. ''Enough and more.''

Wordlessly he swept her away again with the fierceness of his lovemaking, their passion this second time still burning white-hot in its intensity. Yet long after he'd buried himself in the sweetness of Damaris's body, and she'd fallen asleep curled beneath the shelter of his arm, Jonathan still couldn't tell whether he had found himself in her love, or instead been lost forever.

* * *

It was still dark when Damaris realized that Jonathan was gone.

Halfway between sleeping and waking, she had stretched and reached for him beside her, and found only the hollow his body had left in the feather bed. Instantly she was awake, upright in the bed with the counterpane clutched up over her nakedness. Swallowing her panic, she touched her palm to the sheets where he had lain; they were cool, and damp from the sea air. So he had left after all, exactly as he'd sworn he would.

She saw the movement in the shadows near the window and gasped before she found his profile, picked out in the moonlight. He was holding the mourning gown up to the window, staring at it intently as he rubbed the fabric between his thumb and forefinger. "Jonathan?" she asked hesitantly, not quite sure what to ask. "Is thee— Is there something I might do for thee?"

He neither turned nor apologized for waking her. "How did you come by this gown?"

"Roger ordered it for me to wear at Evelyn's burying. He found my own clothing wanting, and because of his grief I thought it best to please his whims." She paused, thinking again how false Roger's bereavement now struck her, and how Evelyn had deserved better. "The mantua maker fussed over the haste, but Roger agreed to pay her double, and the gown was delivered this morning."

She hugged her knees and waited for his explanation. She knew she was inexperienced with worldly men, but this conversation still struck her as passing odd. This night they had made love twice, and confessed it, too, and yet here was Jonathan wanting to discuss a gown. Perhaps he, like Eben, disliked the plain clothing she preferred. The farandine gown was deep mourning, true, but with its sweeping skirts and narrow, tapered bodice, it was far more fashionable than what she usually wore. Beauty should come from the soul, not from bright silk ribbons, Damaris reminded herself sternly, though of course Jonathan wouldn't see with a Friend's eyes. She tugged at a snarl in her hair, and wished he would speak.

Jonathan stroked his fingers across the distinctive twill of the black cloth, remembering. *Foucault's shop was tucked in an alley near the wharfs in Bridgetown, the windows so dirty that the light inside was gray even at midday, and filled with dancing motes of silk and wool and cotton that came from the linen-wrapped bolts stacked high on the old Frenchman's shelves. Foucault had shoved aside a yellow tomcat as he'd spread the farandine across the front counter, noting how elegant, yet durable, it would be on widows in New England. He'd complained about Spanish marauders to try to drive the price higher, but Jonathan had held firm at what was fair, and taken fifty ells of the stuff on the Sparhawk account.*

"I didn't steal it, Damaris," he said, his voice filled with bewildered joy. "I paid for it, or leastways put it on account in my name. Amounts to the same thing, doesn't it? Jesus, I didn't *steal* it!"

"Steal what, Jonathan?" asked Damaris, completely lost. "What did thee pay for?"

"This selfsame farandine, sweeting, come from Lyons by way of Barbados, and now some blessed seamstress in Thames Street!" he exclaimed, waving the gown over his head like a banner.

"But thee has been here, at Nantasket—"

"Hold now, lass and listen," he said excitedly. "The man I met in the tavern said my cargo had been confiscated, marked for stolen. But I'd swear by all that's holy that this farandine came in my sloop with me from Bridgetown, and that I paid for it, paid dear, too, knowing Foucault. God in heaven, what I'd give to know if the rest of my cargo was honest, too!"

"So someone in Newport has stolen from thee." Damaris frowned and shook her head. "That's not right, Jonathan. Thee must learn who it was, and go to the magistrate."

"Not if I want to stay a free man, I won't. Your magistrate takes one good look at this pretty fellow, and I'll be in irons in a blink." He chuckled softly to himself, shaking his head as he scratched his jaw. "I was a damned fool as it was to parade about before the gentry at Mistress Evelyn's burying, and I won't make that mistake twice. 'Tis better to keep low until I can remember more."

To Damaris, there seemed little enough in what he said that was worth laughing at. "Faith, Jonathan, I can't see why that should make thee so gleeful!"

"First things first, love," said Jonathan as he bounded onto the bed. The ropes creaked in protest at his weight. With a great, happy sigh, he settled back against the bolsters. "To you it may seem slight enough, but I've done at least one thing that's honorable and honest, and I remembered it. Pray God that more will come, but it's a beginning, Damaris. It's a beginning.''

He lay there shamelessly, gloriously naked against the pillow biers, his arms folded behind his head and his smile ghostly in the moonlight, and with a little lurch of her heart, and another place somewhat lower, Damaris decided she'd never seen him look as handsome. Despite all that had passed between them, she herself had shyly kept the counterpane tucked up under her arms.

"I told thee from the first that thee wasn't a wicked man," she said softly. "If thee was, then thee wouldn't care so much about learning otherwise. Perhaps when thee remembers more, thee will find that those other... other bad things, can be explained, as well."

His expression darkened. "Nay, sweeting, I doubt that." Even she couldn't explain away dead men, but he wouldn't think of that now. "But you believed in me when I doubted myself, and for that alone I'd love you."

She slanted her eyes at him suspiciously. "For that alone, and nothing more?"

"Oh, I warrant I'd consider your squash pie and lamb stew into the bargain, too," he admitted lazily, pretending to yawn.

She yelped indignantly and reached out to strike him, but instead he caught her wrists and pulled her up onto his chest, and the counterpane slid to one side. He kissed her gently this time, teasing her lips apart with his tongue as she sprawled across his body. Deep in her throat she made a sound halfway between a chuckle of happiness and a moan of desire, and his hands circled possessively around her waist. Even as they kissed, she could feel his blood quicken, and his arousal heavy against her thigh.

Her eyes widened as his lips feathered against her cheek. "Again, Jonathan? Three times in one night?"

"I could love you three score times a thousand, and still not tire of you, my own sweet Damaris," he whispered into her ear as his hands eased down her hips.

And this time, when he loved her, he realized that what he'd lost had not been worth keeping, and what he'd found was worth more than gold.

"Master Allyn must be a-turnin' an' a-twistin' in his grave wit' that bastardy half brother o' his darin' t' come to Nantasket again," said Ruth contemptuously under her breath as she and Damaris watched Roger ride into the yard and toward them. "Ye forbid him come, but here he be, bold as brass an' worth naught but lead."

"Hush now, Ruth," said Damaris testily. Nearly a week had passed since she had quarreled with Roger and left his house, a week in which she'd thought and done little beyond loving Jonathan, and being loved in return. For a week they'd been able to hold the world at bay, but now it seemed that the world, in Roger's elegant person, was determined to intrude.

Ruth spat in the dust. "An' him wit' the blood o' his poor little wife still on his hands!"

"Hold thy tongue, Ruth!" Damaris watched as Roger tied his horse to a fence post, brushed the dust from his cloak, and came toward her, tugging his glove from his hand, and smiling pleasantly, as if he had every right to expect a welcome. She drew herself taller, keeping her face stern. She didn't care if he had come to apologize. She couldn't forget what he'd said and done, and besides, she was more than a little afraid of him. Her fingers tightened on the long handle of the wooden pitchfork in her hands. It wasn't exactly Eben's musket, but it would do well enough. Why had Jonathan chosen today of all days to inventory the hogsheads in the cave?

"Good day to you, Damaris," said Roger, his hand outstretched to take hers. "I trust I find you well?" But his brother's stiff-backed widow only watched and waited in silence, wielding that farmer's fork like some kind of vengeful Quaker fury. Roger let his hand drop to his side and fought back his irritation. Foolish, stubborn woman, considering what he'd come to offer!

Ignoring him, Damaris turned and plunged the fork deep into the kettle of simmering red dye and stirred down the woolly fleeces that bobbed to the surface. Any night now, she was expecting another shipment from de Vere, and uneasily she wondered if somehow Roger had learned of their smuggling, or, worse yet, had come seeking Jonathan. She could sense Ruth's nervousness, too, in the way the older woman was fussing with the fire beneath the kettle, tossing in sticks that weren't needed.

His patience fading, Roger sniffed audibly at the acrid smell. "What in God's name are you doing, Damaris?"

"Dying new wool with dandelion roots. The color's taken by now, so it's likely the mordant that offends thy town nose. Thee might recall from thy childhood what's used from horses to set the dye—"

"Aye, I recall," said Roger hastily. He hadn't come clear out here to discuss horse urine with her. "But look at your hands, your clothes! You're the mistress here. Why don't you leave such tasks to your Negro?"

Damaris saw how Ruth shrank back, her fear transparent on her face. "I'll remind thee again, Roger, that Ruth is my tenant, not my slave," she said, her voice frosty. "As for thy concern for my position at Nantasket, I don't worship empty titles. I'll warrant that my hands and clothes shall wash as readily as Ruth's."

Roger took a deep breath, knowing he must contain his temper at all costs. Since Evelyn's death, the creditors had been gathering like vultures, and there were even rumors that he'd be recalled from the bench until his debts were clear. Damaris was his last hope. "Damaris, I wish to talk. To apologize, truth to tell. We didn't part on comfortable terms, and I wish that to be put to rights. I vow I won't leave until you listen." He smiled winningly, and Damaris didn't doubt he meant to stay. "In the house, out of the sun? Out of the hearing of your... ah, tenant?"

"Nay, there's nothing thee might say to me that Ruth—" Damaris began, then paused. If she took Roger into the house alone, then Ruth could go warn Jonathan to stay away until her brother-in-law was safely headed back to Newport. Today she saw no sign of Roger's temper, and besides, it would be worth the risk to save Jonathan. With a nod, she handed Ruth the fork, praying the woman would understand and go to the cave.

"Very well, Roger, if thee wishes," she said as she led him into the front chamber. "But thee mustn't dawdle with thy words. I've too much to do to sit idle for long."

Roger bit back a reproof as he dropped into his father's oak armchair. After the bright sun, the house was every bit as dark and chilly as he remembered from his boyhood. He'd tear the old stone walls down the first chance he got, and put up timbers and plaster. The front room seemed smaller than he recalled, too, the beamed ceiling lower, but much of the furniture was new, as were the silver-framed mirror and the heavy candlesticks on the mantel, and all of it far better than he'd ever expected Eben to afford.

But what caught his eye at once was the white clap pipe and tobacco on the table across from Damaris's knitting, and the man's greatcoat tossed carelessly over the back of a chair. Ned had told him all about the stranger on horseback, how he seemed at his ease at Nantasket, and he'd claimed that when he'd followed Damaris back to the house he'd heard her and this man rutting like weasels in her bedchamber, but until now Roger hadn't really believed it. Eben's saintly widow, playing Mistress Laycock with some vagabond cripple!

Damaris remained standing, her hands folded over her apron. "Thee has something thee wishes to say, Roger?"

"Aye, Damaris, I do." He spread his fingers across the lace of his neckcloth, considering how best to begin. "I shall be direct, for I know you have little use for frivolous language, and so do I. I'm well aware of what's transpiring here. I'd be a fool not to, wouldn't I? But because I believe we can be of use to each other, you and I, I'd like to propose we join our fortunes instead. A partnership, if you will, Damaris."

Damaris felt as if the floor had been yanked from beneath her feet. How had Roger learned of the smuggling? Rapidly she ran over the names of her customers, wondering which had betrayed her. Jonathan had warned her this could happen, and he'd been right. But who could have guessed that Roger would want to become a partner?

Roger looked at her closely. She hadn't flinched, but she'd turned pale as death when confronted with her indiscretions. He had her now, no mistake. Pleased, he continued. "You're no silly maid, Damaris, and I'm no green youth. Surely you know such arrangements are made every day, to the profit of both parties."

"How much does thee know, Roger?" she asked, unable to keep the agitation from shaking her voice.

Roger shrugged carelessly. "Enough, my dear. There's no need to tatter your reputation any further, is there?"

"And if I refuse? Nay, I know well enough what thee will do." She stared down at the floor. "I never believed it would come to this, nor, I'm certain, did Eben, and if there had been another path open to me, I would have taken it."

Roger cocked an eyebrow. "It's a bit late to consider poor Ebenezer's feelings now, Damaris."

She sighed heavily. "What will be thy share, Roger? What must I give thee to buy thy silence?"

"God's blood, mistress, such high drama!" Irritably Roger pulled his snuffbox from his pocket. "You'll give me what's standard under the circumstances. First your hand until the banns are cried, then the rest of your person, along with your goods and property. In return, you'll have the protection of my good name and my position, and a household that's the envy of half the ladies in Newport. If you've a mind, you'll even be able to put that meddling old gossip Elisabeth Willet in her place. No more toiling at this wretched farm, living out here alone. You'll never have to stir another cauldron full of wet wool, I'll swear to that! And as my wife—"

"Thy *wife!*" cried Damaris in disbelief. She was too stunned to be relieved that he didn't know about the cave. "Evelyn's not a fortnight in the ground, and thee comes to ask me to be thy *wife?* Does thee judge me to be as mad as thee thyself must be?"

She rushed across the room, plucked Roger's hat and gloves from the table where he'd placed them, and hurled them out the open door into the dusty yard. "Take thyself and thy shameful proposal out of my house and back to Newport! Thy *wife!*" In her contempt, she practically spat the word. "Thee is just as Eben said thee was, always eager to covet what was his, whether thee truly wanted it or not. But thee won't have me, and thee won't have Nantasket!"

Roger rose slowly to his feet. His mouth was rigid as he slowly came toward her. "I wouldn't be so hasty to refuse my offer, Damaris. You won't get a better one. And I'd advise you to be careful who and what you call shameful, not as long as your own behavior is worthy of the most common trull on Thames Street."

"Faith, thee surely knows how to come a-wooing with honeyed words!" Damaris's cheeks were flushed, but not from shame but from anger, and her hands were defiantly on her hips. "I would no more wed thee, Roger, than the vilest, lowest serpent in all creation!"

"My God, how did Eben tolerate your shrewishness?" Not even Evelyn had dared speak to him this way. He'd forgotten all about claiming Nantasket. "But you'll learn your manners from me, my girl, just as you'll learn the price of talking tart to me!"

He raised his arm back to strike her with the back of his hand, and he was pleased to see how she gasped, her hands flying to her mouth. But in that half second he noticed, too, that her gaze was fixed not on him, but on something beyond his shoulder. He noticed, and he wondered, and then the blow caught him in the side, bending him in half before he flew sprawling across the floor.

Chapter Thirteen

Roger's face scraped over the wide pine planks before he came to a stop, and, half stunned, he lay there, watching Damaris's shoes and petticoat hem scurry back, away from him. With the wind knocked from his chest, he was still struggling to breathe when he felt himself jerked back upright and onto his feet.

"Strike a woman, will you?" roared Jonathan as he seized Roger by the front of his coat and shook him as a terrier might worry a rat. "Of all the cowardly, bullying tricks, that's the lowest and the meanest, you double-blasted son of a whore!"

"Nay, Jonathan, don't!" shrieked Damaris. With both hands, she grabbed Jonathan's arm, and was appalled by how little impact she had on him. "Let him go, I beg thee! He did me no harm, and he was leaving anyway!"

"Damaris, this jumped-up cur isn't worth your pity! Whatever I do to him's still a sight better than he deserves!"

"But not here, not in my home! Please, Jonathan, respect my beliefs this once!"

She was pleading—begging, really—and Jonathan couldn't ignore her. By now he knew her feelings all too well, and though he didn't agree with them, a woman like Damaris shouldn't have to beg for a villain like this one, even if he was kin by marriage. With a final shake, he reluctantly shoved Roger out the open door and let him go.

Roger stood unsteadily, shaking his head to clear it before weaving in the direction of his horse. Ned had said the black-haired man was crippled, yet no cripple he'd ever seen could hit this hard. After the man had appeared at the funeral, Roger had tried to learn his identity, but no one knew him or where he'd come from—an uncommon mystery on an island. Roger clung to the stirrup for support and touched his fingers to the blood trickling from his split lip. Only Damaris's intervention had kept him from being killed, and for that Roger hated her nearly as much as he hated the man she'd stopped. But, humiliated though he was, Roger had sense enough to leave now, while he still was able. There were other ways to even the score besides fists and brute strength.

Painfully he pulled himself up into the saddle, his head spinning as he fumbled for the reins. "Think on what I've said, Damaris," he called out thickly, "for I won't repeat it. And think, as well, on the consequences if you refuse."

Damaris felt the heavy weight of Jonathan's arm across her shoulders, his strength protectively drawing her closer. "Thee shouldn't have come back to the house," she said as she slipped her own arm around his waist. "Didn't Ruth warn thee to keep away?"

"And leave you to face Allyn alone?" His lips brushed lightly across the top of her hair. "What the devil was he talking about, anyway? Did he threaten you?"

"Nay, not exactly. He asked me to marry him."

Jonathan began to swear, violently and graphically.

"Jonathan!" Damaris waited until he fell silent. Part of her was still reeling from what he'd so quickly done to Roger. She couldn't understand his sudden bursts of violence, with the sailors in the orchard, with de Vere, and now with Roger, and they frightened her. She denied to herself that he was the murderer he claimed to be, and yet when she thought of how he'd flown at Roger, her doubts grew.

"Thee knows very well I didn't accept his proposal," she continued. "I don't love him, and I don't wish to wed him, but I also don't want to be the second wife who comes to grief in his house." Haltingly she told Jonathan all that had happened the day of Evelyn's funeral, and this time, when Jonathan swore, she didn't try to stop him.

"Jesus, I should have throttled the bastard while I had the chance!" he cried, fuming. "Why didn't you tell me any of this before?"

Damaris sighed. "Because once I was back here with thee, it didn't seem to matter," she said softly. "Loving thee seemed far better than dwelling on Roger's hatred."

He couldn't be angry with her, not when she gave a reason like that. "Loving you is better than anything else on God's green earth, sweeting, but a man like

Allyn wouldn't understand that. I don't want you going anywhere by yourself, mind? Not to the fields, or the cave, or the beach, and especially not Newport. You don't leave this house without one of us with you. Promise me you won't, Damaris. Promise me because I love you."

Though she wasn't cold, Damaris shivered, and drew herself closer to Jonathan's warmth. Why couldn't Roger leave them alone? Finally she nodded, and then raised her mouth to Jonathan's to seal her promise with a kiss.

In the weeks that followed, her promise seemed an easy one to keep. If Jonathan himself was not with her, then Ruth or Caleb found tasks that kept them close. The spring planting was finally done, and so was the lambing, and both had gone so well that Damaris could dare consider that, by harvest, she could end the smuggling, though when she remembered the trip to Providence with Jonathan, she was almost tempted to continue. And not once in those days of early summer did Roger trouble her again, or dare to come back to Nantasket. Damaris secretly hoped he'd accepted her refusal, and found another widow to pester.

Late on a Friday, she was fixing supper, alone in the house with the door bolted. She was rushing to finish a batch of Portugal cakes as a surprise for Jonathan, who could eat a dozen by himself. The tins were greased, the loaf sugar beaten and sifted and rubbed into the sweet butter with the flour, and ten eggs whipped, before she realized she had no currants. She could make the cakes with almonds and rose water alone, but Jonathan liked them best with currants, and Damaris knew she could borrow enough from Ruth.

She held her hand in the oven beside the fireplace, counting until she could stand the heat no longer and jerked her hand out. By the time she ran to the Turners' house and back, the oven would be ready. She left her apron on the table, rolled down her sleeves, and hurried out the back door. The fog had rolled in early today, obscuring the line between sky and water, and drifting in wispy patches from the beach. Damaris walked swiftly, her hands tucked beneath her arms for warmth, following the familiar sandy path over the two hills and through the bayberries, and past the tall, angular jumble of rocks that rose straight from the sea.

That was where Jonathan saw her, silhouetted in front of the stones, on his own way back from the Turners' house, where he'd gone to return an axe to Caleb. Damaris stopped when she saw him, a slow smile spreading across her face and her whole body glowing with love. She was dressed in slate blue, and against the gray rocks and the wisps of fog her hair seemed like spun gold, and he knew he'd always picture her like this, smiling shyly at him, and so beautiful that it hurt. As he climbed the path to take her in his arms, he wondered if he'd ever come to believe his good fortune in having her as his own to love.

"Don't chide me for coming here alone," she said, her chin ducked low like a guilty child's, though the way she looked up at him through her lashes was anything but childish. "Thee can see well enough that no harm's come of it, and besides, I need currants."

"Currants?" he repeated as he lifted her chin up with his thumb, staring down at her with mock severity. "You'd risk the life of the woman I love for currants?"

She tried to pretend to be equally severe, but succeeded only in giggling behind her hand like a foolish maid. His teasing had always had that effect on her, and she hoped it always would. Faith, she had laughed more in the time since he'd been washed ashore than she had in the whole twenty-six years before. Tonight, she decided happily, tonight she would tell him. "Oh, aye, for thee would never forgive me if I baked thy precious Portugal cakes without currants."

From the corner of his eye Jonathan caught the dull glimmer of gunmetal against granite, gray against gray, moving, aiming at them. Instinctively he grabbed Damaris by the arms and threw her down into the tall, dry grass, rolling on top of her as the shot rang and echoed against the rocks. The ball had missed them, but not, he guessed by the sound, by much. A marksman, one who knew his business.

He felt Damaris struggling beneath him, saying his name as a question, still unaware of what was happening. But there was no time to tell her, and he shoved away from her and rushed toward the rocks from which the shot had come. He reckoned he had the thirty, maybe forty, seconds that it would take for reloading. If he didn't reach the man by then, Jonathan knew he could consider himself dead, and likely Damaris with him.

His boots sank into the sandy path, slowing him up the hill, until he could throw himself at the face of the rocks, grabbing a hold wherever he could as he struggled to reach the top. Damn, but his leg hurt, the scarred muscle unwilling to support his weight at this angle, and he clawed at the granite with his fingers, trying to make up the difference with the strength in his arms and shoulders. He had no sense of how much time was left, and he was too desperate to worry about it. Finally his hands found the crest, and as he pulled himself over the top he fleetingly considered how it would feel to be shot with a musket at point-blank range.

But the red-haired man on the other side of the rocks was still kneeling, driving the ramrod into the musket's barrel, and when he saw Jonathan lunging toward him, he flung the half-loaded gun aside in favor of the long knife he drew from the sheath on his belt. Instantly Jonathan's own knife was in his hand. He eyed the other man, guessing at his strengths and weaknesses. His rough smock was loosely belted, his red hair was braided like a savage's, and on his feet were worn leather moccasins. He was smaller than Jonathan, but wiry, and he hadn't just climbed up a pile of granite with a bad leg, either. From the ease with which he held his bone-handled knife Jonathan guessed the man would be as deadly at close fighting as he'd been with the musket. But he would soon learn he'd met his match.

It was the summer he'd turned nine, and as he lay in the clearing in only his breeches, his whole body hurting, he didn't think he'd ever move again. He drew up his knees and curled his arms protectively across his chest, and felt the stickiness of blood, his own blood, from the cuts that crisscrossed his skin.

"Get up, Jon," his grandfather ordered, his full white hair at odds with his angry expression. Beside him stood an Indian boy Jonathan's age, his chest heaving and his own body marked with blood, but his knife still gripped tightly in his hand.

The sun glinted off the old man's polished breastplate, and roughly he prodded Jonathan with his toe. "Get up and fight, damn your hide! Sparhawks aren't cowards! You've got half a stone on Attawan here, but you've given him nary a scratch. You're born an Englishman, lad, but if you don't learn to fight like these red-skinned rascals, like Attawan here, you're going to find yourself in an English grave before your time. Now find your feet, you mewling little milk-fed babe, before I find 'em for you!"

With effort Jonathan jerked his thoughts back to the present. By the end of that summer, Jonathan had learned enough from the Indian boy Attawan to win their fights, and what he'd learned then, so long ago, would guide him now.

The redheaded man danced lightly from side to side on the balls of his feet, and then, tired of waiting, lunged at Jonathan. Easily Jonathan raised his arm at the last moment, and deflected the other man's wrist. But the smaller man was agile, and he twisted around, catching Jonathan off balance. All his weight came down on his scarred leg, and it collapsed beneath him, sending him flat on his back. So already the other man had discovered his weakness. The knowledge, and the fear that came with it, cut through Jonathan's concentration, and he struggled to regain it. He felt the cold of the stone beneath his back and heard the labored harshness of his own breathing, and was that Damaris's voice calling to him? Nay, too many distractions, damn them all, and he tried to blot them all out, to focus all his energies instead on the knife in his hand.

With an unearthly yell, the man threw himself on Jonathan, but this time Jonathan was ready, and quickly he seized the man by the arm that held the knife. His hand shook with the effort of trying to break Jonathan's hold, but here Jonathan's strength and size favored him, and with a grunt he slammed the other man over on his back. The man kicked and tried to break free, but Jonathan held his forearm like an iron band across the man's chest, the tip of his knife pricking at the hollow of his throat. With his other hand, Jonathan twisted the man's wrist until he gasped and swore with pain as his fingers opened and the bone-handled knife dropped harmlessly to the rocks.

"Who sent you here?" demanded Jonathan, as he met the undisguised hatred in the smaller man's eyes. "His name, by God, or I'll gut you here and now!"

"Don't know it." Sweat beaded the man's stubbled upper lip. "Not that I'd tell ye if I did, ye black bastard!"

Jonathan's blade dug a little deeper into the man's throat. "You're lying, and you're wasting my time. Either one's reason enough to take your wretched life."

The man's Adam's apple jerked convulsively in his throat. "I told ye, I don't know! The one what hired me didn't tell. Jes' said t' claim th' gold piece I had t' shoot ye an' yer harlot, an' then clear out o' Newport."

Suddenly the man twisted beneath Jonathan and drove his knee hard into the damaged muscle of Jonathan's thigh. As the pain shot through Jonathan he loosened his grip enough for the man to break free. Rolling across the flat rock, he reached the half-loaded musket and grasped it by the barrel. He scrambled to his feet and came back to Jonathan, swinging the musket over his head like a club.

But before he'd taken two steps, the redheaded man let out a startled little gasp and dropped the musket as he stared down at the hilt of Jonathan's knife, all that showed of the blade buried deep in his chest. His eyes were already clouding with death as he turned clumsily away, and his life was done before his body toppled over the edge of the rocks to the beach below.

Slowly Jonathan pulled himself up on his knees, his hands splayed on his thighs and his head bowed, breathing as heavily as if he'd just run to Newport and back. Now that the excitement of the fight was fading, all he had left was a wasted, empty feeling. Where was the fierce glory in surviving that he'd always felt before? He was getting too old for this—tomorrow he'd likely be too lame to work—or maybe deep down he realized how close his luck had come to abandoning him to the fate he deserved. And what did it all come down to, anyway? One more dead man to add to his tally, one more killing that Damaris would neither accept nor understand.

He was still there when Damaris came around the rocks by the hillside. Her cap was gone and her hair half-down, and she ran to him with her arms outstretched.

"Oh, love, how I feared for thee!" He could feel her tears on his cheek as she wrapped her arms tightly around him. "Thee might have been shot, lying here in thy own blood, and I did not know!"

Wearily he rested his head on her breast, letting her fill the emptiness inside him, and linked his hands loosely around her waist.

"I couldn't bear to lose thee, Jonathan," she whispered, almost crooning the words as she held him. It was the one way she knew to reassure herself that he still lived, that he was still hers. He would never know how frightened she had been for his sake. "Not thee, Jonathan, not thee."

He told himself he should comfort her, that she needed him to be strong, and finally, reluctantly, he rose to his feet, bringing her with him. "There now, lass," he said gruffly. "You can see for yourself I'm well enough. You of anyone must know I'm damned near immortal."

With a small concerned frown, she stepped back, holding him away from her to study him. When she was satisfied that he was well enough, her frown turned to puzzlement. "But there was another man. I heard the gunshot, and thee fighting with him."

Her gaze swept across the outcropping, stopping at the musket near the edge, where the redheaded man had dropped it. Before Jonathan could stop her, she walked swiftly to the edge and looked over, already knowing what she'd find. The tide was nearly in, and the water eddied and swirled around the man's body, tugging at his clothes and drawing out his pigtail like a streamer. But even the tide couldn't wash away the dark stain on his chest, or the knife that centered it.

"I had no choice, Damaris," said Jonathan as he came to stand beside her. He slipped his arm over her shoulders, but she held herself stiff and away from him, staring down at the body in the water. "He would've killed us if I hadn't stopped him."

"Does thee believe this was Roger's doing?" she asked, too evenly, as she dragged her loose hair back from her face with one hand.

"Aye, though the man wouldn't admit it." He tried to turn her face away from the dead man, but she held firm, shaking her head. "This has gone too far, Damaris. It's time you went to the constable in Newport and told him how Roger's threatened you. That, on top of what you've said of his wife's death, should be enough to see him into the gaol. We'll take this—this, as evidence. Mayhap someone can recognize him. I'll haul him out of the water—"

"Nay, Jonathan, don't touch him." She was shaking her head harder now, whether denying Jonathan's suggestion or the other man's death, she didn't know herself. "Leave him as he is, and let the tide claim him."

"But Damaris, the knife…"

"Leave it," she said fiercely, her hands knotted into fists at her sides. "I won't have constables or magistrates or any other such at Nantasket. Thee forgets that Roger is one of them. Does thee truly think they'd take our word against his! And thee—what would they make of thee? If thee admits to this murder, what of the others thee says thee has committed? They'll know the truth, Jonathan, or they'll make it their task to learn. And then thee will be hung."

Jonathan let his arm slide from her shoulders. He had saved her life, but he had lost her just the same. "I did it for you, Damaris," he said miserably. "Can't you see I had no choice?"

Instinctively she knew he was speaking the truth. One had died, and two had lived, and if Jonathan had been the one to be killed, she would have gone mad with grief. But everything she'd ever believed in told her this was wrong. She tried to find in herself and in her faith an answer she could accept, and found nothing. She was lost and scared, and with her mouth twisted with anguish, she turned back to Jonathan.

"Mistress Allyn!" called Ruth breathlessly as she rushed up the path toward them, her baby jostling on her hip. Close behind came Caleb with a musket, and the three other boys, armed with hatchets and a scythe. "Praise God ye be unharmed, then! We heard th' shot, not believin' for a moment that it be ye an' Cap'n Sparhawk in trouble!"

"I thank thee for thy concern, Ruth," said Damaris as she gave the other woman a shaky smile. "There's been some small trouble, but Jonathan tended to it, and we are, as thee can see, quite unharmed."

Ruth sniffed. "Ye don't look unharmed t' me, mistress," she said doubtfully as she gave Eli her knuckle to suck to quiet his fussing. "Ye be pale as a gull's wing, an' Cap'n Sparhawk, he be lookin' like he been thumped somehow fierce. If there be some rogue or rascal hidin' 'round my house, I'll want th' men t' take him proper."

"No rogue nor rascal will trouble thee, Ruth. Thee has my word." Eli let out a full-blown yowl, leaning out away from his mother toward Damaris, his arms held out. Thankful for any distraction, Damaris took the child, shushing him and rocking from side to side as she held his small, plump body.

Standing apart from the others, Jonathan watched how easily she comforted the baby. Of course, he'd seen her before with Eli, for the child clearly adored her, but this time he was struck by the tenderness with which she cradled the little boy in her arms.

The woman was small with thick, dark hair that she wore loosely tied with scarlet ribbons, and she carried herself like a little queen, proud and straight, with her dimpled chin held high. Her eyes were a gray like quicksilver, tilted up at the corners, and when they met Jonathan's, he was all too aware of their power to bewitch. They were sitting side by side on a high-backed bench in the shadow of two huge beeches.

"So you're off to sea again, my pretty sailor boy," she teased, her voice gently bred and almost musical. *She held her hand linked comfortably through his arm, and the breeze gently blew her skirts across his outstretched legs. "You scarcely stay long enough for*

us to recall your name, and wave fare-thee-well when
you leave.''

A small, grubby boy hurled himself into Jona-
than's lap and began searching through his coat
pockets for the peppermints that Jonathan always hid
for him to find. The woman laughed.

''Though, to be sure, Joshua never forgets you,
does he?'' she said as she gently swatted the little boy
on his shoulder for his greediness. ''The little scoun-
drel is more like you every day, Jonathan. The same
hair, the same eyes, the same lack of any gentlemanly
graces.''

''The Sparhawk blood is powerful stuff, sweet-
ing.'' Jonathan laughed, too, and reached out to pat
the obvious roundness of the woman's belly. ''But to
help square the odds, my dear Dianna, I'll pray this
next one is a lass that favors you alone.''

God in heaven, he was married. He had a wife
named Dianna, a son named Joshua, and likely at
least one more child by now. He felt as cold and dead
inside as the stone beneath his feet.

God in heaven, what had he done to Damaris?

She was curled on her side when she awoke to feel
his lips on her shoulders, his breath warm on her skin.
He was caressing her, his hand circling the curve of her
hip and waist, higher, to her breasts, and then back
again. This was better, she decided drowsily, the way
it should be between them. Ever since he'd killed that
man that afternoon he'd been silent and withdrawn
and unwilling to talk or listen, almost as if he were

afraid to touch or talk to her. But he wasn't afraid anymore.

Still pleasantly somewhere between waking and sleep, she pressed herself against him, and felt him already hard and ready. She lifted one thigh over his hip, and he eased deep inside her, his hands spread over her hips. Softly she moaned his name as they rocked together, her body arching back to meet his movements, and as he reached around to touch her more deeply, she felt herself beginning the rapid spiral toward pleasure.

"Whatever happens, Damaris, remember that I love you," he whispered fiercely into her ear as she cried out. "Never forget that I loved you best of all."

Afterward, she drifted back to sleep, with their bodies still joined and his arm draped protectively around her waist. She slept deeply, without dreaming. Why should she dream, when loving Jonathan was her reality?

When she woke again, the morning sun filled the room, and there was something rustling beneath her cheek on the pillow. Jonathan's side of the bed was empty, and she wondered why he'd let her lie abed so late and gone to tend to the animals alone. In her sleep she had traveled across the bed to his pillow, unconsciously seeking Jonathan, and drowsily she reached up to brush away whatever was poking her cheek.

It was a crumpled, folded paper, and, curious, she shoved her hair back from her eyes and sat up against the bolster. As she turned the yellowed paper over in her fingers, she recognized it as a page torn from a book, the last page of a collection of sermons from Eben's desk. How had it come to be in her bed? she wondered, frowning, as she unfolded it. Then she saw the familiar handwriting that slashed across the unprinted side, and she felt her heart nearly come to a halt.

He wrote that he had left for her sake. He was sorry for the pain this would bring her. He had betrayed and dishonored her beyond forgiveness, but she must believe that he had not known. He was married. He had one son, perhaps another, or a daughter.

He would never see her again.

Damaris stared down at the paper, the words swimming before her eyes. What hurt most of all was how he'd so forcibly crossed out every endearment and mention of love, every word that might have softened the message, and left it as the last bit of him she was ever to have.

Faith, she didn't want to cry. She had laughed more since knowing Jonathan, but she had wept more, too, and she didn't want to let the tears begin again. Tears would mean she'd accepted what he'd written, and she refused to do that, because in her heart she didn't believe a word of the letter. She couldn't. This had to be one more awful trick of his battered memory. Jonathan couldn't love her the way she knew he did and be wed to another woman. Not her Jonathan.

Damaris flung back the sheets and rushed to dress. He would have gone to Newport, to sail with whatever vessel would take him, and somehow she must find him before he sailed. If he could tell her to her face that he didn't love her any longer, and that she had no place in his life, then she would believe him, not before.

It was all a gamble, but one she had to take. He *had* written "love" and "sweeting" and "my own Damaris" before he'd struck them out, and before he'd left he had sworn to her that he loved her best of all. Suddenly she felt light-headed, and she clung to the bedpost until the weakness passed. Haste or no, she'd have to take time to eat something or risk fainting on the road, and she pounded on the wooden post with frustration.

No matter what happened, she wouldn't beg or weep to try to change his mind. Nay, she wouldn't even tell him the one thing that would surely sway his decision, the one she'd kept to herself with secret delight for the past weeks, until she was sure. She wanted him to come back to her freely, because he loved her, not because he was the father of her unborn child.

Chapter Fourteen

Jonathan had no trouble finding Tom Cooke in Newport. Tom was in the same tavern where Jonathan had met him before, in a far worse, if more blissful, state. He had lost his mates, and most of his money, too, by the time Jonathan paid his reckoning and hauled him out onto Thames Street. Midnight was long past, and even this near to the docks the streets were empty except for cats, rats, and a handful of sailors and apprentices not quite able to find their way home. Thankful that there was little audience for Tom's joyful off-key singing, Jonathan hauled him toward the harbor, and the one sure way he knew to sober his former second mate.

"It be like ol' times, Cap'n Sparhawk, ye comin' t' fetch me back t' the *Leopard*," he said, slurring happily as he stumbled onto the beach. "We've missed ye powerful, Cap'n, 'specially once we'd known ye wasn't true dead."

"You'll miss me less in a moment, Tom," said Jonathan dryly, "and less still come morning."

Holding Tom firmly by the back of his coat, Jonathan thrust the man's face down into the cold water, then yanked him back out, sputtering and choking. After the third dunking, Tom had swallowed a sufficient amount of salt water to unsettle the rum and ale already inside him, and by the time he'd finished vomiting, he was sweating and miserable and very near to being sober. Jonathan guided Tom's shaky steps back up the beach to a pile of parceled lumber waiting on the wharf, and let him sink down to rest, clutching his belly.

"You never did have a head for spirits, Tom, and it doesn't seem likely you'll grow one now," said Jonathan as he sat on the planks beside Tom, who only groaned in reply. "Still and all, if you had enough blunt to spend on drink, then they must be paying you well regular on the *Leopard.*"

"*Tiger,*" said Tom weakly. "She's called th' *Tiger* now, Cap'n, an' they repainted her cat wit' stripes instead o' spots. One o' them Newport wits what owns her did it, not givin' a care-all for th' ill luck that comes from changin' a vessel's name."

Ill luck—Jesus, what more of that could he have? Against his will, Jonathan thought again of Damaris, and how he'd left her, smiling in her sleep with her pale arm thrown back across her head on the pillow in the moonlight, and then he thought of his wife and the little boy with black hair and green eyes that mirrored his own. "*Leopard* or *Tiger,* it's no mind to me, Tom. When's she sailing?"

"Day after next, Cap'n. Tonight be my last bit o' leave. She's all fitted out proper, an' Cap'n Graham only be waitin' on his papers." Uncomfortably Tom glanced up at Jonathan. "Beggin' yer pardon for sayin' so to ye, sir, but Cap'n Graham do be her master now.''

"Would your Captain Graham still have a berth for me, d'you think?" asked Jonathan with studied carelessness. It was far from the wisest plan he'd ever considered—for all he knew, this Graham might be his worst enemy—but it was the only way he had thought of that might lead him back to the family he barely remembered. With those knowing silver eyes and those red ribands in her hair, Dianna seemed so different from Damaris. Likely she hadn't objected at all that he'd been a pirate, and privateering would be much the same with her. Damaris, now, Damaris would have told him—but what Damaris thought or said didn't matter any longer. "I've half a mind to try my own hand at taking on the Spaniards."

Tom's mouth dropped open with hazy bewilderment. "Oh, Cap'n Sparhawk, sir, d'ye mean t' throw in wit' us, then?"

"No more 'Captain Sparhawk,' Tom, and no more 'sir,' " said Jonathan firmly. "I'm likely a damned fool for even considering this, but I warrant just now I'd rather be among friends than strangers, even if I risk my neck doing it. This Captain Graham doesn't need another captain on board any more than a cockerel needs two heads, so I'll thank you to watch your tongue, and tell the others that know me likewise."

Briefly Jonathan considered telling Tom how little he still knew of his own past, but he thought better of it. He'd gotten into the habit of speaking his thoughts to Damaris, but any man who drank as ineptly as Tom would make a poor confidant. Besides, thought Jonathan wryly, while confession was reputed to be good for the soul, in his experience it accomplished precious little for the body, and someday he might need Tom more to obey his orders than he needed him to listen to his troubles tonight. He slipped his shoulder under the smaller man's arms and hoisted him to his feet. "Up with you now, lad. It's time we found this sloop before she changes her name and her colors again."

With difficulty, Jonathan discovered a waterman, dozing in the stern sheets of his boat, who crossly offered to row them out to the *Tiger* for double his fare, on account of the hour. Reluctantly Jonathan agreed, tumbling Tom between the boat's benches, where he fell at once to snoring.

With her repairs and provisioning complete, the *Tiger* was moored at the mouth of the harbor, near Goat Island, and as the waterman's oars began cutting smoothly through the water, Jonathan's shoulders slumped with unhappiness, and he sighed to himself. False dawn already had paled the clouds to the east. Soon Damaris would wake, and find his letter. God in heaven, how he'd wronged her! Wearily he rubbed his hands across his eyes, and tried not to think of her alone in the big bed at Nantasket.

"There be the sloop *Tiger,* sir," said the waterman at last, "directly t' yer larboard."

With little interest, Jonathan glanced in the direction where the waterman cocked his head. His thoughts were filled with other things, and he'd learn soon enough what manner of sloop the *Tiger* was, and the whims of her master. Yet when his gaze found the sloop, swinging gently against her moorings with the waning tide, he felt the sudden shock of recognition.

It was like discovering an old friend in a foreign land. As he stared at the sloop's familiar lines, he felt all the pieces, all the mysteries, rapidly resolving themselves into the real, tangible past that was his own life, and he found himself clinging to the bench as everything he'd feared forever forgotten came rushing back to be remembered.

With a cargo of sugar, molasses, cotton and French goods, the Leopard *had made an easy passage from Bridgetown. They'd been within a day of Saybrook when Jonathan had seen the boat with the survivors of the shipwreck, and brought the sloop round to rescue them. But as soon as the strangers had come aboard the* Leopard, *Jonathan had seen his act of kindness go horribly wrong. There had been guns everywhere he looked, knives and tomahawks, too, and the strangers had thrown themselves without mercy on his own unarmed crew. In that awful instant, Jonathan had cursed himself for a witless fool, a sorry, pitiful excuse for a captain, to be taken in by such an old pirate's game. Then he'd fallen back on his instincts, fighting to stay alive and to keep what was his.*

He twisted sideways and grabbed the barrel of the pistol thrust into his ribs by the pirate captain. With both hands the pirate tried to jerk the gun free, but Jonathan's strength held it fast. Panicking, the man fired anyway, the bullet flying somewhere over the side. Jonathan wrenched the spent pistol free and swung the brass-plated butt against the man's forehead, and with a little grunt the dun-haired man toppled lifeless to the deck.

As he fell, the cutlass the man had hidden beneath his coat slipped free, and Jonathan snatched it up by the haft. Quickly he glanced around, appalled by the carnage: five of his men already down, and oh, God, there lay the tumbled body of his cabin boy near the companionway. It was easy for Jonathan to kill then, grimly slashing the life from another attacker as he remembered the scattered corpses of his crew, his friends, and the Wickhamton boy who'd never see his twelfth birthday.

But then a pistol's ball found Jonathan's thigh, and as the pain came, worse than anything he could have imagined, the deck suddenly angled wildly, and he just managed to catch himself from sliding overboard. The helm was untended, the Leopard's *rudder swinging free as the wind in her unmanned sails drove her listing sharply to starboard. Waves dashed over the railing and up the deck. They'd be beam ends and lost if he couldn't head her back into the wind. He had to get aft to the helm, thought Jonathan desperately as he struggled to find a handhold and claw his way across the angled deck. His wounded leg would not support him, and he felt his strength slipping, fading...*

Damnation, no! He was the Leopard's *captain, and she'd come to this pass through his own fault. He would save her. He was almost to the mizzenmast now, not so much farther to go. He reached for the capstan as the* Leopard *lurched again. His fingers clutched at empty air, and he slipped down the slanting deck, crashing toward the lee rail, toward the waves, and then toward nothing but black oblivion.*

"Steady there now, sir," warned the waterman sympathetically as he caught Jonathan by the shoulder to steady him. "Didn't peg ye as half seas o'er like this other lad here."

Jonathan only grunted in reply. Better to let the man believe him drunk than to have him know the truth, that his mind was spinning so fast he doubted he could put two sane words together. So while he wasn't a man afraid of a fight, he wasn't a pirate, either, but rather a victim of pirates. How easy it had been to misconstrue the few facts he'd had! The bullet wound, the old scars, his quickness with knives and guns, that first conversation with Tom, all made sense now. Even the rakish red coat that he'd been wearing when he'd been lost, and shunned ever since, had an explanation so simple it was painful: he'd worn red because he liked the color.

He stared up at the sloop before him with a mixture of longing and bitterness. The *Leopard*—damnation, paint or not, he wished she was still what he'd named her—had come from the best yard in Saybrook not two summers ago, a joint venture between himself and his older brother, Kit. By now the sloop must have been given up for lost, and it grieved Jonathan to think of his family all mourning him in the big house at Plumstead: Kit, and Kit's wife Dianna, and their boy Joshua, and—

Dianna Sparhawk. Oh, God, that was who it was that he'd remembered—his brother's wife. His shoulders sagged even lower, and he shook his head, unwilling to believe the truth.

He'd never understood the love and contentment his brother seemed to find in marriage, and each time he'd come home he'd bragged of remaining the perpetual bachelor, one of the consolations and joys of being the younger son. At least he hadn't understood until he'd been washed ashore on the beach at Nantasket. He thought of the cold formality of the letter he'd written to Damaris, and the unnecessary pain the words would bring her, and unconsciously he turned his head back toward the shore, as if he could see the stone-ended house he'd left behind.

It wasn't too late. He could still go back and beg for her forgiveness, and return to the happiness he'd found in her love. He could see that Tom was safely on the *Tiger*, leave with the waterman, and abandon his notion to join the sloop's company himself. He could be at Nantasket before noon.

Yet at the thought of the sloop, his head slowly turned back toward the ship. His heart ached to rejoin Damaris, but he knew he had no real choice. If he was to be the man she deserved, he had to try to recover the sloop—*his* sloop—and his pride with it. But how the devil was he supposed to do it by himself?

The sloop's lookout finally hailed them, and the waterman called back as he pulled the final strokes towards the *Tiger*'s steep sides. In a very few moments he'd be back on her deck, and the more he could learn before then, the better.

"What do you know of this vessel?" he asked the waterman swiftly in a low voice. "Of her history, her owners?"

Sensing Jonathan's urgency, or perhaps merely flattered to be asked, the waterman slowed his oars. "She be a queer bird, this one," he began, shaking his head sagely. "Brung into harbor as a prize, but since she don't be Spanish, an' she weren't set up fer privateerin', well, we all asks, what kind o' prize do she be? Her cap'n was killed, an' th' wrongs an' rights o' the matter never were set out proper, like they should've.

But since them that has an interest in her now be gentry, well, it be best not t' talk too much.''

Jonathan nodded impatiently. He already knew the sloop's capture had been suspicious, and that he could expect no assistance from the Newport authorities. ''What do you know about Captain Graham?''

''Not much t' tell,'' the waterman admitted reluctantly. ''Andrew Graham's an Indies man, not Newport-bred, an' brought in special by th' new owners. They say he be a prime fightin' captain, specially wit' the Spaniards. All I heard was grumblin' that Graham's been lingering about these waters a mite too long, considerin' there be no Spaniards in Connecticut, an' that he might have taken a prize or two that weren't quite deservin', just t' keep a hand in, if ye follow me. Them that be good at privateerin' be likewise good at piratin', 'specially if they don't care overmuch to learn th' difference. But then I'll be poor, an' he'll be rich, an' that be the way o' this world, don't it?''

But by then it was time for Jonathan to judge Graham for himself, as the boat nudged gently alongside the sloop. Half pushing, half pulling, he managed to get poor Tom up the side, then followed with the small canvas bag that held his few belongings.

In one unhappy instant, Jonathan saw the changes that had been made to the sloop. The look of her sides, where ports had been cut for the guns, and the way the deck had been rearranged to accommodate their weight, were the most obvious changes, but in countless smaller ways—that spot of tar on the deck, or this sloppy turn of a coiled line—Jonathan could see the effects of a captain other than himself. And it wasn't just in the timbers and canvas, either. Tom had told him that the survivors of the old *Leopard*'s crew had joined the new *Tiger*'s people, but Jonathan found no welcome among the sullen hands on the night watch, and he realized he'd do well to watch his back. As familiar as the sloop was, he wasn't home yet.

Despite the hour, Jonathan was led to the captain's cabin. The seaman knocked timidly, waiting only until the rash of oaths began from the other side of the door before he fled, leaving Jonathan to open the door on his own.

"What the holy hellfire do you want, you great dumb ox?" demanded Graham, turning in his desk chair to glare at Jonathan. He was older than Jonathan had expected, with gray streaked through his dark red beard, and though he wore his hair long and untied, it couldn't quite hide the scar where his ear had been sliced away long ago.

Jonathan stared at Graham's mutilated ear, certain he'd seen him before. Among the pirates who'd stolen his sloop had been one with an ear like this, a man who'd taken great care to hide his face behind a red handkerchief and false tears, and it took all of Jonathan's willpower not to fly at the man now before him.

"Answer me, you great fool!" ordered Graham. "Are you deaf, as well as dumb?"

Still struggling to control his temper, Jonathan took as long as he dared before answering. Graham didn't seem to recognize him in return. It was possible Graham hadn't seen Jonathan clearly on that stormy March night, or that he simply assumed that the *Leopard*'s true captain was long dead. Jonathan wasn't willing to bet on either possibility.

"Tom Cooke says you're looking for men," he said finally, adding "sir" as an afterthought. He'd been his own master at nineteen, and answering to a sorry rascal like Graham didn't sit easy with him. "You won't find a better sailor than myself, sir."

"Sailors come cheap in this wretched place, ten to the groat," declared Graham scornfully. Although it was June, he wore a heavy coat over a long waistcoat, both buttoned to his chin, and his feet, in heavy woolen socks, sat on top of a pierced tin box made to hold coals, the kind that ladies took to meetings in New England winters. "Why come to me, anyways?"

"To make my fortune stripping Spaniards blind, God rot 'em, sir." *And,* added Jonathan to himself, *to take back what's my own.* When he looked around at the cabin that had been his—the books and charts carelessly strewn about and crumpled, rings from wet tankards on the polished woodwork, the tarnish on the brass fittings—he felt his anger rising all over again.

"What, a great cripple like yourself?" Graham sniffed scornfully. "Don't deny it, I saw how you came up halt in the companionway. Trip over your own feet, do you?"

"Nothing that honorable—sir," said Jonathan, with unfeigned sullenness. "A lead ball at close range—sir."

Graham slapped his palm down on the desk and guffawed. "My God, I like your spirit! Don't tell me now, you're outrunning the law, or some husband with a new pair of horns? Either one makes you more than welcome here, more than welcome!"

Laughing still, Graham bent lower, as if overcome by his own wit. Suddenly he twisted about with a movement that was unexpectedly fluid, and the knife he'd drawn from his waistcoat struck with a vibrating *thunk* in the bulkhead as Jonathan simultaneously whipped out his own knife and ducked, with time to spare.

Angrily Jonathan reached up to jerk the other captain's knife from the woodwork. At least he knew now that Graham didn't remember him, otherwise he would have thrown the knife to kill, not merely to test. "Tortuga welcome, that's what I'd call this," he said as he slapped the knife on the desk. "What's it to be next? Pistols or swords, or are fists alone more to your taste?"

"You'll do, you'll do, my black-haired rascal!" Graham exclaimed, plainly delighted. "Lame or no, you won't shame me, and I'll see you get your share of that fortune. I've got the law in my pocket on this cruise, and the queen's share'll come second, see if it don't. No niceties or dainty scruples here!" He picked up a pen with the end of the barb bitten off. "Your name, lad, to add to the book."

"Russell," he said slowly. "Jonathan Russell." When the *Leopard* reclaimed her rightful name, then so would he, and not before.

Later, Jonathan wondered if Damaris would consider this lying. And he wondered, too, if he'd ever see her again.

Chapter Fifteen

With each roll of the ketch, the hammock swung in a wide arc from side to side, and as Damaris clung to the damp bedding, she felt her stomach begin to lurch yet again in the opposite direction. Quickly she squeezed her eyes shut and swallowed hard, wondering how she could feel both hot and cold at the same time. Maybe if she couldn't see how the hammock rocked one way and the bulkheads the other, she wouldn't feel the motion quite so much.

When she had sailed with Jonathan to Providence, she hadn't had even a twinge of seasickness. But that had been in the bay and the river, not in the ocean filled with whitecaps and a stiff wind from the northeast. Nor had she been with breeding then, either. And, of course, Jonathan had been with her as well, not off convinced he was a pirate and an adulterer and God only knew what else.

She flopped over in the narrow hammock, and nearly rolled out onto the deck. She still couldn't quite believe she'd come this far. When she'd reached Newport, there had been no sign of Jonathan, and the only vessel that had sailed that day was a privateer bound for the Caribbean. The privateer was said to be fast, very fast, and the only other ship she could find bound for the Indies was not scheduled to sail for another three weeks.

In despair she had returned to Nantasket, only to learn that Captain de Vere had sent word he'd arrive that night. Anxiously she had waited on the beach with a little trunk of her belongings and a heavy bag of coins to convince the Dutch captain to take her at least as far as New York. Ruth had waited with her, her arm linked with Damaris's, while the men unloaded the barrels from the boat.

"I pray ye find him, mistress," Ruth had said staunchly. "Yer precious Jonathan be a big man, but that ocean be a powerful sight bigger. Think on all th' men it's swallowed up! Yer own father, t' begin with, an' my old master Captain Wilkinson, an' his two boys, too, an'—"

"I'll find him, Ruth," Damaris had said, with a conviction she wished she felt more strongly. "He's always been a mariner. He'll know how to take care of himself."

"And what about yerself, mistress?" Ruth had asked, her golden eyes filled with concern. "Ye don't be a sailor, an' ye be too good an' kind t' be much use lookin' after yerself in th' big world. Why, ye even be trustin' that old Dutch goat de Vere! Ye be careful o' him, mistress, even wit' th' coins sewn into yer stays. He'd rob his own dead mother, that one."

"Hush, Ruth!" Uneasily Damaris had glanced back to see if de Vere had heard her. "Thee won't change my mind, no matter what thee says."

"Then what o' yer babe?" Damaris had looked at her sharply, but Ruth had only nodded. "Oh, aye, ye didn't have to tell me. Likely I've known before ye did yerself. 'Twas only time, anyways, th' way th' pair o' ye carried on fer all th' world t' watch. Not that I fault ye, nay, not wit' a fine-made man like that one!"

She'd laughed softly, then squeezed Damaris's arm. "Ye mind yerself, Mistress Allyn, ye an' yer babe both. I know I've never trusted Master Sparhawk, and maybe I still don't, because no man on this earth would be good enough fer ye. But I believe he'll do right by ye. Aye, I do. Else he'll have t' answer t' me, see if he don't!"

They had both wept and clung to each other, while the men looked away, embarrassed. From the deck of de Vere's ketch, Damaris had stared back at her beach and the sharp roof of her house, long after they had disappeared below the horizon. But if she found Jonathan, it would all be worth it. Nay, she had reminded herself fiercely, she meant *when*. When she found Jonathan.

She pressed her damp palms against her cheeks, and listened to the sailors laughing raucously on the deck overhead. In the two days since they'd left Nantasket, it seemed to her, the men had never once stopped making merry, while she hung down here in this wretched hammock, wishing she would simply die and be done with it.

But suddenly she noticed that the voices of the men overhead had changed. There was more shouting, though she couldn't quite make out the words, and their footfalls raced back and forth across the deck. To Damaris, it didn't seem that the ketch's motion had changed, but perhaps there was some sort of emergency she should know about. Captain de Vere wasn't accustomed to passengers. If the ketch was foundering, would he remember to come find her?

Panicking, Damaris tumbled out of the hammock, her legs tangled in her petticoats, and threw open the door to the tiny mate's cabin she'd been given. The companionway was empty, and from the shouting she guessed that every member of the crew was topside already. Then came another sound, a dry, percussive explosion from across the water, and the shouting turned to swearing, empty bravado colored by a palpable fear. They were scared, those jolly, laughing Dutchmen, and Damaris knew at once that she should be, too.

Another pop, this one louder, closer, followed almost at once by the sharp crack of splintering wood. Instantly the ketch listed to starboard and veered off course, throwing Damaris against the wall of the companionway. Rubbing her shoulder, she hurried up the narrow steps to the deck, only to stop halfway to stare at the wreckage that now littered de Vere's once-tidy deck.

The mainmast itself had been shattered, its top dangling limp, like a broken branch. The large square mainsail had been split, as well, and the rent edges fluttered out like banners in the wind. Lines and cables that before had stretched taut now sagged limp, their blocks swinging like pendulums. With hatchets and knives, the men swarmed over the tangle of canvas, wood and hemp, as they struggled to cut the little ketch free. None of them noticed Damaris as she picked her way through the wreckage, back to where de Vere was trying to guide his battered vessel without the mainsail.

"Captain! Captain de Vere!" she called, shading her eyes against the bright sun with the back of her hand. "Faith, what has happened?"

De Vere glowered at her furiously. "What in God's holy name do you think has happened, woman? We've had our mainmast shot clear away by their god-damned warning shot! Pirates, that's what they are, thieving, whoreson pirates! Look for yourself!"

Damaris's gaze followed his pointing finger, to the tall sloop now bearing down on them, her guns still run out and trained on the ketch. *Pirates.* She remembered all the warnings she'd had from Roger and from Captain de Vere, all the times Jonathan had tried to tell her how pirates robbed and sank other ships and killed their crews, but she'd never really believed any of it until she saw the black-mouthed guns pointed at her, and the crowd of men rowing toward them in the sloop's boat, the sun glinting off the swords and pistols in their hands. She stared at the sloop, unable to look away as unconsciously her hands slid over her abdomen, protecting her tiny unborn child. *God in heaven, what would they do with her?*

As a new man, untried and unknown, Jonathan had been left behind on the sloop with the gunners while the others had crowded, whooping and hollering, into the boat to capture the ketch. Not that he'd minded, though he'd had sense enough to keep his disgust to himself when they'd fired without warning on the other vessel. Privateers be damned, they were pirates, pure and simple, and the more time Jonathan spent among them the more certain he was that he'd fallen in with the same band who'd stolen the sloop from him in the first place.

"Will you look at the mewling, raggedy-arse cowards!" cried Graham scornfully from the quarterdeck. "No fight in 'em at all, excepting their captain! Don't think I'd bother fighting for a minnow like that, either. Scarcely worth the bother to haul her into Newport to be condemned. I'd— Damnation, there's a woman on board!"

As the men crowded to the rail, Graham peered through his glass for a better look. "Gold hair like an angel she has!" he crowed. "Be gentle with her, lads, that's the way, bring her back to me safe and sound. Don't that green apron mark her as one of those infernal Quakers? Quaker, hah! I'll quake you soon enough, my pretty little chick, and have you begging for more of dear Captain Graham!"

Jonathan's head jerked up. God in heaven, it couldn't be her! At once he climbed up the standing rigging to prove to himself that it wasn't so. Even half hidden as the woman was by the men rowing her back in the boat, Jonathan could see the sun shining off her taffy-colored hair and the straight, stiff, frightened line of her back, and he knew it was Damaris. He tore his glance away from her and squinted back at the ketch, recognizing it now as the Dutchman's, and soundly cursed de Vere to the grave and beyond for taking her away from Nantasket.

He lowered himself back down to the deck as Damaris's frightened face appeared over the side, and, lost in the crowd, he watched as she tried to compose herself, her hands clasped low over her apron. For the first time he wished she'd worn her prim little cap with her hair pinned tight under it instead of the way she looked now, as if she'd just tumbled out of bed, the loose braid down her back half unplaited and stray wisps blowing around her cheeks and throat. All around him he could feel the other men watching her hungrily, and he knew the only reason they kept back from her was that Graham, standing before her with his thumbs tucked in his belt, so clearly wanted her for himself. His anger rising, Jonathan watched the captain reach out to chuck Damaris beneath the chin, his dirt-rimmed thumbnail pressed into her smooth skin.

"You'd be wise not to harm her, Captain," Jonathan said loudly as he shoved his way past the other men, and this time he forgot to add the "sir."

With a wordless cry of welcome, Damaris turned eagerly toward the familiar voice. She had avoided the eyes of the crowd of men on the deck, never dreaming that Jonathan would be among them. Yet this was hardly the joyful reunion she had envisioned. Jonathan was purposely avoiding meeting her gaze, and the way his arms were folded across his chest offered little encouragement.

Suddenly she realized he was one of *them,* accepted as an equal by the other pirates in their crew, just as he'd always claimed. She hadn't believed it before, and she didn't believe it now, and uncertainly she smoothed back her hair, watching him, praying he'd say or do something that would explain his behavior.

As she waited, Graham swiveled around to meet Jonathan, his expression a mixture of anger and disbelief. "You dare counter your master, Russell?"

Evenly, Jonathan returned his stare. "Begging your pardon, sir, but I know the wench, and tempting as she seems, she'll be worth more to you unharmed. She's Roger Allyn's sister-in-law, the Roger Allyn that's the magistrate in Newport."

Graham's eyebrows rose high on his forehead as he scratched the place where his ear had been, thinking. Slowly he smiled, his grin broken by the gaps of missing teeth. "Allyn's sister, y' say?" he asked. "Can you swear to it, Russell?"

"Aye, sir, she is, and I can." Silently Jonathan begged Damaris's forgiveness. "And she's dearer to him than any sister. 'Tis said he's taken the woman for his mistress. Everyone in Newport's seen them together, living under one roof, though his wife's scarcely cold."

Damaris gasped and pressed her hands to her mouth, shocked. Why was Jonathan saying these things, destroying her good name and linking it with Roger's in this shameful way? Didn't he realize she'd come here to find *him?*

Finally Jonathan allowed himself to glance at Damaris, knowing that to avoid looking at her completely might strike Graham as odd. What he found in her face in that moment cut straight to his heart. The bright glow of her cheeks was gone, and her blue eyes were dull and lined by gray shadows. She looked pinched and worn and ill, beyond tears or recriminations. She couldn't hide her feelings to save her life, and now he understood her pain at his betrayal, as keenly as if she'd spoken. Yet if he wanted to save her, he couldn't falter now.

Instead he let his gaze wander freely over her with the same crude directness of the other men. "Aye, Roger Allyn won't want her damaged, and he'll be willing to pay good money to guarantee it."

"Aye, that he will, the stinking whoremonger!" shouted de Vere angrily. He stood weaving near the rail, his arms pinioned tightly behind his back, angry bruises already swelling one eye closed, and blood from his mouth staining the long end of his mustache. He, too, was doing what he could for Damaris, and Jonathan very nearly grinned, realizing de Vere was one more man he could count on in a fight. "Allyn hired me to take this woman to New York for him. The tongues clacked too fast for him in Newport, eh?"

Jonathan snorted derisively, playing off de Vere. "And how long do you fancy he'd be able to keep from running after the fair creature, d'you guess? There's some that say the wife didn't die an honest death."

Suddenly Damaris understood. This was like Providence and the Madeira, a trick to deceive the others. Jonathan loved her, and he was trying to save her, and so was Captain de Vere, and she barely stopped herself from laughing out loud with happiness. She would play along with Jonathan and de Vere, the same way she had in Providence, and pretend to still feel wounded and betrayed. She would do whatever Jonathan wanted, for the odds were still very much against them. Taking a deep breath, she pushed her way between Jonathan and Graham.

"It's not true, none of it!" she cried wildly, appealing to Graham. "Roger wouldn't give a farthing for me or my safety! Aye, he asked to wed me, but that

wasn't from love or caring! Will thee believe these—
these *rogues,* or will thee believe me?''

But Graham only laughed and gently shoved her
away, brushing at the place where her hand had
touched his sleeve. ''Nay, madam, I'll believe Russell. He has nothing to gain by lying, and you do, or
at least your brother does. If he wants you back, he'll
pay handsomely, and all your pretty tales won't change
my mind.''

He laughed again, and his laughter was echoed by
the men circled around them. He reached out to clap
Jonathan on the shoulder. ''You've already proved
your worth, Russell. To have such a tasty little plum
drop into my mouth! Now take the chit down to my
cabin for safekeeping.''

Jonathan nodded to Graham and reached out to
take Damaris's arm, but she shrank away. ''Thee
knows I can't escape,'' she said unsteadily, staring past
him, her hands tightly clasped. As long as she imagined how she'd feel if he didn't love her, she knew
what to do. ''If thee leads the way, I'll give my word
to follow.''

All too aware of the others watching, Jonathan
frowned darkly and gripped her arm, and though this
time she let him, he could feel the tension and fear that
made her body almost rigid. With as much gentleness
as he could risk showing in front of the others, he
guided her down the sloop's companionway, her skirts
blowing across his boots.

He held open the cabin door for her to pass inside,
so close to him he could again inhale the undefinable
fragrance that was special to her. He thought of how
different this moment could have been. If the sloop

were his, he could be welcoming her to his own cabin as his wife. *His wife.* Odd how it came to him just like that, and odd, too, how nothing else seemed as right, or as impossible. He wondered if he'd ever be able to win back her love.

She stood in the center of the cabin, her shoulders straight and her back to him, not trusting herself to look at him. Much as she longed to throw herself into his embrace, she feared that Graham was close behind. No matter how much she pretended, the danger to them both was still very real. *Not yet, love, not quite yet.*

"Naught in that ketch to make her worth the gunpowder spent," grumbled Graham as he pushed past Jonathan into the cabin. He dropped heavily into the armchair and propped his feet up on the edge of the desk. "Stay now, Russell, I want you here as a witness that I've left this little chick unharmed. She's the only thing of value that the Dutchman carried."

He frowned at Damaris, turning his finger in the air. "Let's have a look at you now, lovey. Never thought Allyn'd take on a Quaker, but then there's a certain fillip to debauching a decent woman. Sometimes the ones with the gospel in their mouths have the most fire between their legs, eh, Russell?"

Blushing, Damaris looked uncertainly from Graham to Jonathan's impassive face as he agreed. This had been almost a game when they were still on deck, but now the rules seemed subtly changed, and she wasn't sure what came next.

"I would thank thee, Captain, for the kindness that thee has shown me on thy ship," she said, forcing herself to smile. As long as Jonathan stayed, Graham couldn't hurt her. "I shall be sure to tell my brother-in-law."

"Ah, lovey, you're fair enough when you smile," said Graham, preening and puffing out his chest. His eyes narrowed, and he smiled wolfishly. "I swore I wouldn't harm you, but I can't account for what those jackals 'fore the mast might do to you if they found you unattended. But I might take closer care of you, my little chick, if you was to show your gratefulness."

Damaris stared at his dirty hands and his missing ear, his tobacco-stained teeth and the greasy splotches of old food that marked his bulging coat, and she felt the seasickness returning.

What the hell was she doing? thought Jonathan desperately. Any other woman he'd suspect of trying to hurt him back by flirting with another man, but not Damaris, and not with Graham. Yet Jonathan knew that if he tried to defend her, Graham would immediately suspect him.

"Come now, lovey," coaxed Graham, leaning eagerly toward Damaris. He had sucked one side of his trailing mustache into his mouth, and he chewed on it lewdly, working it between his lips and tongue. "Allyn won't miss a kiss given to the captain that saved you."

It wasn't Roger she thought of, but Jonathan, in the doorway behind her, and she wished he would say something to guide her. Was this what she had to do to save them both, smile and dally with this awful man?

She swallowed her queasiness and fixed the smile back on her face. Jonathan had always liked her hair loose, and likely Graham would, too. She reached back to pull apart her braid, combing her fingers through the waves as she shook them free over her shoulders. She was shaking so much she wondered that he didn't notice.

Unconsciously, Jonathan's hands had tightened into fists. He could consider himself dead the minute he struck Graham, but he couldn't bear to stand here and watch him defile Damaris.

With a throaty grunt of anticipation, Graham reached up to take her hand and roughly jerked her into his lap. "There you be, lovey, where you belong. Allyn won't miss a slice from a cut loaf, eh?"

But even as Damaris stiffened, the cry of "Sail t' th' larboard! Aiming to come alongside!" came from the deck overhead. Swearing, Graham was on his feet at once, roughly setting Damaris back on hers as he slid her from his lap.

"Keep watch on her, Russell," he ordered, breathing hard as he thrust a pistol into his belt. "Though God help you if you lay a hand on her yourself."

The door had barely swung shut before Jonathan had seized Damaris by her shoulders. "What in God's holy name do you think you're doing?" he demanded, anger driving his voice well above the whisper he intended. "That old goat would have you on your back with your petticoats up over your eyes before you could blink!"

"I did it for thee, Jonathan," she said unsteadily, close to tears. "I thought thee wanted me to—to please him."

"Because *I* wanted you to?" asked Jonathan incredulously.

She clung to his arms for support, unsure she could stand on her own. "I thought this was like that man Samuel Collins in Providence. I thought thee wanted me to do what Captain Graham wanted to help thee and Captain de Vere."

Jonathan stared at her, appalled by what might have happened. "Oh, Damaris, love, I would never expect you to do that for me. Never, mind?"

She nodded and melted against him with a sigh of contentment. He had called her his love, and he would keep her safe.

"Damaris, listen to me! I don't know how much time we'll have before Graham comes back," said Jonathan urgently, pushing her gently away and forcing her to meet his eyes. "I remember everything. Everything, mind? I'm no pirate, lass. My name is Jonathan Sparhawk, and I was born at a place called Plumstead, near Wickhamton, ten days' journey from Saybrook. My father's name was John and my mother's was Amity, and I've three sisters living and a big bullhead of a brother named Kit. This sloop is mine, or was, until these thieves stole her from me, just as I mean to take her back. If I'd told you so before the others, they would have had us both for supper. Hell, I shouldn't be telling you now, except I can't bear not to."

"Thy sloop, and thee her captain?" Damaris asked breathlessly. "And what of—what of thy wife and thy children?"

"Damaris, sweeting, I'm not married, and never have been. The woman I remembered is my brother's wife, the boy my nephew."

He drew her closer, realizing again how dear and precious she was to him. "You're the only woman I love, Damaris, and the only one I'd want to call wife. I'm sorry, sorry for everything that's gone wrong between us, but I want it to be right, and the devil take me if I don't try my damnedest to make it so. There, I don't know what else I can say."

She closed her eyes and pressed her cheek against the linen of his shirt to hear the muffled rhythm of his heartbeat. He loved her. He wanted to marry her. Faith, she'd never dared dream that, not once.

"Nothing else," she murmured into his shirt, so softly he wasn't sure he heard her.

He stroked her hair with a kind of reverence for the simple gesture he thought he'd never make again. "Nothing else, Damaris, except that I love you, and I always have," he whispered into her hair. "I never did forget that."

He thought she might be laughing softly to herself, the way she did when she was too happy for words. He never knew for certain, because Graham kicked the door open, his eyes near blind with a killing rage, and his pistol now cocked and primed in his hand.

"I told you how it would be with the pair of them, Graham," said Roger Allyn grimly, the plume on his hat sweeping against the doorway as he came to stand beside the captain. "Once a whore, always a whore, but never in my bed."

Chapter Sixteen

Angrily Damaris turned to face Roger, Jonathan's arms still linked around her waist. "Thee is precious fast to throw the first stone, Roger! I'd scarce think thy own conscience would countenance thee accusing me of anything, considering all that thee has done."

"Stop your yammering, woman!" ordered Graham, waving the pistol toward her. "Stiff-necked Quaker cant's got no place on this vessel, and Master Allyn here don't want to hear it any more than I do."

"Leave her alone, Graham," said Jonathan sharply, his arms tightening protectively around Damaris. "She's no threat to you."

Damaris folded her own arms across her chest and lifted her chin defiantly. "Thee can say or do what thee pleases, Captain Graham. Thy threats and guns mean nothing to me, for I have the truth to protect me."

Behind her, Jonathan sucked in his breath. Jesus, she would tempt fate! "Damaris, don't," he warned, "or we may both find out just how little protection your truth can be against a lead ball."

"Thee doesn't hear Roger deny what I've said, does thee?"

"I haven't denied it, because it's too ludicrous to acknowledge," said Roger. He took off his hat, frowning at the damage done to the beaver by the salt spray. "And as the owner of the vessel in which you are now standing, I feel even less inclined to defend myself."

"Owner!" repeated Jonathan incredulously. "The hell you are!"

Roger sighed wearily. "Graham, don't you have someplace to take this man while I speak to my brother's relict alone?"

"I'd lief flog the life out of him, making a fool out of me like he's done!" declared Graham furiously. "Standing there all damn-your-eyes while he's already lain with the chit!"

"As you're still short of men, I think you'd do better to put his able body to good use," said Roger dryly. "His main faults seem to be outspokenness and lust, neither of which have hindered *your* career."

Grumbling to himself, Graham uncocked his pistol and beckoned to the three seamen waiting in the companionway. Instinctively Jonathan tensed, ready to fight, while his thoughts raced on. Thank God he hadn't spat out who he was, though he'd come close enough. As long as Graham and Allyn didn't know the sloop had been his, he still had a chance to retake her and to save Damaris, as well. His best course would be to go now without a fight, to save his strength, and his wits, too.

He gave Damaris a quick kiss before the seamen grabbed him by the arms. "Think twice, nay, thrice, before you do anything foolish, Scheherazade," he whispered to her rapidly. "And remember how much I love you."

Damaris nodded, not trusting her voice, as they led Jonathan away. He had told her again that he loved her, which she'd known, and that he wanted to marry her, which she hadn't. How could she have come this far to find him, only to lose him again before she could say yes? She hadn't even had the chance to tell him about his child, their child. Woodenly she stood staring at the door after Graham slammed it shut and locked it, her hands folded across her apron as she prayed that Jonathan would be all right. He had to be.

"So what am I to do with you, dear Damaris?" asked Roger irritably, jerking Damaris's attention back to him. "I thought you were safely at Nantasket."

"Thee thought nothing of the kind, Roger," said Damaris, her clasped hands tightening into the mussed lawn of her apron. "Or has thee forgotten the man thee sent to kill me?"

"It's clear enough the rascal failed," said Roger sourly as he tossed his hat on the desk. "If he hadn't, you wouldn't be here to plague me now."

Troubled, Damaris shook her head, not wanting to believe what he was so easily admitting. Jonathan had tried to tell her Roger wished her dead, but even now, hearing it from his lips, she still found it hard to accept. "But why, Roger? I didn't wish to wed thee, true, but did thee really wish me dead because of that?"

Roger's sudden laugh held little humor. "Quaker or not, you're as vain as any other woman to believe I'd wed you for yourself alone, Damaris. Couldn't you see it was Nantasket I wanted? By rights it should have come to me when Eben died. Marrying you was the only way I had left. That, or waiting until you died. You'll admit I did try the more honorable path first."

"Thee calls murdering one wife to take another honorable?" she asked, stunned by his callousness.

"You sound like every other shrew in Newport!" he said heatedly, and struck his fist down hard on the desk beside him. "If Evelyn had shown her loyalty to me, her lawful husband, none of this would have happened."

Restlessly he began pacing the narrow cabin. "I loved Evelyn when we wed. I loved her, and gave her everything she could ever want." He was talking as much to himself as to Damaris, and gesturing emphatically in the air. "She loved me, too, and that's what cut the old man. Cut him deep. He set about to destroy me, to take her back. You know he wouldn't even invest in this sloop, the surest way to make a fortune in Christendom? He'd rather see me disgraced as a bankrupt than grant me what he owed me! Refused to receive me at his countinghouse, as if I were some common, begging tradesman, instead of his own son-in-law! And now he's turned the town against me, claiming I murdered his daughter."

Abruptly he wheeled around to face Damaris, his face livid above his lace-trimmed neckcloth and his eyes furious. Uneasily Damaris shrank back. He had been like this the day of Evelyn's burial, but then she had been able to flee. This time, in the middle of the ocean, she had nowhere to go.

"But you believe it, too, don't you?" he said, once again striking the desk. "You believe I murdered her!

But I cheated you all, didn't I? Hah! If I didn't have a man like Graham waiting here, I'd be in the gaol now!''

With effort, Damaris kept her voice and manner calm. "If thy credit is so bad, Roger," she began, hoping to shift his thoughts from Evelyn's death, "how did thee come by this sloop?"

Roger smiled at her indulgently, as if she were a child asking an obvious question. "I am still the magistrate of the colony's naval courts, Damaris. Because I condemn lawful prizes for the Crown, I'm in the position to seize opportunities that present themselves, and this Spanish-owned sloop, when Graham brought her in this spring, was a very pretty opportunity indeed."

"But her owners were English, not Spanish," said Damaris plaintively, stopping just short of identifying Jonathan. "Graham lied to thee. If thee cares at all for thy good name and thy honor, thee must make it right. She's owned by Englishmen, men from Massachusetts."

But Roger continued as if he hadn't heard her. "And now that I'll finally have the cove at Nantasket," he said, his eyes dreamy, "we'll be able to bring in any prizes we take, strip 'em clean before they show at Newport, and only declare the worth of the vessels themselves. There'll be no creditors at my door then, damn their greedy souls!"

Damaris listened, and understood enough to wish Jonathan were there to listen, too. She knew it would be dangerous to cross Roger now, but her love for the farm wouldn't let her keep silent. "Roger, Nantasket's still mine. It doesn't belong to thee, and it never will.''

He looked at her, surprise arching his brows up toward the stiff curls of his wig. "Oh, aye, it will, and soon, for I mean to outlive you, Damaris."

"Eben left Nantasket to me, Roger," she said carefully, "and when I died, it would go to my children."

Roger snorted. "Six years you were wed to Eben, and I doubt even my brother, dry old stick that he was, left you to yourself at night. He never did manage to plant a son in your belly, did he? You're barren as a stone, my dear, the same as Evelyn was."

"Nay, Roger, that's not true." Even with Roger she couldn't suppress her happy little smile. "I'm with child now."

Rapidly Roger's gaze appraised her body. "If you are, then you're not long gone," he said disdainfully, "nor would the brat be Eben's. It's just as well it's come to this, Damaris. Nantasket or not, you really wouldn't have suited me as a wife. One moment spewing your pious hypocrisy, the next spreading your legs for some vagabond sailor. Not that it matters. When you disappear, no one will know you took his bastard with you."

Damaris's smile faded. "Then thee truly does mean to kill me," she said softly.

Roger plucked at his cuffs and shrugged carelessly. "Not by my own hands, no. One night you'll simply be lost over the side, trying to escape, and that will be an end to you. Perhaps I'll ask Graham to see it done off Long Island. I've heard your wretched sect's there, too, and you'll be more likely to have a decent burial if you wash up among your own kind."

Damaris felt cold all over, icy cold, as if the salt-water had already claimed her. "I don't believe thee, Roger," she said slowly, rubbing her arms. "I don't believe thee could do it."

"Believe it, sister dear," he snarled as he grabbed her by the shoulders and shoved her toward the cabin's door. "I've never meant anything more in my life."

Caught off balance, Damaris screamed and stumbled forward, striking her cheek hard against the doorway. Even before she touched her hand to her face, she could feel the blood trickling from the cut. Roughly Roger's fingers twisted into her hair as he jerked her back to her feet.

And as he did, something deep inside her finally shattered, breaking through a lifetime of peacefulness, of trusting in goodness to prevail. Roger Allyn wanted to kill her and her child, and there could be no arguing right or wrong. If she didn't stop him, she would die.

Instinctively she twisted around and threw her whole weight against Roger. Swearing with surprise, he toppled backward to the deck. Yet still he managed to hold fast to Damaris's hair, and she tumbled down on top of him. Tangled in her own petticoats, she struggled to break free, clawing with her nails at his face and hands as he grasped her wrists. At last she pulled herself to her knees. With a dry sob, she grabbed the chair beside her and pulled it down onto Roger's chest as hard as she could, driving the breath from him, and with a loud grunt, he released her at last.

She scrambled to her feet, shoving her tangled hair back from her eyes. Salty tears stung at the cut on her cheek. Here she'd been crying, too, and hadn't even known it. As her fingers fumbled frantically with the lock to the door, she heard Roger moan on the deck behind her. She had to find Jonathan. All she knew was that they'd taken him below, but where was below on a ship?

She swung open the door and ran into the companionway, toward the narrow steps that would, she prayed, lead her to the lower deck, and to Jonathan. Behind her she heard Roger brokenly call her name, then Graham's. With one hand on the line that served as a railing, and her feet already on the narrow steps, she turned back fearfully to see if anyone had heard him. But as she did, she forgot to duck, and when her head crashed into the oak beam, the blackness swallowed her in an instant.

"You're sure of this, de Vere?" asked Jonathan incredulously as he peered at the shadowy features of the Dutch captain. Deep in the hold, where they all were locked, the only light was filtered through the padlocked grating to the middle deck overhead. "This Graham is the one who killed Mistress Allyn's husband?"

"Oh, aye, there's no mistaking a man with one ear like that," said de Vere bitterly, and around him his crew rumbled in agreement. "The devil take my luck to run afoul of him twice!"

"But why didn't you report the bastard in Newport?" demanded Jonathan. "The navy coasters would have run him down in a day!"

"Ah, Captain Sparhawk, you forget we're not all stout, honest Englishmen," said de Vere, laughing painfully through his torn mouth. "In my line, 'tis best to avoid your queen's navy, eh? And what good would it have brought to pretty Mistress Allyn? Her husband would still be dead, she would have lost the gold she gained from my wines and my brandies, and she would never have met you. No bargain for her in it anywhere."

Jonathan sighed impatiently and raked his fingers back through his hair. "Are you with me or not tonight?"

"That's different, Captain," said de Vere sharply, his bantering manner vanished. "Now Graham has stolen from me, and I mean to have my *Henrickje* back."

"Good." Satisfied, Jonathan settled back against the bulkhead. With his own reason for fighting, he felt de Vere could be trusted, and when he remembered how swiftly the Dutchman had moved that night on the beach, he was glad. "I've six men left from my own that I can count on, and with your ten, we'll have a chance."

"And the little widow." De Vere leaned nearer, the faint light through the grating catching his yellow blond hair. "She's an innocent, that one, a rare thing in a woman. I've tested her sore, aye, but she's always treated me fair, and I want her taken back to Nantasket unharmed. I don't know how you've used her, Sparhawk, but—"

"I've asked her to be my wife," said Jonathan tersely. "Is that good enough for you?"

They all heard the footsteps overhead, and as a man's dark outline leaned over the grating, Jonathan retreated farther back into the shadows.

"Cap'n Sparhawk, sir?" whispered Tom Cooke tentatively. "I told th' others t' be ready tonight, during th' night watch."

"Good lad." Jonathan rose, and linked his fingers through the grating as he stared up at Tom. "Have you found where they've stowed Mistress Allyn?"

"Aye, sir, aft o' th' galley."

Despite the other men around him, Jonathan couldn't keep the urgency and longing from his voice. "Go to her, Tom, and tell her this . . ."

"He told thee *what?*" croaked Damaris. Uncertainly she tried to focus on the thin young sailor who crouched beside her, wishing he had two eyes instead of four, and that they'd stay in one place on his face. Gingerly she touched the bump on the side of her head where she'd struck the beam, and then the ripe bruise beneath the cut on her eye. No wonder she felt as if she'd been kicked in the head by a cow!

Sympathetically the young man handed her the broken tankard of water she'd been left, but she shook her head, winced at the motion, and closed her eyes again. If only this little storeroom had even a breath of air, or didn't stink so much of stale fried codfish! Just the thought of adding anything to her stomach made it rebel, and she swallowed hard, pressing her hands across her belly. As foolish as her fall had been, she hadn't lost the child, thank God.

"Cap'n Sparhawk said for ye to keep safe an' away from th' others until th' sloop be his agin," said Tom slowly, repeating the message he'd so carefully memorized, "an' he would come fetch ye himself."

Unsteadily Damaris pushed herself up to a sitting position, clutching at the filthy wool-stuffed mattress until the man's face stopped spinning before her. She wondered if she should be listening to him at all, or if his visit was some new trick of Roger's. But the message sounded very much like Jonathan at his most high-handed, or Captain Sparhawk, as she supposed she should be calling him now. "So I am to stay here, cowering and useless, waiting for thy captain to come rescue me? Those are his orders for me?"

Tom nodded solemnly.

"Then damn thy Captain Sparhawk's orders!" she declared indignantly, and understood at once the satisfaction that men derived from blasphemy. "I won't sit idle while he risks his life for mine! From what thee has told me, it seems that Jona—I mean, Captain Sparhawk—relies overmuch on Captain Graham sleeping soundly. What if he wakes, and raises an alarum? Nay, it would be well to distract the man instead."

"Cap'n's orders said ye was t' stay here, ma'am."

Damaris looked at Tom with the same stern frown she reserved for Daniel Reed. "Has thy Captain Sparhawk told thee, too, that he has asked me to be his wife? When I wed him, I will be thy mistress, and thee wouldn't wish to cross me already, would thee?"

Though Damaris herself wasn't sure if she would in fact have any position on board as the captain's wife, Jonathan would become master of Nantasket, and that seemed reasonable enough. At least it worked for poor Tom, who hung his head miserably, his untanned, unwashed neck showing grimy and pale above his neckcloth.

"Now tell me true, Tom Cooke," she asked, holding her head as high as she could. "How ill do I look?"

The reluctant regret on the sailor's face was answer enough.

"Then I warrant I must count on Captain Graham's desire for me being stronger than his eyes." Damaris sighed deeply, once again tracing her swollen cheek. "Now mark me well, Tom Cooke—before thee releases thy captain and the others, thee must come to me first, and lead me to Captain Graham's cabin."

She smiled crookedly, imagining what Jonathan would say if he knew what she planned. But she had never in her life sat by idle while others worked, and she didn't intend to begin tonight, when so much was at stake. "And mind," she added fiercely. "Not a word—not even a hint!—of this to Captain Sparhawk."

"The devil take you for robbing me of my peace, whichever son of a pox-faced bitch you be!" bellowed Graham from inside the cabin when Damaris knocked timidly on the door. "Well, in with you, then, or are you waiting for an invitation from Her Majesty to make it nice?"

Once again Damaris smoothed her hair, and took a deep breath to try to settle herself for what she was about to do. For a fleeting moment, she considered retreating to her storeroom prison and waiting for Jonathan, the way he wished. No one except for Tom

Cooke would know otherwise, and she'd never have to suffer the touch of Graham's unwashed hands on her skin. *Coward!* her conscience hissed back at her. *Your squeamishness could mean Jonathan's death!* Swiftly, before she could change her mind again, she pushed open the door and slipped inside.

A single candle guttered in the swinging lantern, and by its shifting light she saw the shadowy figure of Graham in the bunk. To Damaris the cabin seemed unbearably close, the windows sealed shut and the warm air stale with the smell of burning tallow, spilled ale and old tobacco, yet Graham lay fully dressed beneath the coverlet, an earthenware jug of rum or whiskey on the deck within his reach. Slowly he pulled himself upright, and Damaris realized then that in his hand was a pistol, cocked and aimed at her.

"Now who set you free, little chick?" he asked curiously, though the gun remained level across his bent knees. "Did your bullyboy send you 'round to slit my throat, or was it your fine brother-in-law, eh? You know I don't trust a one of 'em, nay, nor you, neither. Come, confess your business before I send you back to your pen."

Damaris forced herself to smile. At least in the candlelight he wouldn't notice her cheek, or how she shook with nervousness. "I came by my own wishes, not theirs. I wanted to see thee again, alone." Faith, but she was wretched at this!

"Alone, you say." Damaris saw the spark of interest in Graham's eyes as he tugged on his beard, judging her. "You turned coy enough this noon. Why should I believe you now?"

"What else would thee have me do before the others?" She stepped closer to the bunk, nearly within his reach. Her ears strained for sounds of a fight overhead. Tom had told her Jonathan meant to recapture the sloop by surprise, not force, but shouldn't there be some noise to tell her they'd begun their attack? Perhaps she'd been wrong to trust Tom, after all. "I'm not by nature as wanton as thee would believe."

"Ha! There's not been a woman since mother Eve that's claimed otherwise," said Graham scornfully, but now he uncocked the pistol and lay it on the coverlet. "But you've laid your gold on the right cockerel for this fight, lovey. Allyn's no use to me in disgrace, damn his cheating soul, and your other fellow will ne'er keep you in ribands and laces."

The unkept fringes of his beard twitched upward as he smiled, and with one hand he patted the mattress beside him. "Come along, then, don't keep your captain waiting. Enough of your sham modesty! I'm not a man that wastes his time on idle niceties, but I wager you won't go away wanting, nay, you won't!"

Reluctantly Damaris inched closer. From the eager way Graham watched her, she knew she'd succeeded well enough in distracting him. If she had to, she would let him take her hand, at worst even kiss her. But what if that wasn't enough?

"Come to me, lovey, be a good girl," coaxed Graham. "Along with you now."

Suddenly he reached out and grabbed her around the waist, hauling her back to the bunk. Before she could protest, he had trapped her against the mattress with his body. She remembered the pistol, and desperately her fingers groped blindly across the cover-

let. But with a low growl Graham realized what she
sought, and with one hand caught both her wrists and
yanked them over her head.

Gasping with panic, she twisted and fought beneath him, but he held her fast, the horn buttons of his
breeches grinding against her thighs. He tore open the
front of her bodice, roughly squeezing the soft flesh
of her breasts upward, and she cried out with fear and
revulsion when she felt the wetness of his mouth and
tongue and the sharp bristles of his beard against her
skin. He jerked at her skirts, ripping her petticoat in
his urgency, and then she felt his hand on her bare
thigh, thrusting higher.

With her head muffled by the tangled bedding, Damaris only half heard the splintering wood as the cabin
door flew open. Instantly she was free as Graham
rolled to one side, and she scrambled off the bunk to
the deck, clutching at her clothes.

And then there was Jonathan, standing in the
doorway with his legs widespread and a battered sword
in his hand, his face rigid with anger as his eyes swept
rapidly from Damaris, crouched on the floor, to Graham behind her.

And, with sickening clarity, Damaris knew the worst
still lay ahead.

Chapter Seventeen

"Don't glare at me like that, Russell," sputtered Graham. "The little slut came to me on her own."

"Are you unharmed, Damaris?" asked Jonathan, his eyes fixed on the other man. Though she knew he wouldn't see, Damaris nodded, still too shaken to speak. She had never seen Jonathan like this, wound tight as a watchspring with a ruthlessness he barely controlled. The blade of his sword was smeared red with blood, and his mouth was hard and set. *God help them both, what had he done in her name?*

"Your life's already mine, Graham," continued Jonathan, "but if you've hurt her..."

Graham made a little snort of disgust. "For all love, Russell, look at the proof of her whoring ways with your own eyes!"

"She's no whore, you bastard," said Jonathan, slowly, evenly, "and my name's not Russell. I'm Jonathan Sparhawk, master of this sloop until you stole it from me, and this night I mean to take her back."

Graham's laugh was a misplaced cackle that made Damaris glance sharply back at him. He was kneeling on the bunk, his back against the bulkhead and his hands buried in the coverlet. She remembered the pistol the same moment Graham found it, raising it swiftly with both hands to aim at Jonathan.

"Jonathan!" she shrieked as she grabbed the earthenware jug from the deck beside her and swung it up at Graham. The jug smacked the gun from Graham's grasp, sending it flying harmlessly across the cabin, as the jug crashed and shattered against the bulkhead. Jonathan charged forward, his sword raised high, but Graham was surprisingly agile for a man so heavy, and he deftly rolled off the bunk and seized another sword that hung from the back of the desk.

They were even now, thought Jonathan grimly as he twisted the hilt in his fingers, forcing his wrist to relax. He'd be a fool to underestimate Graham; the man couldn't have survived as long as he had without cunning and skill. Jonathan shifted sideways, testing and appraising Graham's reflexes, and the older man matched him as neatly as if in a mirror.

Oh, they were even, all right, maybe worse than even on his side, though Jonathan didn't like admitting that. He'd already fought three other men that night, while Graham was fresh. In such close quarters Jonathan's height was a disadvantage, too, and he was forced to stand with his shoulders bowed to clear the beams overhead. He wished they'd met on the deck, with room to move and only the stars above them. Here in the crowded cabin, they were scarcely a blade's length apart.

As the two men inched around the boundaries of the narrow cabin, Damaris scrambled back up onto the bunk to avoid Graham. Not that he or Jonathan noticed her now, the air was so thick with tension between them. The lantern swung gently with the rocking motion of the sloop, casting strange, wavering shadows of the two men. In the cabin's silence, Damaris could finally hear shouts and calls from overhead, the rushed scuffle of feet on the deck above. If the sloop was back in Jonathan's hands, was this fight really necessary?

"I beg thee both, stop now!" she cried, her hands working in her apron. Briefly she considered throwing herself between them, but then she remembered her child. "I beg thee, please!"

"Save your breath, Damaris," said Jonathan without turning. "The world won't miss this bastard at all."

"But to kill him . . ."

"Damaris, he'll be doing his damnedest to kill me as well. He has the blood of dozens of men on his soul already!"

"Perhaps 'tis I she favors, Sparhawk," taunted Graham. He spread the fingers of his left hand and rested them across his breast with feigned modesty. "She'll make a fair enough prize to warm the sheets of whoever wins, eh?"

Jonathan lunged forward, the blade of his sword scraping harshly along the length of Graham's as the other man deftly met the first thrust. Over and over the steel blades clanged together, until suddenly Jonathan twisted sideways and rammed his shoulder into Graham's midsection, below his sword arm. The impact threw Graham crashing against the bulkhead. His boots outstretched before him, he gasped to find his wind.

Breathing heavily, Jonathan raked his hair back and wiped the sweat from his forehead. He knew he should end this now, run his sword through the man and send him to hell, where he belonged. The fight had been fair enough, and God only knew how much longer he could count on his scarred leg. So why the devil didn't he just kill Graham?

Damaris.

She didn't say a word, but he could sense her there behind him, waiting, judging, ripping to shreds any concentration he'd managed to hang on to. Savagely he tried to remind himself that her kind of goodness had no place in a world like this. Men like Graham didn't deserve mercy. At last Jonathan raised his sword.

But he'd waited too long. Graham scrambled back to his feet, holding the hilt of his sword with two hands as he swung the blade in wide, deadly arcs that were harder and harder for Jonathan to deflect. He knew he had to stop thinking of Damaris, or he would be lost. Graham's sword swung high, and Jonathan barely ducked in time. Jesus, he was losing already....

Her eyes round with horror, Damaris watched the two men. Graham was going to kill Jonathan, she could feel it, and everything she loved most would die with him. "Thee must stop!" she wailed. "I want no killing for me! Both of thee must stop now!"

"Damaris, listen to me," said Jonathan hoarsely. "De Vere swears that Graham killed your husband."

But all he heard was her strangled little cry of anguish. Dear God, he hadn't meant to hurt her again, and without thinking he turned from Graham toward

Damaris. In that half second he saw with heightened clarity the fear frozen on her face, and how her mouth was open, his name on her lips, and he realized how very much her love meant to him, and the strength that knowledge could give him.

Then came the whistle of Graham's sword as the blade sliced through the air toward him, and this time Jonathan was ready. He turned abruptly on his heel, holding his sword so the blade pointed out behind him, and thrust sharply upward with all his force, beneath Graham's ribs and up into his heart. The man's final words were a mumbled curse, and then, held upright only by the sword angled through his chest, he sagged against Jonathan's back. Jonathan jerked his sword free, and the body slumped to the deck, leaving a bright trail of Graham's blood across the back of Jonathan's shirt.

Eagerly he looked to Damaris, and his heart sank. Her blue eyes were staring, still too full of the horror of what she'd just witnessed. There'd be time enough for explanations after the shock had passed. Besides, until he knew his men had found and captured Roger Allyn, he didn't dare consider the sloop fully his.

Damaris stared past Jonathan's outstretched hand at the body on the deck. She stared at the wound that went clear through the chest, the blood that stained his clothes and puddled on the deck beside him, the glassy look of his unclosed eyes, and saw not Graham's body, but Eben's. Graham had killed her husband, and would have killed Jonathan if he could, and she had done nothing to stop him. Worse than nothing— she had come close to being raped by her husband's murderer.

Numb, she let Jonathan lift her over Graham's body, and when he held her and asked if she was unharmed, she nodded mutely and followed him through the cabin door and into the companionway. She gasped when she saw the blood that stained the back of Jonathan's shirt. What would she have done if she'd lost him the same way she'd lost Eben, if her child had been born without ever knowing its father?

She stopped on the steps, unable yet to follow Jonathan as he bounded across the deck to the men clustered at the rail. The wind off the water was cool on her cheeks, salty and fresh after the stale air below. To starboard lay the eastern horizon, pinkish-gray with dawn, and dully she realized the sloop had changed course and was headed back to Newport, back to home. So Jonathan had won after all, and there would be no privateering, no piracy, no voyage to the Caribbean. At the rail beside Jonathan she recognized Captain de Vere's long yellow hair streaming in the wind, and Tom Cooke, too, and beyond them in the distance she could make out another ship racing toward them with every sail set. She leaned her elbows on the edge of the hatch and closed her eyes, letting the wind play across her face and through her hair.

Confused, she felt someone grab her arm and roughly shove her up the last steps to the deck. *Roger.* His face was behind her, but she knew him from the carnelian ring on the hand that was locked around her waist, and the fine lace on the holland-linen cuff. She tried to face him, and felt the chilly barrel of a pistol pressed along her cheek. Before her she saw all the faces of the men turned from the sea toward her instead, a crew of men as still as statues. In the center stood Jonathan, his legs widespread against the sloop's roll, and Damaris wondered if the others saw his fear as clearly as she could.

"Let her go, Allyn," ordered Jonathan. "You'll gain nothing this way. Graham is dead, and his men with him."

"And that ship you all find so fascinating is the *Prince William,* come to fetch me back to the gallows," said Roger grimly. "Oh, I know her well, and I'm flattered to be judged grand enough quarry to merit one of the queen's own vessels in pursuit. But the *Prince William*'s a sluggish sailer, and her master's a cautious old fool. You'll have no trouble at all outrunning her, Captain Sparhawk."

"The *Leopard*'s an honest ship again," said Jonathan firmly, "and we're not outrunning anything."

"Either you don't believe I'd really harm Damaris, or you don't care what becomes of her." Roger's arm tightened around Damaris's waist. "One of us is gambling, Sparhawk. Maybe both of us. But even if the chit's life means nothing to you, I'd think you'd care what became of the brat she carries in her belly. Unless, of course, it isn't yours?"

Across the deck, Jonathan's face mirrored his confusion, and, miserably, Damaris wished she'd been able to tell him herself. "It's true, Jonathan," she called, and immediately Roger jabbed the pistol into her cheek to silence her.

"So there you are, Captain, you've heard it from my dear sister-in-law's own lips. What will your wager be, I wonder?"

Jonathan didn't waver for a moment. "Turn her about, Ned," he said heavily to the man at the helm, "and signal to the *Prince William* that we've changed our mind. There now, Allyn, will you let her go?"

Stunned, Damaris could not believe it. That after all Jonathan had done to retake his sloop he would give it all over in an instant for her sake was unbearable. This time, she wouldn't fail him. She had broken away from Roger before, and she could do it again. All she had to do was reach Jonathan.

Swiftly, before her courage could fail her, she shoved the pistol from her face and twisted sideways out of Roger's grip. It was easier than she had thought, unbelievably easy. With her skirts bunched high to keep herself from tripping, she ran across the deck, laughing. She was close to the safety of Jonathan's arms, so close, when she felt the bullet strike her arm, and the impact and the pain drove everything else from her mind as she fell into Jonathan.

"Jesus, Damaris, why did you do it?" Jonathan kept saying over and over, rocking her against his chest. "Why did you do it, love?"

To her, why seemed perfectly obvious, but she was too tired now to explain. When she glanced back to where Roger stood, she saw that he wasn't standing anymore, but lay instead crumpled on the deck, his fine holland shirt now crimson. Captain de Vere stood over him, a pistol in his hand. For the first time Damaris smelled the acrid gunpowder on the sea spray, and remembered the dry pop of the two guns, one after the other. Gingerly she touched her arm below the shoulder, and her fingers came back red.

"Stop thy yammering, Jonathan," she whispered, her voice too weak for anything more. "If I forget who I am as thee did, at least thee shall be there to tell me."

And then she stopped remembering, and welcomed the darkness that followed.

Epilogue

Plumstead
May 1709

"You know we didn't believe Jonathan would ever marry," said Dianna Sparhawk. Her voice was lowered confidentially, even though she and Damaris were alone in the chamber Damaris was sharing with Jonathan while they visited Plumstead. Dianna paused as she threaded her needle, biting on the tip of her tongue while she concentrated, until finally the silk slipped through the needle's eye. "He always swore that no single lady would suit him, that no such proper paragon of womanhood existed. Until, of course, he found you, or rather, you found him. At least he wasn't too fuddled to realize his good fortune."

Damaris smiled shyly at her new sister-in-law. Dianna was not at all the way Damaris had pictured a duke's granddaughter to be, not with her skirts always smudged with her children's sticky handprints and flour from baking, and when they'd first met, three days before, Damaris had half expected Jonathan to admit that the ducal grandfather had been one more of his jests. But there was an understated gentility to Dianna that didn't need elegant clothes to show itself, and Damaris had quickly realized that here in the wilderness was the elusive "quality" that Roger and Evelyn had so vainly strived to achieve.

From habit, Damaris touched the ripple of the scar beneath her sleeve, thinking sadly of Roger and Evelyn. Though now no one would ever know for sure, she still wanted to believe Evelyn's death had been an accident, and that it was grief, not greed alone, that had made Roger so desperate. One week after his death, a ship Roger had given up for lost had finally returned to Newport, and the profit from the voyage would have cured many of his difficulties. Ironically, the courts had declared Damaris to be Roger's heir, and when at last his estate was settled, she had been regarded by all Newport as a very wealthy widow, and Jonathan a most fortunate man.

Yet now that she'd seen Plumstead, she realized that in regard to fortunes, Newport had figured it all wrong. The *Leopard* was only the beginning. The Sparhawks owned lumber mills and grist mills, and more land than a man could ride in two weeks, and the house where they'd been born was as grand as any she'd ever seen. Not that the worldly goods meant much to Damaris. For her, the grandest fortune of all was Jonathan himself, and she still couldn't quite believe he was hers forever.

She glanced up at Dianna, her smile widening. "From that first night, I think Jonathan knew he'd been lucky to land at Nantasket. Even though he was so sorely wounded and his thoughts were all twisted about, Jonathan was still—well, still Jonathan."

"Meaning that even halfway in the grave he still tried to seduce you!" Dianna tipped back her head and laughed so hard that tears filled her eyes, and she reached out to squeeze Damaris's hand affectionately as she, too, began to laugh. "Don't forget I'm married to the other Sparhawk brother, and I doubt there's any mischief Jonathan's tried that Kit didn't do first. Though you know, of course, Kit and I remarked the changes in Jonathan as soon as he stepped through the door."

"Changes?" repeated Damaris with concern. "I thought he had recovered completely, but then thee knew him before. Pray, tell me, what kinds of changes does thee see?"

"The usual ones," said Dianna, not quite keeping the merriment from her voice. "Foolish grins for no reason, lying abed with the curtains drawn at midday, a strange desire to stay by his own hearth instead of roaming every tavern in every port. All the changes that generally occur when a man falls so far in love."

They were laughing still when they heard the men's voices in the kitchen below, and swiftly Damaris tucked away the half-darned sock and smoothed her hair. Always her heart beat faster whenever Jonathan was near, and she was somehow certain it always would. She was smiling before he came through the door, and she marveled again at what a handsome, perfect man her husband was. His eyes looked very green in his sun-browned face, and his grin very white, and cradled gently in his well-muscled arms was their daughter, Sarah, her serious face all eyes beneath the the dark curls she'd inherited from her father.

"We saw robins and mockingbirds and a butterfly or two, didn't we, young miss?" said Jonathan as he bent to kiss Damaris. Sarah smiled and gurgled at the sight of her mother, but showed no wish to leave her father's comfortable embrace, and Damaris couldn't blame her. She loved to see the two of them together, loved to see the tenderness her great, strong husband could show with his tiny daughter. But close as father and daughter were, there were some comforts that only Damaris could offer, and as Sarah began to rub at her eyes with her fists, she squawked with hunger and turned her face to her mother.

"Now lookee well, Kit, and swear you've never seen a fairer child," said Jonathan proudly as he handed Sarah to Damaris. "Mark my words, in sixteen summers Sarah Sparhawk will be the prettiest girl in the colony!"

"I don't doubt it, little brother," said Kit amicably, and Damaris smiled to herself. As a larger, blond version of Jonathan, only Kit would dream of calling her husband little. "Likely you'll have every buck in Newport sniffing 'round your door. Seems only fair, Jon, considering how much of that you did in your day."

Damaris could feel Jonathan bristle behind her. "The devil take your Newport bucks! You're forgetting we spend as much time on the *Leopard* as we do at Nantasket!"

"Then Sarah will have her pick of sailors, too." Kit shrugged and slipped his arm comfortably around Dianna's shoulders. "You'll be in your dotage by then, Jon, and your pretty little daughter will dance circles around you. You'd do better to give the lass a brother or two to watch after her virtue. Here you've been wed nigh on a year, and only one babe to show for it.''

"Nor are they likely to have another, sweetheart, if we don't leave them alone,'' said Dianna as she tugged the reluctant Kit toward the door. "Come, it's time we learned what our own son is doing to destroy the kitchen garden.''

"A wise little woman, Dianna,'' said Jonathan as Damaris gently laid Sarah, now asleep, into her cradle and tucked the coverlet around her tiny body. "Not so wise nor fair as my own sweet wife, but Dianna does well enough for Kit.''

Damaris circled her arms around Jonathan's waist, relishing the feel of the lean muscles beneath the linen. He had been gone from her no more than an hour, but she had missed him still. "I like thy family, Jonathan, and I won't listen to thee say such foolishness about them.''

"They're your family now, too, if you want to claim 'em.'' He sat on the edge of the bed, bringing Damaris with him. "But enough of Kit and Dianna, sweeting. I'd rather think of how much I love you.''

He pulled her on top of his chest. "Do you know what day this is, Damaris?'' he asked as one by one he pulled out her hairpins, until the rich golden waves spilled loose over them both.

"Second Day?'' she answered lazily, and lowered her lips onto his.

He groaned with happiness, tangling his fingers in her hair to hold her face. "Nay, don't confuse me with your Friends' days! The rest of the world calls it the seventh of May. And if you'd stop being so damned contrary, sweetheart,'' he murmured, his hands caressing the soft curves of her hips as she lay over him, "you'd likely remember that on this day one year past we first made love. Well, maybe that's too proper for what we did, but at least it's not something I've forgotten, the way you seem to have."

"Oh, I haven't forgotten." Her voice was husky as she traced the outline of his lips with one finger. "How could I, when thee's so willing to remind me each night?"

"And afternoon and morning." He rolled her, laughing, onto her back. "Whatever time pleases you."

"Whenever thee wishes, Jonathan," she whispered happily as his lips met hers. "Whenever thee wishes at all."

* * * * *